Resilience

DIANA RICHMOND

ISBN
978-1-957378-90-9 (Paperback)
978-1-957378-89-3 (eBook)
978-1-960197-71-9 (Hardcover)

To the inspiration of Cataract Falls

Table of Contents

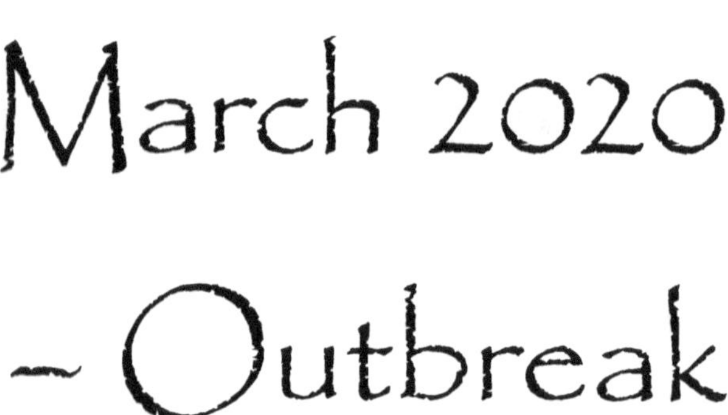

March 2020
~ Outbreak

The traffic on the autostrada was even worse heading back toward Milano than it had been on the way north. A Ferrari grumbled just a few feet behind her own car, its pent-up frustration breathing proverbially at the back of her neck. Already tense from the change of plan, Fran raised her left hand from the wheel to relieve her neck and glanced to her right to find an opening in the next lane to escape the Ferrari. Just as she was about to swerve to her right to catch a space in the lane, Liliana's voice distracted her.

"Why did we have to leave so soon, Mama?"

Fran took a deep breath to find an answer. At that second, a motorcyclist sped up between her and the cars to her right, zooming at Italian speed. All she saw was the flash of a neon green cycle as the cyclist wove unevenly between the two lanes of cars. She gasped despite herself, almost coughing in a double inhalation.

"Lili, it's hard to explain, but everyone has to return to Milano." It wasn't an explanation, but it was a response, and Lili fell quiet for a few miles. Fran found an opening and moved to the slow lane. Here she felt less aggression; it was as if resignation flowed through the slow lane, and she could drive more comfortably. She wondered if she had repacked the groceries she had just unpacked at the lake cottage. Glancing backward, she caught sight of the plastic *Esselunga* bag on the rear seat and took the tiniest comfort in knowing she would not have to shop again as soon as they arrived home. Lili's little red overnight bag and her own dark blue satchel sat next to the groceries, testaments to a presence of mind she did not feel.

"Mama, tell me a story." Lili knew better than to ask this while Fran was driving, but this was not a usual day. She wracked her mind for a story to tell, to relieve Lili from her sense of disruption. All the familiar storybooks flitted through her mind by title, but none felt like a story she could retell from memory.

"*Non posso*, Lili. I'll read to you when we get back home."

Not four hours earlier, Fran and Lili had been on this same route headed North to their lake cottage, to escape the eeriness of a nearly deserted Milano. All the schools had been shut down since the beginning of the week, and containing the four-year-old's energy in their apartment had been trying. So they had taken off for their cottage at Lago Maggiore, a drive of less than two hours on most days. It had been such a good idea. Lili had burst out of the car and literally run around the perimeter of the cottage several times while Fran unpacked the groceries. She'd had time to open a bottle of Pinot Grigio and sit in the swivel chair to gaze out at the dark water, mesmerized as always by the random glints of sunlight on the waves. When Lili burst in, Fran got up to turn on the television and pour herself a second glass. She peeled a *mandarino* for Lili, who took it delicately and sat down on her own small chair in front of the television, knowing she would have to sit through the news before her mother would insert a movie for her. An *emergenza* alert flashed: Milano was to be cordoned off to contain the further spread of the coronavirus that had already gripped its urban lungs. Fran threw herself into reverse, screwing the cap back onto the wine bottle, repacking the groceries, and turning off the television, only glancing back at the lake. "*Andiamo, cara mia*, we have to go back home."

The traffic slowed even more, and Fran could discern flashing red lights ahead on the left side of the highway. Gradually, two lanes melded into one, and she caught sight of the angry Ferrari ahead of her on the left about six cars ahead. At least she would not have to wrestle with him for a space in the line. About twenty minutes later, she inched past the ambulance scene on the left. A neon green motorbike lay crumpled at the roadside, its rider sprawled on his back, one leg bent at an unnatural angle. That was all she could see in the moment it took to pass the accident scene and the traffic picked up quickly. All Fran could think of was how often she had joked about organ transplants in the offing when she saw a motorcyclist drive between lanes. If Lili had not interrupted her, she might have been the one who had smashed the cyclist.

⬤●⬤

In "Out of Africa," it is Isak Dinesen's ability to tell stories that enchants Denis Finch-Hatton. In the film, the candle burns down altogether over a dinner that becomes her first story-telling session, as the fire in the hearth provides the last light. Their mutual fascination begins that first evening, and, when he departs with his friend the next morning, he gives her a pen, which she hesitates to accept, as a gift that may signify an obligation.

What need did he have of stories? His life itself was the 'stuff of tales,' hunting and exploring an African terrain that had not yet been scarred by roads, where herds of Cape buffalo roamed and lions hunted. He would go for days and weeks without seeing another human being except his Kikuyu hunting crew. Perhaps he could not understand the language of the stories they told themselves at day's end around a fire.

————•◦•————

For four days Alice had been coughing, but with lozenges it had been relatively easy to hide. A winter cold, she'd tried to tell herself, nothing more. Her retirement community was already on virtual lockdown, with all the common areas closed, no movies or recitals in the auditorium, the exercise classes cancelled, and the lounge and dining areas closed. The only times she saw her fellow residents were when they lined up at the buffet, their food dished out by the dining staff into disposable paper boxes that they had been instructed to toss into large garbage bins posted near the elevators. After eating dinner in her apartment, she lacked the energy to put the used paper box onto the flat surface of her walker, walk back to the elevator area and toss it into the bin. So the paper containers accumulated on a counter in her apartment.

What she missed most was the domino tournaments every Monday evening after dinner in the resident lounge. Harold and she had played together, on the same team and then sometimes at different tables, in order to stir up more variety. Her friend Hertha had a long memory and was quick at calculating numbers, but she was also very competitive, a trait Alice had never liked. Her own mother had trained her that it was graceful to yield, not to compete. Hertha and Harold were both now gone, Harold of congestive heart failure and Hertha of a sort of incremental crumbling, ending in fatal pneumonia after she fell and broke her hip. Now Alice played with two women in their seventies, Jackie and Susanne, both the age of Alice's son Mark, whom she'd lost in the Vietnam War, and with Jack, who was her own age and as courtly as a suitor. He always pulled the chair out for her and offered to fetch her some tea, the almost courting of old age.

A week ago, Alice had played a surreptitious game of dominoes in Jackie's apartment, and Susanne had brought a small box of See's chocolates for a snack. She didn't feel strong enough to manage that now, and her cough was getting more annoying. Alice sank into the sofa pillow on the left side of her bed and stared at the familiar assembly of family photographs atop her dresser. Mark was nineteen, proud and clear-eyed under the brim of his Army helmet. Harold and she posed stiffly in their wedding portrait from 1951, she with her long veil draped artfully around the hem of her white gown, and Harold in a tie and black suit, carnation in his lapel, looking sternly at the camera, as was expected in those days. To the right was Carol, in a hinged grouping of photos, one of her in her nurse's uniform at her graduation, another with her own husband and two children, all grinning at the camera, another of Carol holding her first newborn Sean, and another of her second, Shirley, tap dancing in a competition. Carol had offered to come out this week to stay with Alice, but with the quarantine, no outside visitors were allowed.

Usually at this time, after dinner, Alice watched a movie on the television, but nothing appealed to her on the regular schedule and she was too tired to get up and insert one of her favorite DVDs. Without undressing, she pushed the sofa pillow aside, slunk under the covers and dozed off. She woke again a few hours later and was able to get herself to the little bathroom to pee. She thought then that she should take off her clothes and put on her nightgown, but doing so seemed like too much effort. Besides, she was feeling chilly and the sweater over her blouse helped.

When she woke again, a bright light shone in from the east window. She had failed to pull the blinds last night and a bright stream of light splayed diagonally across the room. Her clock read 8:20, almost too late for breakfast. Alice got up unsteadily with the full intention of washing her face, changing her clothes and walking down to the buffet, but it was too much of an effort, so she phoned the dining area and asked to have her breakfast delivered. The dining attendant – Alice thought it was Graciela – asked, "Are you not feeling well?"

"Just a little tired, honey, can you have my breakfast brought up?"

"The rule is that you should schedule it in advance, but if you tell me what you want, I'll have it brought up for you."

Alice ordered orange juice, corn flakes and milk, a bowl of prunes and a cup of Lipton's tea, and then she sank back under the covers. She really was feeling cold, despite the sun in the apartment. She heard the knock on the door a few minutes later but could not bring herself to answer it. Thankfully, the attendant – this time it was George from the kitchen – brought in the tray and laid it before her on the bed.

"Not up to par this morning, Miss Alice?"

"I guess not, George. Can you bring lunch today also?"

"Sure thing." He smiled at her and left.

Alice drank all of her orange juice, but it made her even more chilled, so she focused on drinking her tea and taking a bite of her cereal every few minutes. She wondered if she would be able to finish her meal and if she could carry the tray away, but her thoughts drifted. When she opened her eyes again, the staff nurse Ellen stood before her, wearing a face mask and plastic gloves.

Ellen took a thermometer out of her pocket and thrust it gently under Alice's tongue. Alice had to concentrate to hold the thermometer long enough under her tongue. When Ellen looked at it, her face revealed no reaction, but she excused herself to the hallway, where she called for direction.

The next time Alice looked up, her tray was gone, but a team of first responders rolled a cart up to her bed. Each of them wore the white plastic suits Alice had seen on the television when the coronavirus had struck China and then Italy. "We need to take you to the hospital."

Alice was the first to contract coronavirus in her retirement community.

———•◦•———

In Tahar ben Jelloun's *The Blinding Absence of Light,* twenty young Moroccan soldiers who had followed orders without knowing they were participating in a failed coup were sentenced to indefinite punishment in an unlighted, secret underground prison in the Moroccan desert. The prisoners had no way of knowing where they were or how long they would be kept there. Their existence and location were known only to their reluctant keepers and to an unseen commanding officer. Plagued by moldy, meager food, no blankets or beds, and even an infestation of scorpions, only a few of them survived the ordeal. They organized themselves with assignments: one man had an inborn sense of time and his task was to announce the time and date each day; another recited their collective prayers; and another became the designated story-teller. Each day he would conjure tales that he recited in the night hours. One of their cohort started to rave furiously during the sessions, and he eventually succumbed to his madness and died, leaving the survivors to their stories. Miraculously, word got out to Amnesty International and four of the men lived to emerge into daylight and tell their ghastly tale.

———•◦•———

As soon as they re-entered the limits of Milano *citta*, Fran and Liliana found almost no traffic, at least by comparison to normal. *Normal,* Fran thought, a new normal was upon them. Today they could have found parking on the street, but they eased into their space in the garage. With

Liliana carrying her own pack, they managed to unload the car in just one trip upstairs to their apartment. Liliana unpacked her red backpack, put her clothes back in the drawer and hung the pack on its hook while her mama cooked a simple *spaghetti e olio* meal in their little kitchen.

"Why did we come back so soon?" The question would not go away.

"We had to return to our own bubble," Fran began.

Liliana tilted her head inquisitively. "Is this a story or real?"

"You decide. Remember 'Jack and the Beanstalk' and the giant at the top of the beanstalk?" Liliana nodded.

"Is this a good giant or a wicked giant?"

"This is a wise giant who wants to take care of all the people inside Milano." Dipping an imaginary stick into an imaginary bottle, Fran waved her arm to spread bubbles from the stick. As she did so, Liliana sneezed so violently her head jolted. Involuntarily, Fran brought her hand to Liliana's forehead, as though to wipe aside her hair but actually to feel for fever. Her head felt normal.

"Your sneeze broke all the bubbles so I have to start over." Fran dipped again and this time swept a long, slow arc over her head. "This is the giant's very, very big bubble. He is blowing it over all of Milano, to keep us all inside."

"Why does he want to keep us inside?"

"To protect us."

"From what?" Fran paused.

"From the bad air outside. The giant saw the black smoke from a huge factory and wanted to keep it outside of Milano, to keep our buildings clean and our lungs clear with good air."

"How long will the bubble last?"

"That's a surprise. Want some gelato?" Fran leapt to the freezer to see what they had. "*Cioccolata o nocciola?*"

<hr>

Georgea had a new client on her calendar for tomorrow, which was to be the first day that Magnin and Fourier LLP was to operate virtually from its San Francisco law office. Georgea had a personal rule that all first meetings with clients were to be in person, so that she could see every nuance in facial expression, every shift in body posture, every hesitation and change in tone. She wanted for her clients to have a feel for her as well, in a way that a telephone or even Skype call could not. In a personal meeting, she could sense whether she and her prospective client would be a good fit, in a way that a remote connection could not afford. So she telephoned Janice Goodman and explained the new firm quasi-quarantine procedures. Janice immediately asked whether Georgea could come to her home. They both knew that Janice's husband Don would not be home, since Janice had already informed Georgea's assistant he was in assisted living in a local retirement community. Georgea immediately agreed; Janice had herself suggested what Georgea would have proposed. Besides, it would give Georgea the bonus of seeing where Janice lives. Before the meeting Georgea emailed Janice the intake form she always used for new clients; besides basic contact information, it included the names and birthdates of any children and the prospective client's own birth date. It continued to astonish Georgea how much she could read about a person based on whether their actual and visual age coincided. Many people aged prematurely from the emotional lives they had led; some appeared younger than their actual age. Yet another data point for the observant attorney.

Janice answered the door of her luxurious Kentfield home, ushering Georgea to a study lined with bookshelves and to a rosewood table with two upright matching rosewood chairs with dark green velvet seats. Georgea declined her offer of tea or coffee. Janice moved with the grace of an athletic forty-year-old as she pulled out her own chair. She brushed back her luxuriant auburn hair and donned eyeglasses. Her skin and hazel eyes gleamed as healthily as her hair. She wore leg-hugging jeans over her slim legs and a pale blue sweater. Georgea had to glance again at the intake sheet and could not quite believe that Janice was fifty-four. "Are we alone in the house?" Georgea asked, knowing Janice had a teen-aged son and wanting to ensure their privacy. Janice assured her that her son was at school and had his cello lessons afterward; he would not be home for another two hours.

"How can I help you?" Georgea began with the most open-ended question she could summon, in order to let her prospective client shape the first meeting.

"I don't know if I want a divorce, but I want to know what would be involved if that happened."

Georgea assured Janice that such foresight was always wise and would afford her the opportunity to make a more informed decision, whatever it would be.

"I am afraid my husband will divorce me, and I want to know if he can do it and what the grounds are." Georgea explained that in California anyone could obtain a divorce simply by checking a box asserting 'irreconcilable differences.' Divorce was automatic and no evidence of fault was permitted.

"What makes you think he will seek a divorce?"

"Four years ago Don had a stroke that left him with no use of his right side at all. His right arm -- which was his dominant arm -- hangs limply and he no longer has the use of his right leg. He used to be able to walk with a walker, but he no longer can. I was away at work when his stroke hit, and he lay without any remedy for more than an hour; by lucky chance a Viacom repairman came by appointment, let himself in by prior arrangement, found him and called 911. So vital recovery opportunity was lost in the first hour. He had aggressive physical and speech therapy, but it was of little use. He can talk, but only slowly and it's difficult to understand what he tries to say.

"For the first two years I took off work and tended to him myself. We've been together twenty years now, and I did what anyone would want their spouse to do. I helped him in and out of bed, I dressed and fed him, I took him to all his medical appointments, I did all the shopping and cooking and took care of our son Adam. I retired from my own job – I was a hospital nurse – because there was no way I could manage working on top of all I was doing at home. Don used to be a gourmet cook and avid golf player. Now he was idle at home."

"That must have been very difficult for you," Georgea inserted.

"Not difficult -- it was impossible. After two years I realized I would go mad if I had to continue like that. " Janice paused, sighing slightly, and continued. There was no self-pity or resentment in her voice. "I began to speak with him about moving him to a residential treatment center where professionals could care for him. I will never forget the look he gave me when I first brought it up. 'After all I've done for you?' was what his eyes said, though he never said it out loud.

"I was married once before, to an alcoholic who sometimes hit me. It took me more than a year to convince myself that I had to go it alone. Only after I left did I realize the freedom from sex on demand and the generalized fear in that marriage. Don was the director of the hospital where I worked; when he took an interest in me, I had to leave that hospital and find work somewhere else. But he has always been caring, generous and wise; he was the one who made all the important decisions in our family and they were good decisions. I have always trusted and relied on him. After he retired – he's twenty years older – he began to make all of our dinners at home, which was a huge treat.

"When I finally decided we needed outside help, he insisted he could stay at home and have nursing care on almost a 24/7 basis. And we did that for nearly another year. But even managing the nursing schedule, with vacations, illnesses and other interruptions, and still being the only functioning parent, was difficult. I began to research placements where he could get the care he needed and I could begin to have a life again. At my insistence, we went for an interview at The Evergreen Community, and I persuaded him to move there. Fortunately, it's only a twenty-minute drive from our home, and at first I visited him every day, in the afternoon, just before I had to pick up Adam from school.

"Do you still visit him every day?" Georgea asked, realizing this was the time Janice described as her typical visiting time.

"No, I can't visit him now at all; The Evergreen is on lockdown and no visitors are allowed." Janice took another deep breath. "But even before the lockdown, I was falling off. It became every other day and shorter visits; I had to make up news to give him and his inability to speak, or his not wanting to speak much, doesn't keep a conversation going. It's a chore now and he knows it, I'm sure."

"How is his mental functioning?"

"Oh, he's just as sharp as he ever was; he reads several books a week, keeps up with politics; he voted this month -- for Warren, dear man; but he doesn't seem to want to talk to me."

"Does he have other friends where he lives?"

"Sometimes when I visit I see him playing chess with another man who lives there. And occasionally I interrupt a visit from one of the women who live there. They are all closer to his age or even much older. They have many ninety-year-olds at The Evergreen." At this, Janice smiled ironically.

"Do you want to divorce him?" Georgea asked in a very soft voice.

"I don't think I could do that; I could never forgive myself. I feel responsible for him and doing that would be totally disloyal."

"Do you want him to divorce you?" Janice gave her a fleeting, penetrating glance.

"What would happen to me if he did?"

Georgea began the list of questions about their assets and income. The Goodmans' biggest asset was this home, now worth several millions and free of the mortgage that had existed at the time of the marriage. Janice knew that Don had owned it since before their marriage, but didn't know if title remained only in Don's name or whether she had been added to title. No, the home had never been refinanced; the original mortgage had such a low interest rate. Janice and Don lived from Don's generous hospital pension and medical care provisions. Janice was still licensed as a nurse but didn't want to try to return to work until after Adam left for college. "He starts at Oberlin this fall," she added with undisguised pride.

Georgea explained that Janice's interest in the home depended in part on how title is held and how much equity was built up during this marriage, that the pension was community property to the extent earned during this marriage, that spousal support would depend on the amount of Don's and her incomes and would likely last for an indefinite period, but that child support would end with Adam's upcoming graduation unless Don agreed to support him during his college years.

"How long could I continue to live in this home? Does it have to be sold?"

"Do you want to keep living here?"

"Until Adam leaves for college, for sure. After that, I don't know."

"Well, you don't have to decide now." Georgea paused before broaching the next subject.

"You know, if you are worried about Don thinking you are abandoning him during this corona crisis, you could send him cards or notes every day. That might make him feel more cared for."

The barest downward tilt of Janice's lips provided her answer.

"I suppose I could."

Janice was agitated after Georgea left, not quite aware that Georgea had provoked her to consider whether to cultivate or terminate her marriage. Thinking tea would calm her, she put a bag into her mug and stared out the window, waiting for the water to heat in the kettle on an unlit burner. She stood at the window for some minutes before realizing the tea kettle was cold.

━━◆◆◆━━

Helen, who was Fran's mother and, more happily, Lili's grandmother, was to have flown from her home in San Francisco, where Fran had grown up, to Milan to help out. Helen made her reservations in the brief interval between Milan shutting down its schools and Milan shutting its own municipal boundaries, and before Italy itself was shuttered to international travel. Fran had been in tears in her Face Time call with Helen when she'd begged her to come help with Lili. Helen had eagerly agreed to come.

Unraveling her travel plans proved far more difficult than making them in the first place. She'd booked on Alitalia, using Orbitz to get a competitive fare, and it had cost her less than usual. More a loving grandmother than a lover of Italy, Helen had become a frequent flyer to Milan. Going to the Orbitz website, Helen logged in the itinerary number, readily found the scheduled flight, and pressed the button to manage the flight, then the 'cancel flight' option. At that point, the website announced that something had temporarily gone wrong in the system and that the user should try again later, which of course Helen did three times before resorting to the 800 number provided. After the usual automated telephone prompts, a recording advised her that due to the unusual call volume, the website would be a better remedy and not to wait on line unless the caller's intended travel was scheduled for the next seven days. Helen waited on line for forty-seven minutes before giving up. The next day she called the Orbitz number a little after four a.m., when she awoke and could not go back to sleep. After following all the prompts and putting her cell phone on speaker, she got dressed, carried the phone into the kitchen, where she made coffee, prepared and ate her yogurt and granola, fetched the *San Francisco Chronicle* from the front door and read it, checked her wait time on the phone which then read 1:37, and began the daily crossword. At almost precisely 2:00 wait time, a thickly-accented woman's voice came on and Helen responded with the eagerness of discovering life on a desert island. The voice, after listening to Helen's request to cancel, asked Helen very politely to wait a bit more since the voice needed to check with Alitalia on their refund policy. Helen's reasonable fare was explicitly nonrefundable, but she had also purchased travel insurance, so she waited, with the optimism of early morning, while she continued to do the crossword. The polite voice returned after ten minutes to inform her that, since her travel was not between the interval of February 25 and March 8, no refund would be provided.

"But the whole country is shut down!"

When Helen asked to use her travel insurance, the voice became even more polite and informed her that such insurance covered the traveler's own illness but not 'the present circumstances'.

"So there's no insurance for pandemics," Helen burst out sarcastically.

"No, ma'am," the voice responded with a musical lilt.

Helen hung up the phone before starting to snarl at the poor operator whose unhappy job it was to deal with thousands of customers like her.

Boccaccio wrote *The Decameron* in Florence in the middle 1300s, just after the outbreak of the Black Death that killed nearly one hundred thousand Florentines. The plague began with swellings in the groin and under the arms, *gavoccioli* or *buboni,* which grew to the size of apples and then spread throughout the body. In Boccaccio's own words, the streets were littered with corpses, many of them with the telltale black spots that appeared after the *buboni.*

The work begins in these words: "To have compassion for those who suffer is a human quality which everyone should possess…. In my suffering, the pleasant conversation and the admirable consolation of a friend on a number of occasions gave me much relief, and I am firmly convinced I should now be dead if it had not been for that."

The hundred stories of *The Decameron* are the ultimate pleasure distraction for the ten young, privileged Florentines who retreat to one another's palaces in the countryside, where they walk the opulent gardens, dine luxuriously, play music for one another and tell the tales for which the book is famous. Some humorous, some tragic, the tales elaborate on love, its fixations and risks, the hypocrisy of proscriptions of the church, and the pleasures of the body.

In the first week of March, Esta's husband Mark died of the coronavirus in the local hospital near Sacramento. The hospital took over completely the burial arrangements, not allowing Esta any access to his body. He'd been hospitalized for only four days, and she had gone home just to fetch his IPad and electric shaver. When she returned to the hospital, she was not allowed into his room. A flustered nurse wearing a mask and gloves directed her to wait in a private room until a senior physician came to give her the news. He also told her that she herself had tested positive. He directed her to return directly home and to stay there for the next fourteen days. For some moments, she just looked at him blankly, wondering if she had heard him correctly, if this was real.

Esta and Mark had been home less than two weeks after debarking from a cruise to Mexico, where for the first time in two years they had felt carefree, drinking margaritas and sunbathing on deck, sleeping deeply and without anxiety. Two years earlier, their home and entire tiny town of Paradise in Northern California had burned to the ground. They had escaped in their car, literally racing the flames. The Mexico cruise marked their return to some sanity, some leisure.

Esta looked down at the IPad in her left hand and tried to wipe a smudge off its surface. Her car keys clattered to the floor while she was wiping. She had wet her fingers at her lips, wondering after the fact if she were breaking some hospital contamination rule. Mark was gone. He wouldn't need his IPad. She picked up her car keys and stared at them in her hand. Drive home? What else was there for her to do? She continued to sit for some moments longer, staring blankly at the large beach photo on the facing wall. Was that in Mexico? It reminded her of Mexico, wherever it actually was. She and Mark had walked barefoot ashore for a beach barbeque one late afternoon, relishing the warm sand on their feet as much as they had the massage in their room earlier that day.

She got up hesitantly, as if remembering how to walk, then gained purpose as she headed to the elevator and to the garage. She remembered to insert her parking stub into the machine and pay the tab before returning to her car. Mark's baseball hat lay on the seat next to her, the cruise line symbol at its front. She flipped it upside down and started the car, pulling out of the garage and heading home by muscle memory. About halfway home, Esta became aware of the loud vibrating noise of a helicopter. She glanced about, wondering why it sounded so loud, so close, then jumped in her seat as she spotted it looming low directly ahead of her, with its red lights flashing. It turned broadside to her so she could read that it was a police helicopter. A voice blared from it, instructing her by name to head directly home and not to leave once she got there. Alarmed, she pulled into the slow lane and drove more slowly, wondering if somehow she were going to be arrested. In her driveway, a police car was parked adjacent to her space in the garage. As she opened the garage door, two police officers got out, each of them wearing white plastic suits and protruding masks that made them look like zombies. They directed her to stay at home without going out at all for any reason for the next two weeks. They left in a hurry, no doubt leery of exposing themselves any more than necessary, not bothering to tell her how she should get groceries or prescriptions or anything else. She glanced at her front door, which bore a sign. It warned that her home was quarantined; no one could enter or leave it for the next two weeks.

⸺•◦•⸺

On Monday, March 16, 2020, Israel's Prime Minister Benjamin Netanyahu announced that he could trace all those who had come into contact with persons who are carriers of COVID-19. He authorized Shin Bet, the country's internal security agency, to use its vast network of private cellphone data it has been collecting since 2002 to locate and notify private citizens who had come into contact with COVID carriers. If Esta, now confined to her Sacramento home, lived in Haifa, the national system could track through their cellphones all those persons who had come into contact with her in, say, the last two weeks. All such persons would be notified by text on their conveniently tracked cellphone that they had been exposed and that they should immediately isolate themselves for the next fourteen days. A failure to obey could be punished by prison sentences of up to six months. Suppose the Haifa widow who is Esta's counterpart doubts the source of the ominous text. Whom should she notify? Is it real or the prank of a hacker? To whom is she even permitted to speak? Is someone listening in on her conversation? Is it legal? Netanyahu was potentially ousted by a vote on March 2 and the Israeli Parliament that supervises his actions was dismissed December 19, 2019. It did not vote on this action. Did the Haifa widow even know her cellphone had been tracked since 2002? Is she entitled to any privacy during or before this crisis?

No one can touch or embrace either Esta or her Haifa counterpart. No funeral service can be conducted. She cannot sit *shiva* because groups of people are not allowed. There is no comfort for her.

⸺◦●◦⸺

On January 25, 1920, Sigmund Freud's 27-year-old daughter Sophie died of the Spanish flu in Hamburg, where she had been living with her husband and two young children. Freud wrote to a friend two days later that she "had been snatched away in the midst of glowing health, from a full and active life as a competent mother and loving wife, all in four or five days, as though she had never existed. Although we had been worried about her for a couple of days, we had nevertheless been hopeful; it is so difficult to judge from a distance. And this distance must remain distance; we were not able to travel at once, as we had intended, after the first alarming news; there was no train, not even for an emergency. The undisguised brutality of our time is weighing heavily upon us…. The happiness existed exclusively within them; outwardly there was war, conscription, wounds, the depletion of their resources, but they had remained courageous and gay. I work as much as I can, and am thankful for the diversion. The loss of a child seems to be a serious, narcissistic injury; what is known as mourning will probably follow only later."

———•◦•———

"Mom, look at this." Fran interrupted her FaceTime face to play a video Fran had recorded of the front of the apartment building facing her own apartment. Most of the front windows were open and people hung out of them, smiling and singing.

"It started with the national anthem," Fran explained. "What they're singing now is "*Oh, Mia Bella Madunina,*" a song about our city's pride. "Oh, and there's a violin player. I didn't know I had such a neighbor." Fran shifted the IPad to show her mother the corner window, from which she could hear a skillful classical refrain.

"This is happening all over – isn't it great?" Fran stopped the scan of the apartment façade, and Helen could see Fran's beaming face.

Helen chortled her appreciation. "You Milanese are dealing with this better than we are here. I'd go crazy if I couldn't get a daily bike ride or walk."

Fran gasped. "Tell me you're not going out. Please tell me that. You're part of the most vulnerable population, and I don't want to lose my mother. Can't you think of Lili? You need to stay healthy for her. No, no, no, no!"

There was no opening for Helen to say anything and nothing she could say to alter her daughter's opinion. To her daughter, she was old, irredeemably old, and frail because she was old. Helen could not see herself preserved in her home as if in formaldehyde.

———•◦•———

One of Don's daily visitors during the lockdown was the Evergreen's social worker Erythea. Part of him bristled at the supposed expectation that he would somehow flounder if he couldn't have outside visitors, especially his wife. Part of him welcomed Erythea's warm smile and beautiful face. She was as physically captivating as her name, with ringlets of long dark brown hair and expressive eyebrows, and he smiled involuntarily each time she showed her face, even though he knew his smile was lopsided due to the muscle loss on his right side. Besides, he had been too well trained in his years at the hospital to make any comment that could be construed as a come-on or sexual harassment.

Standing at the foot of his bed, Erythea asked Don if he had heard from Janice since the lockdown. He told her Janice called him every day, at the same hour, four-thirty. "Just before she starts to make dinner for herself and Adam." He glanced at his watch. "Should be soon." Erythea excused herself, telling him she would check back with him later. It happened so quickly he couldn't frame the words, "won't take long."

Today it was Adam on the other end of the line at 4:30, sounding dazed and reporting that officially there would be no more school for at least the next month, "maybe all the rest of the year." Don tried to visualize Adam's face. He asked whether classes would be held online so that Adam would not lose the semester. Adam seemed more concerned with his cello lessons.

"Where's Mom?"

"At the store. She tried to go this morning, but the line at Safeway was too long so she decided to go later when she figured more people would be home cooking." Don immediately thought Janice had some other kind of errand in mind, not one he would discuss with his son.

"Okay. Ask her to call me when she gets home, or after dinner if that's more convenient."

Ever since she'd deposited him into this place, Don had wondered whether Janice had a lover. It would be only too convenient, with Adam away at school most of the day and Janice no longer working. In the early days, he used to wonder who it was, conjuring up suspects among their mutual friends. He would even inquire obliquely about some of the suspects when Janice visited, but she never seemed to have any current information about them.

Now the rules were different, since only this week she and everyone else in the six Bay Area counties were directed to 'shelter in place.' For him, it had no effect, since he couldn't go anywhere if he tried, but for her he knew the rule would rankle. She would be the nemesis vector, the one who would spread the contagion by refusing to be confined.

Janice wasn't old enough to remember, but in the late fifties, his parents had built a bomb shelter in their back yard, in case either the Soviets or the Americans were crazy or panicked enough to drop a nuclear bomb on the other. He was only a kid then, maybe ten years old, but the project had seemed insane to him even then. For how long would they have good air to breathe? Would their gas masks have any effect at all against nuclear fallout? And could his parents, who always bickered, last more than a few days in their 12 x 20-foot shelter? He remembered television programs at the time, fictionalizing fights among neighbors who did and did not have their own shelters. And the film "On the Beach," where survivors lasted longer in Australia because the poisonous fallout took longer to reach them.

Don's dinner tray was delivered with predictable regularity at a few minutes after five, in a brown plastic bowl with an oval cover that reminded him only too well of the hospital where he had worked for nineteen years. Tonight it was a thick slice of pink salmon, with a lemon wedge, springs of asparagus and rice with mushrooms, not a bad combination – and a sliver of lemon pie. He had trained himself to eat with his left hand but he needed assistance to slice his asparagus. Rather than wait, he squeezed the lemon over the salmon and flaked a piece of it with his fork, bringing it to his mouth without dropping it. He stabbed his fork into one end of the asparagus and lifted the whole stalk to his face, biting the soft end first and working his way up the stalk.

At that moment, Erythea re-entered his room with her brilliant smile. He dropped the stalk, his face reddening immediately.

"I'm sorry for interrupting your dinner," she began, and he assured her she was welcome. "I have to bring you further news of our quarantine," she said ruefully. "Starting tomorrow, you can't have any resident visitors at all, not even at a six-foot distance. So, I'm sorry that your chess games must stop for a while, and your visits with Hilda."

He noted that she knew his patterns only too well. "What about yourself?"

"I can still see residents, but only from a six-foot distance." He wondered if his relief showed. "Is there anything I can bring you, now that you will have even more time on your hands?"

"Books from the library?"

"It's closed, but let me check. What do you want?"

"Camus' *The Plague*." She looked at him quizzically.

"Really?"

"Yes."

⸺◦●◦⸺

Georgea sat across from her husband Eric the following morning, each of them reading the news on their IPads.

"Can you believe this?" Eric began. These words had become a daily joke between them, since each day brought news they couldn't have imagined before. "Gun sales have surged all over the country, especially in the states hardest hit by the virus. There are long lines outside gun stores, especially those in Asian-American communities in Southern California. And in the Midwest, people are frightened people will rob them for food. And, get this – Donald Trump, Jr. tweeted, 'You don't need it, till you need it,' taunting Democrats who are buying guns for the first time."

Georgea sat still listening, allowing this news to sink in while her professional mind zipped to work.

"We're going to see more domestic violence cases," she pronounced, "as people are stuck home with each other and can't get any release outdoors. With more guns, it'll be worse."

Eric paused to give her a long look.

"It's funny where your mind goes. You might have said, 'we're going to see a population surge, like we did after the New York City blackout', but you went immediately to DV."

"Well, you're the one who brought up guns." She gave him a sudden huge conspiratorial smile. "That doesn't exactly conjure up erotic thoughts."

Now he grinned also. "I promise I won't read the news to you in bed."

⸻ ⬩◉⬩ ⸻

On March 18, Ralph got up at five rather than his usual five thirty, in order to be able to vote before he began work today. He had arranged the day before with his construction crew that he would probably arrive late and the other four men knew exactly how to begin the day. His plan was to arrive at his local polling place -- which had been his high school in Cincinnati twenty years earlier -- when the polls opened at six thirty, so as not to get caught in a long line and expose himself to a crowd of people. He'd heard on the radio the day before that the courts had overruled Governor DeVine's decision to close the polls. Ralph kicked himself for not having had the foresight to vote by mail, but he agreed with the governor's reasoning that residents should not have to choose between exercising their right to vote and jeopardizing their health. He couldn't afford to lose work for this odd virus that was circulating.

He parked in the high school lot, remembering the old Chevie his dad had allowed him to drive to school in his senior year and all the other benefits he'd enjoyed by having the freedom of a car. When he got to the entrance, he was happily surprised to see only three other people at the door, but all of them were reading the sign that said the governor had closed the polls. He silently praised the governor for having the guts to buck the courts that had ordered him to keep the polls open. Heading back to his car, he glanced at his watch and was pleased to note he would still make it to work on time.

After work that day, he saw on Fox News that the Ohio Supreme Court had upheld the governor's decision to postpone the election. As a Democrat in a Republican community, he understood and agreed with much of his neighbors' concerns even as he differed from them on others. He worried that the Democrats would put up a candidate whose progressive plans, like universal health care, would only frighten mainstream Democrats.

He had watched several of the overcrowded debates with increasing anxiety. Biden struggled to get a word in edgewise, Sanders barked, Warren bragged about taking the bark off one billionaire, Klobuchar had a snarky smile, and Buttigieg made sense but looked like a high school kid himself. Besides, he couldn't imagine the election of a gay man. Privately, Ralph had watched Mayor Pete's concession speech and admired his ten 'rules of the road': respect, belonging, truth, teamwork, boldness, responsibility, substance, discipline, excellence and joy. Ralph lived by these rules in supervising his team at work but he found it hard to imagine a political reality that lived by them. He would vote for Biden in the June 2 primary.

What had been a rich and unruly stew had quickly boiled down to a pale broth.

———•◦•◦•———

Arturo worried. As Marta handed him his usual breakfast plate of eggs and refried beans -- he had lately asked to skip the tortilla – she could tell he was distracted. Today was his birthday, and the family always celebrated it together at their restaurant in Novato, but now the restaurant was closed. Blinds down, a handwritten sign on the door in English and Spanish announced that Arturo's was closed until further notice.

Arturo broke the yolk on his eggs and took a few bites, but he had lost his appetite. Today he was 49, on the brink of what was now considered middle age but to him seemed old age. His father had died at 53 in Mexico, of lung cancer that Arturo suspected derived from pesticides on the fields he tended, and he had seemed old at the time. How would Arturo keep his family going? He and his younger brother Pedro ran the restaurant together, and each of their oldest sons worked there, as did seven others. Two of the workers were undocumented, by definition ineligible for unemployment or any other benefits, not to mention the obvious risk of being deported as a consequence of asking for any assistance.

He took a sip of his coffee, which had grown cold. He got up and put his cup into the microwave.

Marta came back into the kitchen, dressed as if for a picnic.

"Where are you going?" he asked.

"Where are *we* going is what you should ask. I just spoke to Pedro and Carla. We're going on a hike and a picnic, all of the family."

Arturo looked at her in disbelief. He hadn't even realized she had left the room. Now she had a plan for the whole family.

"Don't look at me like that. Just tell me where you want to go. We're all going."

Arturo had read of a beautiful picnic area at the top of a steep hike alongside a creek with waterfalls. He'd read a short description of it in the sports section of the *Chronicle* months ago and cut it out, intending to hike it some day when he had nothing better to do. To his surprise, he found the article right away, in a drawer with his jogging shorts. It was dated two years ago but also in March. Besides the beauty of the cascading creek, the article touted the wildflowers to be found in spring and the good exercise of the climb itself. He needed exercise these days.

Arturo called Pedro to confirm details. Each of them would drive their own car in a caravan, with Arturo in the lead. Pedro's son Carlo had already coordinated GPS directions with Arturo's son Beto on their cellphones, and their wives had decided on the food. In a burst of uncharacteristic optimism, Arturo threw on his long jogging shorts and a T-shirt, tying a sweatshirt over his shoulders. He tied the laces on his new hiking shoes that Marta had given him for Christmas but which had gone unused since then. The restaurant took up all his time and energy.

The drive was shorter than expected, and Carlo's directions were perfect. They parked at the edge of a lake. The two families bounded out of their respective cars and embraced each other. So much for 'social distancing', Arturo noted, but there had never been a time that the two families had not been together, either in their restaurant or at one another's homes, only two miles apart. The trailhead was well marked and the two brothers took off in the lead, determined to get some good exercise today. Behind them the two mothers herded the four youngest children. Surprisingly, Beto and Carlo lingered behind them all, bored with the idea of hiking and much more interested in their own private conversation, drowned by the loud music they played on speaker mode on their phones.

Determined to get a workout, Arturo tried to set a fast pace, but the stone steps were so steep that it was inherently slow going. Pedro matched his pace to his older brother by habit, and they spoke of how their families would make it financially in this odd time. Pedro's wife Carla was a hospital nurse, and, so long as she stayed well, her income was not threatened. But Arturo and Pedro's incomes depended entirely on the restaurant. Marta worked two jobs, one of them as a maid in a local retirement home and the other in the laundry of the hospital where Carla worked. Sometimes, when the restaurant was especially busy, she also pitched in there. Her income was also only as secure as her own health.

Pedro told Arturo that Carlo had come up with an idea for the restaurant to do take-out by online orders. As the younger brother, he'd been hesitant to bring up the subject, knowing that Arturo maintained some family machismo, but Arturo looked at him eagerly. He wondered how they could set it up. Pedro explained that Carlo was confident he could set up a web page that would keep them all in production, without violating any of the emergency restrictions.

Spurred by this idea, Arturo stepped up the pace, until they caught up with an older couple on the trail. Surprisingly, the two old gringos cheerfully stepped aside so that Arturo and Pedro could pass and resume their planning. By this time, their wives and children were far behind. Arturo found himself sweating and wished he had brought his sweatband. Soon they came to a turnout in the trail, where they could look up at a waterfall on their right. They stepped off the trail to wait for the rest of their families. They were silent, appreciating the plash of the water alongside them and the pink wildflowers blooming at their feet. The flowers had large clover-like leaves, and Arturo smiled, as if realizing good luck. The two old gringos again passed them, greeting them with smiles and comments on the beautiful day. Soon they heard jaunty rhythmic music that they knew came from Beto and Carlo, who caught up with them.

"Where are the others?" Arturo asked. When Beto reported they were far behind, he asked Carlo about the takeout idea. "Do you know how to set up a website?" Carlo, who had always had an affinity for electronics and was now studying electronic engineering at the community college, explained the idea in enough detail that Arturo was convinced he could do it. He offered to begin setting it up immediately, in consultation with Beto, who was more artistically inclined, and with Arturo as owner. Arturo beamed and hugged both young men.

By the time the women and younger children caught up with them, Arturo and Pedro were energized and eager to set out again, while the women admired the waterfall and caught their breath.

At the top, Arturo and Pedro sat down at a picnic table and waited for the rest of their family. The only other people up here were the two old gringos sitting at the only other picnic table, sipping water from their water bottles, and looking only a little tired. He speculated on how old they were, with their gray hair and wrinkled faces, but obviously fit. Probably in their seventies, he gauged, wondering if he would still have the capacity to hike at their age. In his present mood, he felt as if he would, he felt as if he would rescue his business too, and continue to support his family. He hadn't felt this good in weeks.

When the women caught up with them, they laid out sandwiches and oranges and chips on the table, even a bottle of red wine. Arturo walked over to the two tired gringos. They looked hungry. "We've got more than we can eat," he told them, holding out two of the plump sandwiches Marta had wrapped. They took the sandwiches eagerly, admitting they wished they had planned better. "Have one of these too," he offered, holding out one of the oranges Marta had packed. They grinned back at him as they took it.

Arturo's niece Sabrina stuck a candle into an orange, lit it with a match, and the whole family sang happy birthday to him, first in English, then in Spanish. The two gringos sang along. Arturo thanked Marta for bringing the whole family together once again, and she kissed him, whispering "*como siempre.*"

———•••———

Helen and Fran Face-Timed every day now at eight in the morning, which allowed Helen to get up and make herself coffee and Fran to leave Lili in front of a video before Fran began to make dinner for the two of them. Lili's father Gianlucca shopped groceries for them and sometimes stayed for dinner, but it was a complicated relationship for all three of them.

Helen had just finished her yogurt when her cellphone rang and she touched the button to see her daughter's face. Helen didn't have a chance to ask how Fran was doing; Fran burst into an agitated rant about how she couldn't take this any longer. Lili was bored and demanded to go outside. She saw her father come and go and couldn't understand why she couldn't go with him. Gianlucca's papers that allowed him out for grocery shopping did not extend to her address, only to his own, so Fran worried that he would get arrested.

"Do you believe that people are now calling the police when they see others out on the street!" Fran practically screeched.

Helen still had not uttered a single word. She knew she needed to let Fran rant until the spew of words sputtered to a halt. Fran wasn't even close to finishing. Helen wondered whether to suggest that Fran allow Lili to spend a few days with Gianlucca, or whether the suggestion would render her the opposition, since Helen knew Gianlucca had himself suggested this before. She waited with practiced patience until Fran wound down.

Finally Fran asked how Helen was doing. Without pausing to think, Fran revealed to her daughter that she had been taking exhilarating bike rides through Golden Gate Park and beyond, that the weather had been sunny and that daffodils were in bloom everywhere. Fran practically screamed at her, 'how can you be going out? You're part of the vulnerable population! I can't bear the thought of you getting ill!'

This tirade had occurred before, and was happening again now only because Helen had forgotten to edit herself. There was no point in telling Fran that exercising in the open air was a vital part of what kept her going.

⬥

By the end of March, tracking citizens for the coronavirus also proved contagious on a worldwide basis. While Israel's Netanyahu proposed tracking people's movement from data secretly collected all along, Germany circulated a survey on whether citizens wanted the country to track people's movements. Various European Union countries were developing applications to use in conjunction with cellphone tracking information to enable anyone on request to learn whether and where he or she had encountered someone afflicted with the virus. South Korea was already collecting data from cellphones as to the movements and contacts of those carrying the virus. In some places, penalties were imposed for movement of people quarantined in place because of COVID-19. Personal cellphones would become the replacement leg bracelets on parolees, the radio collars of endangered species. Any movement outside one's residence would become a traceable line. The term contact tracing entered the vocabulary as one of the defenses against the new virus.

⬥

Marta came home at six one evening, exhausted after her shift at the retirement home. Arturo, Pedro and Carlo bent over Carlo's big screen computer with their heads tilted together. All she could think of was their violating social distancing, which was now rigorously enforced at the retirement home. Every employee had to fill out a form at the beginning of each shift, confirming that she did not have a fever or any other sign of respiratory disease, that she would remain masked and gloved at work and keep a distance of at least six feet from everyone else. Arturo looked up at her, beaming.

"I think we got it," he announced. "Carlo has us up and running for ordering take-out from the restaurant. Now we just have to organize the kitchen."

"How're you going to keep everyone six feet apart in that small kitchen?" She knew she was throwing a damp towel over the whole operation, but she had seen the hearses line up at the hospital when she left early this morning to start her second job at the Evergreen. "People are dying."

Arturo got up and put his arms around her, knowing she was beat.

"Sit down, Cara, I'll reheat some enchiladas for you." He bustled efficiently through the kitchen, picking a chicken enchilada off a platter onto her plate, adding beans and rice to the plate and depositing it into the microwave while he fetched salad from the refrigerator. He placed a small bowl of her favorite salsa verde next to her place and took a fork and knife from the drawer.

"Seriously," she persisted. "If any one of us gets sick, we're all cooked."

She caught sight of Beto smirking behind his hand at her unintentional pun. She might have lashed out at him, but by this time Arturo had put the plate of her own favorite comfort food in front of her, and she began to eat without another word.

⎯⎯◄●►⎯⎯

Erythea put on her hospital mask and blue plastic gloves before entering Don's room. Under the new rules, she could not even touch him, even with the gloves, and she knew well from all their prior meetings how much Don craved being touched. She would often lay a hand on his shoulder or touch his hand in the course of their talking sessions together, and she always leaned over to hug him before she left his room. Once she had even kissed him on the cheek, not something she would do professionally, but it had just happened as they hugged. Another time – and this made her smile every time she remembered it – a big lock of her hair had fallen into his open mouth and got a bit tangled as he struggled to say something. After that she had carefully pulled her hair back before leaning down to hug him, or piled her hair on top of her head with a barrette.

Don appeared to be napping, and Erythea sat down to see if he would awaken. This was their scheduled talk therapy hour, and he was a man of disciplined habit. In repose, his face loosened some of its habitual lines, and his jowls hung like empty saddlebags astride his head. His forehead looked like that of a much younger man, with prominent eyes, strong horizontal eyebrows nearly touching at the center, a smooth Greek nose and full lips with a marked oval dip under his nose. She had an innate bias for full lips and distaste for straight thin lips, as if the shape of one's lips denoted one's level of passion. Elissa had gorgeous full lips, so rounded there were almost no corners at either side. Erythea folded her arms around herself involuntarily. How long would it be until she and Elissa could hold each other again?

Elissa was stuck in Genoa. She'd been there for two weeks for painting lessons, and the plan had been for Erythea to join her the day after tomorrow. They'd never been apart this long in all the time they'd been together, some three years now. Erythea smiled despite herself to recall how much they had lived the stereotype about gay women: 'what do gay women do on a second date? Move in.'

Erythea touched people by instinct, Elissa by training. Elissa was a gifted physical therapist, whose touch could identify hidden sources of pain and relieve them by deep probing. At this strange moment in time, what Erythea missed most of all was the way she and Elissa spooned each other at night, the comfort of each other's warmth and the rhythm of soft breathing.

Erythea glanced over at Don, who was still asleep, also breathing in a slow, gentle rhythm, and at her watch. She was twenty minutes into their hour and much more inclined to continue to sit here and ruminate than to do any of her other assigned tasks. When the hour ended, she would join the kitchen staff to help deliver bagged meals to each of the residents. Not only did this delivery task take up gaps in what was usually her time to counsel groups of residents, it also enabled her to gauge the residents' frame of mind in the minute it took to hand over the bagged food.

Don stirred suddenly and a smile flitted across half of his face. What a strange divide his stroke had caused. Seated at his left side, the side he could still use, she noted how handsome he was when he smiled.

Erythea shifted in her seat, straightening her purple tunic as she did so and glancing down at it and the matching dark leggings. Until last night the new tunic and leggings, a special purchase for a treasured trip, had sat inside her packed suitcase. Last night she had torn everything out of the suitcase, lecturing herself that she had held onto this dream for too long. With all the strictness she could muster, she put away all of the suitcase contents and then shoved the suitcase back into the closet where she could not see it. Her passport and Euros went back into the safe. Only after she had rid herself of all physical evidence of this thwarted vacation did she allow herself to go back onto the website of the hotel Elissa had reserved for them in Camogli. Pouring a bit of salt into the wound, she looked at the palm trees silhouetted against the Mediterranean, the turquoise pool and orange umbrellas below at the seaside. The hotel had denied their request for refund but had permitted them credit for their payment against a future date, which granted only distant hope.

The more important issue was how to get Elissa back home. Not only was it difficult to get a flight out of Italy back to the U.S., but even when they found one, Elissa would also have to quarantine for two weeks under terms not yet determined. Elissa had been able to remain at the simple hotel that had been the base for her painting classes, even though she could no longer go outside to paint. But could she stay well? The hotel had closed its dining room and reverted to room service only.

Another glance at her watch told Erythea it was time for her to go to the dining room for her own rounds. Changing gloves as she entered the dining room to pick up a cart with meals for one of the resident floors, she told herself to stop thinking about Elissa. Now was the time for her to be present, really present, for the residents, and try to discern if anyone needed help. Susan took the dinners for herself and her husband with good cheer, trying to engage Erythea in conversation. Simon, an edgy widower whom she knew kept mostly to himself, did not answer the door after several sets of knocks, so she left the bag with his food in front of his door. As she approached Ed and Jerry's door, she overheard them laughing together from deep inside. Their TV was on, and they probably could not even hear her knocks, so she left their bags in front of their door. But Lena in the next apartment called 'coming' as Erythea knocked and took a long time to open the door. When the door swung slowly open, Lena stood in a loosely tied robe and nightgown, leaning against the wall. 'I'm not sure I can carry it, dear, can you put it on my table?' Erythea slipped passed Lena in the hall, maintaining such distance as she could, put the bag on a table littered with napkins, the dirty plate from lunch, and an open magazine. Lena apologized for her messy table. When Erythea asked her how she was managing, Lena admitted, without looking up, 'not too well'. At last she glanced up at Erythea and asked, "What am I going to do?" Erythea promised to call her after she finished her round of meal delivery, closed the door gently and made a mental note to talk to the clinic about Lena.

———◦●◦———

Simon heard the dinner bag dropped outside his door, but he waited until he thought the deliverer had moved on before he opened the door. He was too furious at being locked into his room to talk to anyone, and whoever delivered the meal was not to blame. He slammed the door accidentally as he retrieved his dinner bag. It was too early to eat, too early even for the news hour. When Julie was still alive, they did not eat until seven at the earliest, savoring their martinis over the news hour. He had tried to change his habits once he moved to the Evergreen a year after her death, but change came hard. Dinner hour was the least of it.

He banged his fork and knife onto the table, ignoring the paper napkin delivered with his meal package. Inside a plastic container lay his lukewarm meatloaf, potatoes with gravy and peas. Julie and he had mainly grilled steaks or lamb chops for their dinner, with a fresh green salad from their own garden. That was then. Simon downed his self-imposed limit of one goblet of red wine before even touching his dinner. He accepted intellectually that growing old entailed loss after loss, but these days he felt as if he was dying by the proverbial thousand tiny cuts. Like this dinner. Like not being allowed even to play chess with Don, a cunning tactician confined to his bed by a stroke. Like not even being allowed to hike on Mt. Tamalpais. He tried not even to think about Julie.

———◦●◦———

When her cart was empty, Erythea returned to the dining room to pick up the next round of meal bags to be delivered. On her way, she encountered the Evergreen manager George, who was himself delivering a cart of meals. He asked her to check in with him when she finished for the evening. Erythea glanced at her watch, calculating when she might expect to get home and be able to call Elissa after talking again to Lena, talking to the clinic manager about her and talking to George. Ten thirty was optimal, before she went to bed and before Elissa would get breakfast at her hotel.

She decided to talk with George first. When Erythea saw the clinic manager already seated in his office and she was asked to close the door, she involuntarily shuddered, hoping they did not see.

Alice died in hospital, George told them, their first COVID-19 fatality. Ordinarily, the Evergreen didn't announce resident deaths, except for a small photo on a table in the room where residents picked up their messages. But this was not only a resident's death, it was also a statistic that the news would inevitably pick up. Alice had no family, no children who visited, no friends among the residents that they knew of – facts which simplified tracing people with whom she may have come into close contact. But there was the glaring fact that the enemy had penetrated the barriers of the Evergreen. The fact could not – should not -- be concealed. Yet it would ignite all the latent fears that every resident and every staff person must feel. George had already decided to have every staff person tested along with residents who had had contact with Alice before she had been hospitalized twelve days ago. Anyone who tested positive would be sent home on leave with pay.

But he hadn't yet decided how to announce the death. If he did not identify the person, everyone would be pre-occupied with finding out who had died and distracted from taking care of themselves. Even if he identified the person, residents' anxiety levels would shoot up. He knew he needed to urge people to redouble their sanitizing efforts. Obviously searching for how to comfort the residents, George asked Erythea for her thoughts. First, she suggested, George should televise a remembrance on the internal television channel, with a moment of silence to be maintained by everyone during the announcement. She named two residents who might participate with prior private notice, one a retired rabbi and the other a retired Presbyterian minister. Would you also speak? George almost pleaded.

"Of course, " she said automatically, without any idea of what she might say. "When will we do this?"

"Probably tomorrow," George blurted. "We need to stay ahead of television news, and there's no controlling that."

"Bad idea," injected the managing nurse. "Today is the last day of March, and you can't make this announcement on April Fool's."

George cursed under his breath. "You're right. I'll tell everyone on our inside broadcast tomorrow that they should tune in at nine the following morning for an important announcement."

By the time Erythea finally came home, without even thinking again about Lena, it was ten. She collapsed into her soft sofa, intending to call Elissa in half an hour.

⸺ ◦•◦ ⸺

Within two days, Arturo and Carlo had re-organized their kitchen, converting the dining area to food preparation. Only tasks that required heat stayed in the kitchen, the rest moved to tables pushed together for their new purposes of chopping salad greens, onions and tomatoes, pouring salsa and other condiments into little plastic dishes, and packing meals into boxes and bags. Everyone was legally distanced, except for the persons who had to go into the kitchen to fetch hot food and assemble it. Everyone wore gloves as usual and they had stockpiled a supply well in advance of the crisis, but now they wore masks too – not the N95 ones that supposedly kept out infected air, but ordinary thin white face masks that kept them from touching their own faces or coughing on others. Orders were coming in at an increasing pace, and the two undocumented workers – distant relatives of both Arturo and Pedro – had even begun to sing while they worked, more relaxed now that ICE raids had officially halted and immigrants were arrested only for crimes other than being in this country.

Still, Arturo worried. His only brother Pedro, his business partner and best friend, was not looking well. He denied that there was anything wrong with him. But Pedro sweated more in the kitchen, and he leaned on the counter, drooping like a wet towel. Arturo knew that if any one of them got sick, likely they all would. Arturo also knew Pedro's pride; he might not even admit to himself he was getting sick and he would carry on for what he thought was the good of the family he supported. Take the afternoon off, Arturo told him, you look tired, but Pedro insisted he was fine. That was as close as they got to a conversation about whether Pedro was ill. After two days during which Pedro began to look hollow-eyed in addition to tired, Carlo spoke to Arturo while they were alone in the stock room. Carlo told his uncle he was worried about his dad.

"He takes a big swig of cough medicine before coming in to work, and then hides the bottle back here." Carlo gestured to a spot on the shelf behind a stack of large cans of tomatoes. "He goes to sleep early. My mom's worried too, but she tells me he denies anything is wrong. She asks me what to do with him, and she's the nurse."

"I'll talk to him," Arturo promised. All that day Arturo stewed over how best to do it. When they were boys in Mexico, Pedro had been the one who obeyed all the rules while Arturo partied. Pedro had covered for him with their dad once after Arturo had spent all night drinking and racing around in the desert in their dad's truck with his reckless buddy. Pedro had made up a convincing story that Arturo and his buddy had had to spend the night in a different town where the buddy's sister needed protection from a jilted boyfriend. Their dad had just nodded and not asked any more questions about the incident. So Pedro knew how to cover.

By March 30, deaths in the United States from the coronavirus totaled about 20,000, one-fifth of the number noted by Boccaccio in Florence in his time. All news sources reported that the number of deaths had yet to reach its peak. Marin County, California had 149 confirmed cases, with ten deaths and no recoveries. Five of the Marin County deaths had occurred in nursing homes. Unlike New York and Italy, Marin hospitals had ample available beds. Governor Newsom issued a new order, requiring everyone to shelter in place and prohibiting all public and private gatherings outside a single-family household. The exception for essential activities was significantly narrowed.

April
– Distancing

E rythea jolted awake at the sound of her cell phone and groped for where it was. She located it at her feet, beneath the sofa where she'd fallen asleep. Elissa! What time was it? Too dazed either to read the caller or time, she managed to press the green button and just wait to hear Elissa's voice.

"I'm sorry to call you this early." It was George. "But we need to handle this differently. I hope you haven't spoken to anyone about the memorial plan."

"No. I confess I fell asleep as soon as I got home. What time is it now?" She still felt half-asleep. Missing Elissa was foremost in her mind.

"It's just before seven in the morning, and I apologize for bothering you so early. But I've thought about this through much of the night and now know what we need to do. We do *not* tell the residents. Not the residents, not the staff. We never tell the names of anyone who died and we never disclose the cause of death. It's in the policy manual; I checked it in the middle of the night as I was mulling this over. When and if the media contact us, we stand by our policy."

"Okay." Erythea was still too dazed to think.

"I kept you too late last night, and I can hear you're tired. If you want to give yourself an extra hour this morning, take it. I really am sorry for disturbing you."

Erythea just stared at the dark screen for a few moments. If it was seven in the morning now, it was three in the afternoon in Genoa. She automatically dialed Elissa's number, listening to the different double ring of another country droning into space. Elissa must be out. As she stood up, Erythea looked down at herself, still wearing her traveling clothes for Italy. She smoothed the tunic and noted that indeed it did not wrinkle, the perfect traveling outfit. Except that she could not travel.

Erythea slipped on her flat shoes from the day before and stumbled to the kitchen to make herself some tea. If she were a coffee drinker, this would be the day for a double espresso, but she had given up coffee years ago. Instead she reached for the plastic bag full of her favorite herb tea that she had packed for Italy. She popped one into her favorite mug before stopping in front of the cabinet. No, she thought, taking the tea bag out of her own mug and pulling Elissa's mug from the cabinet. Whatever I can do to bring her closer, she thought. She imagined where Elissa might be but couldn't visualize because she'd never been to Genoa. All she knew was that it had a big harbor, major crime tied to the harbor area, and an old city where Elissa stayed in a tiny hotel. Maybe she was out painting, Erythea thought, before she remembered that Italy was now locked down much like the Evergreen. Being out on the street required papers, Elissa had told her the last time they talked.

The tea revived her, or at least warmed her. Her mind began to work. Had Elissa found a flight home? That was their challenge these days. Even logging in to the airlines, never mind calling them, was nerve-racking, and they had tried it both from Italy and the US. Erythea dialed her again but once more the double tone droned into nothingness. So she took off her clothes, showered and washed her long hair. As she stood drying it, she remembered how Elissa had once dried it for her, running her own fingers through her wet strands before they curled, a smile of wonder on her face. Elissa's own hair was straight and short. She liked to draw her fingers through Erythea's long curls. The two of them defied the stereotype of 'look-alike dykes'. Elissa stood at least five inches shorter than Erythea and she was the fleshier, rounder one, who reveled in good food.

After getting dressed, Erythea made herself some breakfast, a bowl of muesli and yogurt and a slice of raisin toast with a new cup of tea. Gradually coming back to a sense of time and place, she brought her mind back to work. Was it a good idea not to tell the residents they had had their first COVID-19 death? Yes, it would alarm most of them and their families, but they would need to know sooner or later and not telling the residents felt like a major breach of faith. Part of the burden of comforting residents was hers personally, and at this moment she could not decide which choice was better.

Shaking her head at the weird coincidence of this being April 1, she was relieved that today would not be the day to make that decision. She put on her coat and left for work on time as usual.

⊷•••⊶

The Genoese have been sea traders from ancient times. They established the ancient port of Caffa (now Feodosija, Ukraine) on the Black Sea in 1266 by agreement with the Khan of the Golden Horde. To get to and from Caffa, the Genoese merchants sailed through the trading hub of Constantinople. In the spring of 1347 they carried unwonted cargo – the plague – back with them from Caffa, through Constantinople, and Messina on Sicily, before returning home in January 1348. Gabriele de' Mussis, a notary from Piacenza, wrote at the time in his *Historia de Morbo,*

As it happened, among those who escaped from Caffa by boat were a few sailors who had been infected with the poisonous disease. Some boats were bound for Genoa, others went to Venice and to other Christian areas. When the sailors reached these places and mixed with the people there, it was as if they had brought evil spirits with them: every city, every settlement, every place was poisoned by the contagious pestilence, and their inhabitants, both men and women, died suddenly. And when one person had contracted the illness, he poisoned his whole family even as he fell and died, so that those preparing to bury his body were seized by death in the same way. Thus death entered through the windows, and as cities and towns were depopulated their inhabitants mourned their dead neighbours. ....Alas, once our ships had brought us to port we went to our homes. And because we had been delayed by tragic events, and because among us there were scarcely ten survivors from a thousand sailors, relations, kinsmen and neighbours flocked to us from all sides. But, to our anguish, we were carrying the darts of death. While they hugged and kissed us we were spreading poison from our lips even as we spoke.

⸺•◦•⸺

When Pedro showed up for work the next day, he looked even worse, and a glance from Carlo reminded Arturo he needed to act today, now.

"Hey, bro, I need your advice on something," Arturo said in English. He had a rule about speaking English at work. He'd insisted it was good training for them all. Now he led Pedro into the storeroom and closed the door. Glancing at the place on the shelves with cans of tomatoes, Arturo couldn't spot the cough syrup but he didn't need that evidence.

"You're sick. I can see you're sick. You need to go home right now and call Dr. Gutierrez." Pedro was already shaking his head slowly. Arturo reverted to Spanish. "No, man. You're going home, and if you won't call the doc, I'll call Carla and tell her to do it. I haven't spoken to her but I'll bet you a day's profits she already knows."

Pedro pulled up the little chair they kept in the storeroom and sank into it. "I can't let you down." He too now spoke in Spanish. Arturo had got through to him.

"I know you feel that way, but by doing nothing about this you're putting us all at risk. I have no idea if you have a cold or the flu or something else. But you need to find out. Now. If I have to lock you out of here, I will." He tried to glare at Pedro but glanced down. He knew Pedro knew it wasn't anger that drove him.

"Yeah, Carla wanted to take my temperature, but I wouldn't let her."

"Do it yourself, and let me know. Is Carla at home now?"

"No, she's on the day shift today."

"Just do it." Arturo opened the door and let Pedro out, then watched as Pedro went out to his car. Carlo shot him a grateful glance, then slipped into his dad's place at the big stove, where they coordinated almost as seamlessly as if Pedro were there. The day was almost a busy one, and they left at the end in positive spirits.

Arturo dialed Pedro as soon as he got home. No answer. He dialed again, waiting four rings before Pedro picked up.

Rather than saying anything, Arturo waited for Pedro to begin. "You were right; I have a fever, not much, just a little over a hundred. And I have a Zoom call with Dr. Gutierrez at nine tomorrow."

"That means you're not coming in tomorrow." Arturo exhaled. "Good man. You know, Carlo did a pretty good stand-in for you today, he felt like a real partner. Now be sure to isolate yourself at home until you know more. Go sleep in the game room."

"Carla told me the same thing. I've already set up the sofabed in the game room."

———◄●►———

Erythea checked in with George as soon as she got into the building and put on her mask. "Still of the same mind?" she asked as she popped her head into the doorway of George's office.

"Come in. I've been awake much of the night." He launched into speculation about how much discord and anxiety the disclosure would likely cause. "We never tell residents the cause of a death, or identify residents who die except in our monthly newsletter. Luckily, we won't have another newsletter until May 1. But I think we can't hide our first COVID death. The question becomes how to deal with resident anxiety."

"What about the staff? They're going to be anxious too." George wiped a hand over his brow, unconscious of the new training on not touching his face.

"Yeah, let me think on that. But for now no disclosure."

She nodded and left his office for her own, where she was going to call Lena, the identified anxious resident whom she'd promised to call the night before.

Before she could do so, she felt the vibration of her own phone ringing in her hip pocket. She practically lunged for it. As soon as she swiped to answer, Elissa's face beamed in front of her.

"Ryth, I missed your call this morning, but I figured you were working late. I want you to know I've left the hotel. One of my classmates has allowed me to share her apartment, and this is much better. Look." Elissa moved the phone in a slow circle so that Erythea could see the living room of the apartment where she now was. Two easels stood side-by-side facing a large window looking out on a sweeping urban view with the sea in the distance. Suddenly a figure walked across the room, a woman with a butch hair cut, all shorn on the side and straight up on the top, and an ear with a large silver ring. A hand went up in a casual wave. "Ciao, Ryth," wafted the figure in motion before Elissa brought her phone back to her own face.

"Who's that?" Erythea blurted, incensed that a total stranger had called her by the name only she and Elissa used.

"That's my classmate Bea. I need to tell her she can't call you Ryth." Elissa knew automatically what rankled her partner.

"Are we alone now?"

"Yes."

"Why did you move? Aren't you arranging a flight home any day now?"

Elissa explained in extended detail all she had done with Alitalia, then other carriers, especially American and United, thinking somehow that an American carrier might give some preference to citizens returning home. But there were no available flights, at any price. Elissa was in some virtual queue with several airlines, including Alitalia, her original carrier to Genoa, for seats when and if they became available. She explained she had even called the State Department, which at this time had seemed the most sympathetic recourse. "Maybe if I had the virus it would be easier," she laughed hollowly.

"Don't even go there."

"You're right. I'm feeling good. At least here I can paint, and that by itself lifts my mood. You know I'm not a landscape painter, but I've thought of at least five different ways to paint what lies in front of my canvas, so that's a good thing all by itself." Elissa asked Erythea about herself and listened patiently to the details of anxious confined residents.

"I miss you," they each confessed in the same breath.

"You know, Camogli is only 20 miles or so from here. I took the train there almost two weeks ago when we could still go out, and just walked the length of the little town, which fans out across a lovely beach, during *passeggiata*, slurping on a gelato and wishing you…"

"Let me guess, *albicocca*."

"*Si, amore*. You know me." Elissa paused. "You know, I can't go out at all now. Only Bea has a pass for the grocery store and necessary errands. I've never had to live like this – even when my dad grounded me once in high school for two weeks. Then, at least, I figured a way to sneak out and meet my girlfriend. This is something else altogether."

Erythea could hear a siren in the background, approaching and then receding.

"Those are the main sounds on the street these days."

"Stay well, Liss. I love you. I need to get back to work."

They blew kisses to each other and signed off.

•———•◆•———•

Marta asked about Pedro as soon as she came home from work. Arturo told her about his fever and the telephone appointment the next morning with Dr. Gutierrez, who was the physician for their whole family. She nodded her approval and went directly to the kitchen, where Sabrina lunged at her to give her a hug before she went to bed. Leaning over to kiss her thirteen-year-old daughter, Marta asked how her virtual classes were going, and Sabrina showed her proudly the homework she had completed online. Marta kissed Sabrina, assured her she was proud of her and reached for the plate Arturo had prepared for her. Sabrina insisted on heating it for her and sat with her while she ate, smiling at the scarce reality of her mother. Sabrina asked Marta if she would read her a story in bed. Marta looked up quizzically; Sabrina was grown-up for her age, not one to ask for a bedtime story.

"We have a story to read in Spanish, from *Don Quixote*, and I'd like to hear you read it in Spanish to me. You'll get it much better than I do, and I just want to listen. OK?"

Marta smiled her pleasure at the request, and read Sabrina to sleep in Spanish.

She had a more difficult task when she joined Arturo in bed. Marta confessed that she had been the maid for the Evergreen resident who had died. "I heard her coughing before she went to hospital. I thought she had the virus. Now I'm supposed to get tested."

"And all of us have been exposed to Pedro," Arturo added. "I suspect he has it. If he does, it means we're all quarantined. None of us can go to work." They had separately been harboring the same fears. It was unimaginable for either of them not to work. Not in their whole lives, not since they were children in Mexico, and even then they had helped their parents.

Marta gently passed her hand over Arturo's face, closing his eyes, her signal that it was time to sleep, time to leave worries until the next morning. Although he closed his eyes, he re-opened them as soon as he could hear the slow rhythm of his wife's sleeping breath. His remained open for a long time.

If Pedro had the virus, Arturo knew he would have to close the restaurant. Everyone had been exposed to him at close quarters, and it was only a question of time before someone else in their restaurant family would also come down with it. Who could tell if one of them had breathed on food that had gone out to infect others? How would he support everyone when restaurant income ended? He could feed everyone for a time, literally from the storeroom and freezer, but with no income how long could they last? Caught in the swirl of these survival issues, Arturo pulled back the covers on his side so as not to wake Marta and got out of bed. He knew he had to answer at least one of his swirling questions. In his slippers and robe, he padded directly to the closet in the family room where he kept the safe. For years he had followed the tradition of his family and kept any savings hidden at home, in a hollowed-out book or behind a brick in a corner, anywhere but the bank, his father had warned. For his dad, survival had always been an issue, every day. In more recent years, as the restaurant had made them more comfortable, Arturo had a real safe installed, at home at the same time as at the restaurant, keeping a reserve at work but moving his own profits home. He knew Marta had some savings in a bank, but he'd told her that was her money, for herself and the children, he'd keep the family going.

As he opened the safe, Arturo realized it was for the first time not to deposit money, only to count it. What a mess, he thought, as he stared at the mass of envelopes crammed inside. It was as chaotic as the inside of his own head these days, not at all like the orderly life he thought he led. As he pulled out envelope after bulging envelope, he saw that the totals for each envelope were not even the same. What he thought was his habit was to accumulate two thousand dollars of hundred-dollar bills in one envelope, and there were stacks of such envelopes, but the ones in the back had no labels and no such order. After he had removed every envelope, Arturo sat on the floor of the closet, pen and paper at hand, and counted them all, meticulously using bars and slashes to count subtotals of five envelopes and then the odd amounts in the earlier envelopes. Then he neatly restacked, the envelopes, the more recent tidily totaled ones in the back and the older, more ragged ones at the front, labeling each of them with its own total, intending to put them in order one of these days. Ninety-two thousand seven hundred dollars. Not much to show for over twenty years of work. Yes, there was this house, nearly paid for – another lesson from his dad -- never borrow money, but if you have to, pay it back as soon as you can. Arturo reclosed the safe, and tried to stand up, but his legs burned from the awkward position in which he'd been sitting and he had to grab the wall to steady himself. Instead of going back to his bedroom, where he knew he would only toss and turn and wake up Marta, he grabbed the afghan from the back of the sofa and lay down on it.

Where he must have fallen asleep, for the next thing he knew was Marta laying a hand on his brow. "You too?" she asked without saying the words. He shook himself awake enough to speak. "I'm all right, I just left because I was tossing and turning and didn't want to wake you." He glanced up at her, already dressed for work. "What time is it?"

"Time for you to get the kids up and ready for school." He sat up. "What school?" They both knew Sabrina and Tomas had been home from school for weeks now.

"They need to stay on their regular schedule, and tune in on their computers as if they were sitting in class. I don't want them to lose their discipline." With that, she was off.

— ·•· —

With no meal duty this morning, Erythea had the liberty to meet with individual residents as usual, counseling those who had regular appointments like Don or following up with others to check on them. She phoned Lena to ask if she could stop by. Lena answered after three rings, saying the nurse was with her now but that she would be free afterward. Lena's voice sounded more cheerful than it had the other evening, and the nurse visit was something Erythea had requested. She decided to make rounds in the assisted living, starting with Don. He was seated upright in his bed, with his customized slanted worktable that another resident had made for him in the workshop. Braced on the worktable was Don's iPad, and and he appeared to be writing an email.

Don beamed when he saw her. "I'm training myself to write with my left hand, but it's slow. The program corrects my spelling, but it gives me strange words." Even speaking these words took what seemed like a long time.

"Are you writing to Janice?"

"Yes, actually I am. I can't let her forget me." Erythea tried to read his voice.

"Is it an angry note?"

"No, it's more like an elegy – for all the things we shared before. I'm reminding her of our good times. No, that's not quite right. I'm reminding myself of our good times, because it helps me, and maybe telling her will bring her back too." It took him a long time to get out all these words.

"What would you like to hear from her?"

"I haven't got that far. So far, I'm just trying to harness my left hand to get out my own thoughts, and that's hard enough."

Just then the nurse popped her head in the door. Erythea asked Don if he wanted her to come back at their usual time. He nodded.

Erythea followed the nurse to a place in the hallway where they could speak privately. Lena's fine, she was told, only missing her usual companions and a bit at a loss on her own. Erythea thanked her and headed for Lena's apartment. On her way, Erythea summoned all the recent details she could remember about Lena, who fit one of the general prototypes of female residents at the Evergreen – widowed by a successful husband whose needs she had spent a lifetime serving, floundering for a time on her own and then coming back to life with a group of new girlfriends. They ate together regularly, they played bridge, went on museum outings and went together to see romantic plays at the local theater. Her son and daughter-in-law visited on Sundays with their own children. Now all that had come to a hard stop for almost a month. Erythea knocked on Lena's door and heard her call 'come in'.

Lena sat in a sunny corner in a flowery upholstered chair, her thin white hair neatly combed and lipstick on her smiling face, the television remote in her hand.

"I never thought I would enjoy cooking shows, but they are really fun – especially since I don't have to do the cooking." Erythea chatted with her about her new interests for a little, then asked about contact with her family and friends.

"My son taught me how to use FaceTime on my phone, so I can see him and even my grandkids a lot. I talk on the phone with my friends here, but Myrna is the only one who has a cellphone, so I can't see the rest of them. But everybody's well. I do miss our morning exercise classes, though." Erythea remarked on how resilient she seemed, and explained how the exercise classes were now available on the internal television channel. Lena thanked her cheerfully.

Erythea decided to visit Hilde in hospice in her own apartment. Oddly, this was one of her most gratifying work assignments. For the dying who knew what they faced, she could provide some comfort. Hilde's lungs were failing from emphysema, not coronavirus, she had simply come to the end of their functioning. Hilde knew it, felt a bit betrayed by the body that had given her so much pleasure in her life, so much mileage over ninety-two years. Hilde welcomed her with a smile and a flood of words.

"Just the person I wanted to see. I need your help. The hospice nurse assigned to me is cranky and seems afraid to be here, she thinks I have the virus. I don't want cranky in my last days. And I want to go out and see the garden. I was supposed to get a wheelchair but where is it after two days?" She gestured with a wave of her hand. "I don't have that much time, you know."

Erythea knew. What was remarkable was that Hilde wasn't in more physical distress. Most other patients would be seeking morphine by now, the gradual painless path to the end. She promised to try to find a wheelchair today and to speak with the hospice agency. Then she sat silent, waiting for whatever Hilde would find to say. Her wait was not long.

"You know, I'm ready. I've had a rich life, I've had my adventures, I have my children and grandchildren here and I even have great grandchildren. I don't want to live in this rotting body any longer than I have to."

Erythea asked her what she would like in the time that remained. Chocolate, lots of chocolate, Hilde told her. And peace. Too many friends were calling her and crying on the phone. She only wanted to see her family. She had said goodbye to the friends who mattered. Did she want any religious or spiritual advisor? Hilde waved her arm dismissively, absolutely not. After another pause in the conversation, Hilde glanced off into space.

"I would like to know what it feels like on the other side, when I leave this body."

"Would you like to visualize that?"

"Perhaps, but not now. If you could just get me the wheelchair, I could see the spring flowers."

Erythea promised to try, then got up to leave. Ordinarily, she would take Hilde's hand, would have done so as soon as she came in, but now she was masked and forbidden to touch anyone. Hilde blew her a kiss, a graceful gesture, and Erythea echoed the gesture with both hands.

Back in the hall, Erythea felt in urgent need of a break. Flooded with unbidden emotion, she took refuge in a chair in the garden, took a deep breath and felt a tear flow from her wet eyes. Ordinarily, such a visit would make her feel deeply gratified, committed to go on with the more frustrating moments of her counseling work. If she herself were dying now, she thought, the hardest part would be not being able to hold Elissa, not even being able to touch her. In the way April was supposed to flow, she and Elissa would now be vacationing in Camogli. Instead they did not know even whether Elissa could come home, whether either of them would survive the virus, whether Elissa even wanted to come home. That last, dark thought crept in involuntarily, spurred by the momentary video exchange with Bea the other day. Leave that, Erythea told herself, no good can come from that thought. So she tried to imagine what she would feel if she were in Hilde's bed, at ninety-two. It was nearly impossible to take herself there, she realized, since that was more than forty years in the future and she was not someone who plotted her future. If she were dying now, she would definitely feel cheated. She had so many years she wanted yet to live, so much connection with Elissa still to build, so much living yet in them both.

Erythea put her mask back on and went to the kitchen to start helping deliver the midday meals. George himself was loading meal bags onto the delivery tray and invited her to do his route with him. As they rode the elevator up to the seventh floor, he told her casually, "We're not going to tell the residents."

"So there will be a notice for Hilde when she leaves us but not for Alice?"

"That's right. There's no good reason to upset the residents."

Erythea knew when not to question him. With a wordless rhythm, they divided the bags between them as they made their deliveries on alternating wings of the resident halls.

In less than a month, Janice's world had constricted. The seder she, Don and Adam had always celebrated at the Rosses had been replaced with a televised version, a seder on Zoom, with a mosaic of faces the size of postage stamps. She tried to console herself that these were real friends in real time but felt distanced by the medium itself. You don't watch a seder on television, she told herself. Saul Ross had always been a convivial and inclusive host, but the medium weakened his warmth. The medium silenced her, separating her from friends rather than connecting them. Adam had clung to the large screen, hungry for every glimpse of Leah he could get. Saul and Naomi's daughter, Adam's girlfriend for as long as anyone could remember, was no longer allowed out of the house, since she had asthma and her parents worried that she would be among the most susceptible to the virus.

Even Janice's daily walking group had shriveled to one companion. Sometimes they had been as many as five, but nearly always there were at least three, and now only Zoe – the one they teased for being fearless and respecting no boundaries, the one who climbed over fences with 'no trespassing' signs posted on them – would walk with her. Naomi had been the first to announce that, since their daughter was vulnerable by definition, she would drop out of the group so long as the virus threatened. Janice missed her the most; Naomi was the most simpatico of her friends, the one in whom she could most comfortably confide. Susan, the most anxious of the five by her own temperament, had followed by telling them she had a cold and didn't want to worry the group with her sniffling. And Gina had just e-mailed the group that she would be 'absent for the duration' without any further explanation. Janice admired Zoe's confidence even as she didn't share it; Zoe knew Trump would be defeated in the November election and acted as if she knew she was immune to COVID. Janice kept hoping a bit of Zoe's confidence would shed onto her but could feel no evidence of such transmission. Janice appreciated Zoe's energy; it was Zoe who had raised the length and duration of their daily walks.

But even with the endorphins of a daily long walk, Janice returned home to a lugubrious atmosphere. Adam had begun to play his cello obsessively, and his music was invariably melancholic. Usually he practiced one hour each day. Now he seemed to be playing whenever he didn't have online classes. This morning, on her return, she pushed open the door to the study room where he played and saw him in the corner, the cello between his bony knees, bowing expressively with a sad tilt to his eyes.

When he paused, she asked him what he was playing.

"Bach Cello Suite No. 1, the Sarabande section."

"It's sad music, don't you think?"

He nodded. "That's why I chose it."

She tilted her head inquisitively. "Leah?"

"Yeah. Sometimes I walk over to her house and talk to her on my phone, watching her on the other side of the window. But putting our hands together with a window between just doesn't cut it.

"I tried to tell her parents that I was like family and should be allowed in to see her, but they said no."

Janice remembered only too well the intensity of love at seventeen but groped for what she could say to console her son.

"I don't suppose you could play music from *West Side Story* on a cello," she tried, joking. He actually smiled. "You know, there may be some cello music in Romeo and Juliet; I might look that up."

"And then play it outside at her house. I could drive you and the cello over there."

"You know, I might take you up on that once I find the right music." He looked at her with something resembling appreciation.

"In the meantime, can you give Bach a rest?" He nodded, but only after I finish this piece." He went back to playing the Bach piece while she closed the door quietly and went to her room to shower.

Standing under the shower, Janice marveled at Adam's forbearance. At seventeen, she would have been the Leah who climbed out of the window to be with Adam. The biggest celebrations of their senior year – the prom and graduation – had simply been canceled. Diplomas would be mailed. Senior proms are not replicated in college. Janice could not imagine teen-age love in intermission. By definition, it could not wait, it was the most in-the-moment time of life, the most florid in expression, the most immediate. All they could do in this time was to repress and fantasize.

⸻ ◦◉◦ ⸻

Marta left her first job at the Evergreen just after lunch, heading for the hospital laundry room to pick up her second shift of the day. She hoped to connect with Carla, whom she trusted to give her a more accurate report on Pedro than Arturo might. Besides, as a nurse Carla would likely know more. Arriving at the hospital a few minutes early, she texted Carla to see if they could meet. Normally, it was easy for them to find time to share a break and catch up on family plans, but now Carla was overloaded like all the medical professionals and catching one another was trickier. Marta heard a ping, then saw that Carla was on her way down to their meeting place, the staff room adjacent to the laundry. Marta hung up her coat and donned the used mask that hung in her locker. Carla slumped into the seat at the staff room table.

"I know he has it," she said softly, seated six feet away.

"Test?"

"No results yet, I just know."

"Is that my sister speaking, or the nurse?"

Carla's eyes told Marta it was her worried sister, not the nurse, speaking. "When will you hear?"

"In California there's a long line for test results. Never mind that you can get them within an hour in Korea or Germany. Besides, there's probably a longer line when the doctor's name is Gutierrez." Carla tightened her belt impatiently. "Well, so long as we don't know, we can keep working."

"Not me. Every day when I come to work at the Evergreen I have to sign a form that says I haven't had any close contact with anyone who has the virus or even a fever or cough. And they tested me because I had worked with a woman who died there, but I don't have the results yet either."

Carla stared at her intently. Marta just nodded. Neither one of them could say what they knew. It was unthinkable that their whole combined family would be out of work. They each got up and went to work without even giving the other another glance.

When Marta got home that evening, she gave Arturo a similar intent look that they both knew signified they needed to talk, without the children around. He corralled the children and let them know their mother and he needed time to themselves. Beto looked up inquiringly. He was old enough to know this time wasn't because they wanted romantic time together, and a single glance told him it wasn't because his parents were angry at each other. He took charge of initiating a game with Sabrina and Tomas.

Arturo served Marta her dinner as usual, then sat beside her with his arm over her shoulder, his hand gently massaging her neck, which he knew would be stiff. "You first," he said.

"You know this form I have to sign each day now at the Evergreen?" Glancing at her husband, she realized she may not even have told him about it. "In order for us to keep working, we have to sign a form each day that we haven't come into contact with anyone with the virus, or anyone who has a cough or fever." She glanced at him meaningfully. "I can't sign it one more day.

"Also they tested me because I cleaned the room for the woman who died. No results yet."

"What does that mean for you?"

"I get leave with pay from the Evergreen."

"That's good." Arturo paused for a long moment. "I think I need to close down the whole restaurant operation. Whether he has it or not, Pedro's getting sick makes me realize we're all going to get sick, and who knows how much I'm also putting customers at risk." His head sank to the table. "I can't just let everyone go, but without any income I can't pay our workers for very long."

"If you let them go, can't they get unemployment?" He glanced at her in admiration, not knowing she would think of this. "The regular employees, yes, but not M______ and S______. " He mentioned the names of the undocumented workers. "I have to keep paying them." Marta nodded emphatically.

"And then there's Pedro and me."

"But don't you qualify as a small business to get a loan under the stimulus package?" Again, Arturo found himself amazed that Marta even knew about it, not to mention that she understood it. After less than an hour of conversation, he and Marta worked out that he would close the business, apply for federal relief under the new act, lay off all the regular workers so that they could apply for unemployment, and keep paying the two undocumented workers. He told her how much he had in savings and was amazed when she told him she herself had saved twenty-two thousand dollars from her jobs. They agreed he would continue to pay M_____ and S_____ each their fifty dollars per day in cash.

Marta got up from the table and telephoned her supervisor at the Evergreen, leaving a message that she would not be in the next day because of illness at home. When they went to bed that night, Arturo made love to her more tenderly than usual.

❦

Janice opened Don's email with trepidation. Is this how he would tell her? But what she read was not at all what she expected. He recounted their driving trip across the Maremma eighteen years ago when she was four months pregnant with Adam. He described the steep tufa walls of the town of Pitigliano, where the walls of homes perched exactly on the cliff edge, where they'd seen a housewife toss a pot of water out a window and watched the water cascade down only a fraction of the hundreds of feet to the river, staining the pale walls slightly, but not even falling close to the water below. How do they paint the walls of the houses, they'd wondered, or replace a broken window? They couldn't imagine someone suspending himself over the chasm below. They'd driven on to the coast, across a small causeway to the island where they'd found a seaside hotel with its outdoor restaurant on a concrete platform literally inches above the level of the Mediterranean. There they'd shared a simple dinner of grilled *branzino* and a dessert of a perfectly ripe melon, the word for which he couldn't remember. From their bedroom, after making love, they'd fallen asleep to the gentle sound of the sea caressing the rocky shore. And had rich dark coffee and brioche for breakfast in their room as they watched the morning light alter the color of the water below.

"*Carentais*," Janice said out loud, recalling the Italian name of the exquisite melon. She didn't know Don remembered these details, didn't know he even thought about this or their other trips, and especially that he could write so gorgeously about the details. She was immediately tempted to reply with the name of the melon but clearly that wouldn't be enough. She touched the print button immediately, wanting to reread Don's beautiful letter. She wanted to make herself a cup of espresso just to savor it with the letter, but it was now nine in the evening and that much caffeine was out of the question. She got up, made herself some tea, and wandered around Don's study before sitting down again at her desk. Again, nothing but the name of the melon came to her, so she decided to leave it until morning. After showering and distracting herself with a light novel, she fell asleep.

But she awoke before dawn, her mind alert and bursting with memories. That night in Monte Argentario, how she'd wanted to have sex but he'd told her he wanted to protect the baby. And then surprised her by doing more with his tongue than ever before, and how she'd reciprocated with hers. When she was nearly at term and her back ached at night, she'd lie on her side and Don would massage her back so deeply and patiently, first one side and then the other. He would do the same when her back ached from carrying Adam around as a heavy toddler night after night, with endless patience.

How could this many years together create such a distance between them? Was intimacy too much to bear over a span of years? Or was it just his stroke that caused the distance? Why couldn't she bear to comfort him physically?

Pedro's fever burned so much that Carla put him into a bath of cold water and applied a cloth filled with ice across his forehead. He could barely stand by himself as he tried to get out of the tub. Carla told him to lean on her shoulder as she dried him, and then she put him into their big bed rather than the family room pull-out sofa where he'd spent the first two nights. He sank into it gratefully and fell asleep almost immediately. Carla then took the towel with which she had dried him and put it into the washer with her own clothes as she removed them. Then she herself showered, put on her nightgown, robe and face mask, and started the washer before leaving the quarantine area she had created within their own home and walking down the hall to say goodnight to their anxious children. She had forbidden them from coming anywhere near their father from the first day. The family room was now off limits to them. The three of them could use the kitchen and living room freely, as well as their own bedrooms, but they couldn't see or touch their dad. She knew they'd all been exposed, many times over, in the days before Pedro had started to cough, especially Carlo, but none of them could undo that history. Now they could only wash and wash and wash their hands, miss their father and wonder what would happen to them all.

"He's got a high fever but we brought it down in a cold bath and he's sleeping now," she reported to the children.

"Does he have it?" Bettina asked.

"We don't know. He's not having any trouble breathing, and we'll just keep treating him for flu." She hugged them all, despite the house quarantine. They were all family and all in this together. "What you each need to do is go to your rooms and focus on your classes. We all need to carry on."

"Are you going to work?" It was Sabrina again.

"No, for the safety of the hospital, I'm not going to work until we know more." She glanced at Sabrina. "And don't ask me when."

Don propped himself further upright when he saw Janice had replied to his email. With only one working arm, it was awkward, but he didn't want to wait for a nurse to prop him up before he read it.

"The delicious melon was a *Carentais*. Write more."

That was the whole message. Janice was usually the voluble one. This was as strange a message from her as he had ever received. He sat for many moments wondering how to read it until other emails with the daily news distracted him. His phone blasted news alerts several times a day, the pace of death tolls in New York and New Orleans, the contradicting reports from the President and his medical advisors, predictions of the curves of incidence of COVID-19.

When a nurse assistant came to remove his breakfast tray, Don asked him – luckily it was Russell, who was strong enough -- to brace him upright and to set up his writing stand. After bracing his laptop on the stand, he sat for a few moments, but only a few, before another memory took over. "It was such a sunny day in Oslo," he began, "and we walked holding hands as Adam played games at running ahead of us and hiding and then running back and gripping your legs so hard you almost lost your balance. Until we realized he had truly lost us and hadn't run back. You took off to the left to do a big circle and I took off to the right to do the same thing. By our first rounding back, we'd each seen many blond three-year-old boys who looked like him, but they were each with their own parents. You were pale with anxiety, and I must have been the same. We took off a second time, faster and more fearful, until we found a gigantic fountain with several children frolicking in it, all with their clothes off. I found Adam's clothes before I found him. You were racing around the rim staring frantically at each little blond boy.

"We just gripped each other's hands, not wanting to alarm him. When he wanted to come out, we three hugged each other like life itself."

"I'm still here," he ended the message and pressed send.

———•◦•———

Erythea left work on time for the first time in nearly a month. She phoned Elissa at their usual time and Elissa answered on the first ring. "Are you alone?" Erythea blurted. Elissa smiled reassuringly. "Yes, I'm in the bedroom and Bea is out shopping." *The bedroom* was all Erythea heard.

"Nothing yet from the airlines or the State Department," Elissa reported, stifling a cough. Erythea stared at her inquiringly. "I'm feeling punk today, a little achy and I've started to cough. I'm afraid to tell Bea, maybe she'll throw me out." Erythea stifled her impulse to blurt 'that's crazy!' Instead she asked if Elissa had taken her temperature. "Yeah, it's up a little, just a little." Elissa looked hard at her and ran a hand through her thin hair. "Could be anything."

"Tell Bea. Find out what you should do at this stage. See if you can call her doctor." After three imperatives, Erythea finally asked what she could do to help. Elissa just looked at her pleadingly. Neither of them knew. They agreed to call twice a day now to check in.

When Pedro awoke the next morning, he felt spent but not fevered. Carla took his temperature and assured him it was nearly normal, though she knew fevers tended to rise over the course of a day. She brought him breakfast and he ate with a normal appetite. He asked if she and the children were feeling okay and she reassured him. "I'm sorry," he told her, "I feel like I'm letting the whole family down." She ran her hand over his forehead and through his hair. "It's my turn to take care of you." She kissed his forehead reassuringly and left the room to take away his breakfast dishes.

In the kitchen she first washed her hands thoroughly and then washed Pedro's dishes, propping them to air dry separately from the dishes of the rest of the family. After settling Sabrina into her room to study, she called her supervisor at the hospital. Ann, her supervisor, sighed but told Carla she was making a responsible decision. Keep checking in by phone, Ann told her, every nurse is needed.

When she popped her head back into their bedroom to check on Pedro, she overheard him on the phone talking to Arturo about details of filing for unemployment and small business relief. He was sitting up and sounded normal.

After Arturo hung up the phone with his brother, he felt mildly encouraged. Pedro's voice had energy. Today he resolved to call all of his employees to see how they were. He explained to each of them how to file for unemployment, now that Marta had given him enough information to pass on. When he got to M____ and S____, he hesitated. They were by definition not going to apply for or receive unemployment, and he needed to work out logistics for paying them. When he spoke with M_____, he learned that the two young men did not even have a kitchen to prepare food in their tiny apartment. So he arranged that he would deliver them their usual earnings in cash, and he resolved to cook extra food for them and deliver it each day. He questioned them closely about how they were feeling. M______ told him 'okay' but Arturo could hear stifled coughing in the background. He reverted to Spanish.

"Tell me straight. Is S______ okay?"

"Yeah, he's coughing a little but it's just a cold." Arturo asked for more details but M______ was evasive and clearly wanted to get off the phone. "I'll check back later."

When Arturo showed up at the door that afternoon with an envelope with their earnings and a whole platter of beef enchiladas, M______ answered the door. Instead of inviting Arturo inside, his body blocked the entrance. Again, coughing erupted from the rear of the small room but Arturo could not even see past M______'s body. "Does he have a fever?" M____ lifted his shoulders slightly, a familiar vague gesture that could be interpreted however the other person wished to take it. It was the gesture usually used with unfriendly strangers or the police. Arturo gave him a look that asked who he was trying to fool.

M____ stepped outside, the platter still in his hands, but pulling the door closed. In a low voice, he told Arturo that S______ was sick. "I'm worried but I can't take him to a doctor." They both cursed, and Arturo glared down at his own feet. He didn't know whether it was safe for S______ to see a doctor. "Let me call and try to find out," Arturo told him and left.

Before Arturo even started the engine of his van, he called Dr. Gutierrez and left word for a call back without explaining the problem. When he got home, he could hear music blaring before he even opened the door from the garage. Heading straight for Beto's room, he yelled "Turn that down." When he flung open the door to Beto's room, he found Beto at his computer, working out some design in complete silence. Beto looked up inquiringly and Arturo apologized. "It's Bettina," he said as he turned back to his design. "It's getting to me too." Arturo stomped down the hall to Bettina's room and threw open the door without knocking. Halfway into a yell to turn it down, he saw Bettina hunched over her computer watching a conductor lead an orchestra. He glimpsed assorted horns making strange loud sounds with no tune. He wanted to hold his ears. "Sssh, it's our music class," Bettina told him. "Turn it down" was all Arturo said and he backed out of the room.

Arturo's anger had no ready target. He flung open the refrigerator door and grabbed a can of beer, which itself erupted on opening. He grabbed a paper towel and swiped up the wet spot on the floor, then flung himself out the back door. What he really wanted was a cigarette, he thought, a habit he'd kicked years ago. He paced the yard, literally tracing the perimeter of the fence several times before he could sit still.

When Marta found him, he was hunched over the front of a garden chair, elbows on his knees and cellphone at his ear. "No, I won't tell you what the problem is, I need to talk to the doctor." He punched the red button. When he felt Marta's arm on his shoulder, he realized he'd been yelling. She pulled one of the garden chairs over until it faced his and sat down, giving him a penetrating look.

"S______ is sick, with a real hacking cough. I don't know if it's even safe to tell the doctor." He crushed the empty beer can with his fist.

"Ask Carla. She works at the hospital, she'll know." Arturo looked at her gratefully, then wagged his head in reproach at his not even thinking of it. He tossed the empty can in a clean arc into the waste bin a dozen feet away. When Carla answered he told her where he was and that he would put her on speaker so that Marta could hear at the same time. After he described what he knew of S____'s condition, her first question was how close Arturo had got to M______.

"Too close," he admitted. "We stood at the doorstep together. I didn't go inside. But it's been less than a week since we all worked next to each other."

"Okay, just listen," Carla launched. In plain words, she explained that S______ would not be deported as a result of checking into a hospital. "California is a sanctuary state, and even if it weren't, ICE would be afraid to come near right now." S______ could use whatever name he wanted when checking in if it came to that, but after he checked in the family would lose touch with him. No one could visit, obviously, and the hospital would take his phone.

"So you would have no way of knowing his condition until or unless he comes out. There's no one you can ask at the hospital, for privacy reasons, so it's like his dropping off a cliff once he's gets admitted."

Then she explained that Dr. Gutierrez would give reliable advice and keep it confidential, but that S______ should not be traceable to a particular outside doctor or to any other person, just in case. So while Arturo should get general advice from Dr. Gutierrez, S______ needed to call himself. She told them S______ should get whatever over-the-counter cough relief he could find, take Tylenol to keep his fever down if possible, and call 911 if he developed trouble breathing. An ambulance would take him to the Novato Community Hospital. It's a reliable hospital, she reassured him.

M______ would need to be quarantined for two weeks if S______ went into hospital. For now, M______ should keep whatever distance he can from S______ and wear a mask. They're likely in close quarters anyway, and probably need to stay together until you know more. Finally, she asked, "what haven't I covered?" Nothing, they assured her and thanked her.

"How's Pedro?" Arturo asked.

"His fever's coming up again," but nothing else new. "He's stable."

Arturo called M______ back and relayed Carla's advice. "How is S_____?"

"He's got a bad headache that the Tylenol didn't help. And he hurts all over."

"Call me if anything changes," Arturo told him as they rung off.

"Let me help you with dinner tonight," Marta insisted. "I never get to cook at home." Arturo grinned and asked her to brown the meat while he chopped the onions, and they sang together in the kitchen the way they did years earlier, before the restaurant even existed. He stirred the onion and garlic and red peppers, she poured the browned hamburger over it and he dropped in some tomato paste and stirred it around. They took eggs out to warm up before dropping them into the pan while Marta chopped and mixed a salad and dressing and Arturo called the children. Beto glanced between his parents as he took his seat, taking their emotional temperature, while Sabrina set silverware on the table and Tomas laid out napkins.

"How's Uncle Pedro?" Bettina asked.

"He's okay, got a fever and some aches but he seems okay," Marta answered before leading them in their quick dinner prayer.

Arturo apologized to Bettina for barging into her room and being angry, before asking her what was that terrible music she was listening to. "It's a symphony by Charles Ives," she told him, smiling. "You just don't like gringo music."

Her dad just pointed at her with the tortilla he was holding. "You got me."

After dinner the whole family played monopoly, something they had last done so long ago that they had to search for the game board. Tomas bought cheap hotels on the maroon properties and collected big rents every time the other players went around, winning handily. "It's my silver shoe," he bragged, waving his token over his head. They all hugged each other before going off to their own bedrooms to bed. The last time Arturo remembered their doing this – the picnic on Mt. Tam for his birthday less than a month earlier – seemed like another lifetime.

Arturo and Marta fell asleep in an embrace.

His cell woke him at 11:37, and he grabbed for it. Marta jolted up at the same time. "Pedro?" she blurted.

Instead it was M______, sounding close to panicked. "S______ can't breathe. He's gasping."

"Get off the phone and call 911. I'm on my way." Arturo reached for his jeans and a sweatshirt, running his fingers through his thick hair as he lurched toward the bathroom to pee before he took off.

By the time Arturo pulled up near M_____ and S______'s building, the ambulance had already arrived. From his parked car, he watched the EMT team in their otherworldly gowns and boots and masks and gloves wheel S______ out of the building and into the ambulance. He paused after it began to pull away, hesitating whether to follow it or talk to M______. He took off after the ambulance, telling himself he could check back with M_______ later. With almost no traffic on the roads, it was a quick trip to the Novato Community Hospital, where Arturo pulled into the entrance lot and watched the ambulance quickly unload its passenger. He felt guilty not trying to follow S_____ inside, even though he knew no outsider would be allowed into the hospital. When the ambulance pulled out, he turned around to check in on M________.

M________ answered the door immediately, but for the first time Arturo stood six feet back. M told him in more detail how scared S________ was, shivering and gasping for air. M______'s own big dark eyes showed white around the top. Arturo re-assured him that he would check on him every day, continue to bring him food, but that now he needed to stay in, all the time, for at least fourteen days. "No one should come in contact with you. No grocery, no neighbors, no friends. Not even me. I'll drop off your food and anything else you need. You should call me whenever you need something or have a question. And – take good care of yourself. I don't want to see you ride off in one of these things." Arturo knew M______ had hidden away before – he couldn't have made it here otherwise – but his cousin S________ had always been at his side. "You've been through worse before," Arturo tried to reassure him, "I know you can do this."

M______ still stood in his doorway as Arturo started the car, his forlorn silhouette framed by the dim light behind him.

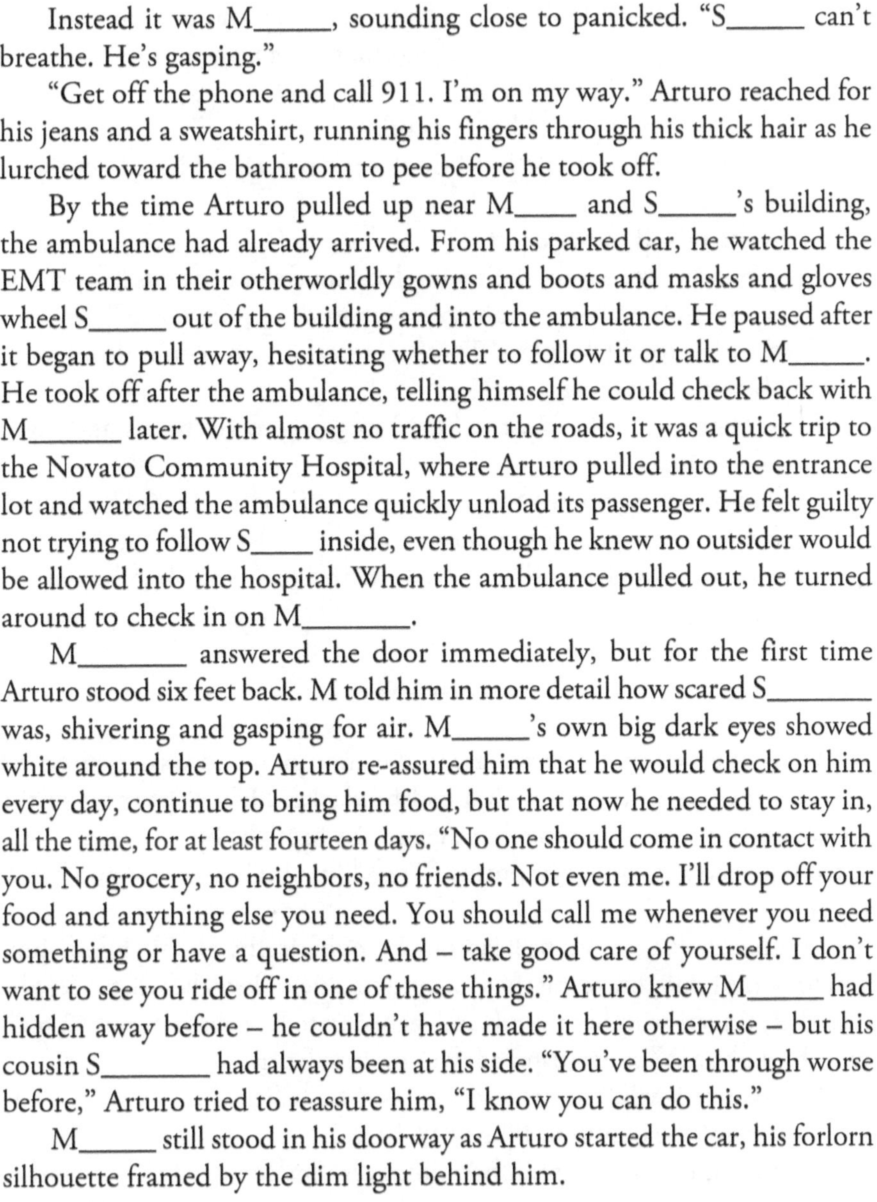

Erythea dialed Elissa immediately after the dinner delivery with George. This time, Elissa answered on the first ring. Since Elissa hadn't initiated FaceTime, Erythea did. What she saw confirmed her fears. Elissa's face was red and puffy. "You look awful, how *are* you?"

"I feel as awful as I look. I've had a fever all day and my bones ache. I haven't got out of bed even to eat. Bea brings me a tray but puts it at least six feet away. I drink but don't eat."

"How is Bea taking your being sick?"

"Better than you'd think, but I think she's sick also. I heard her throw up earlier today."

"Has she talked to her doctor?"

"Yes, but the word is to 'shelter in place' unless either of us has trouble breathing. There's nothing to do unless either of us gets worse."

Erythea felt totally helpless. There was nothing she could do to make this any better. "What can I say?"

Elissa replied simply, "Just tell me I'm going to get better and say it like you mean it."

Erythea could only mouth the words and Elissa's look reflected her failure.

"We should just get off the phone then."

Erythea promised to call her back in the morning, but Elissa had already hung up.

❖

Carla checked in on Pedro late in the afternoon and wasn't surprised to find him feverish, again with a bad headache. He'd slept most of the afternoon but was now miserable. Again, she brought him a Tylenol and asked if he had any other symptoms. "Feels like a bull sat on me and broke my ribs."

"Hungry?" He shook his head more emphatically. She sat beside him and took his hand, knowing the risk, and unable to keep her distance. She traced his fingers with her thumb and leaned in to kiss his forehead. "You'll pull through this," she whispered, willing it to be true.

"Of course I will," he assured her, as if he believed it himself. "Now go take care of the children. I'll be OK here."

As she got up, the nurse in her took over. She removed all her clothes and put them directly into the washer, then showered and dressed in clean clothes. She had shopped earlier that day and bought sole and lemons and asparagus, thinking she wanted anything that wasn't on the menu at Arturo's. Sabrina joined her in the kitchen to offer help. Carla showed her where to break the asparagus stems and how to steam them in pot of shallow water, while she breaded the sole and melted butter into her own pan. Finishing first, Sabrina leaned against her mother's side, her arm around her mother's waist. "Is he going to be okay?"

Carla looked into Sabrina's eyes. "There's no way to be sure. That's what I live with every day at work. We make predictions and sometimes we're wrong. We just do the best we can and hope." Carla reminded Sabrina that, whatever ailed her dad, Sabrina and her brothers should be careful to keep their distance. Sabrina nodded and went out to get her brothers when dinner was nearly ready. By the time she returned, Carla could see that Sabrina had already spoken to them about their dad. When Carlo flipped on the television, which they often watched during a meal, Carla shook her head and Carlo turned it off.

They held hands and prayed together. Carla tossed out a challenge: talk about anything but the virus. Who would start? Luis blurted that he had seen a woodpecker come in and out of a hole in the oak tree in their yard. He'd watched it for some time and found the woodpecker coming back each time with something in his mouth. What was it? Sabrina explained that he was probably feeding the mother woodpecker while she sat on eggs in a nest in the hole. She asked him to show her the hole right after dinner. Seven-year-old Luis pushed back his hair, smiling behind his hand. Carlo asked Sabrina about her classes, and she explained why she really liked biology but found English lit boring, especially Jane Austen. "Emma was such a meddling elitist. Reminds me of Mrs. McFarlane last year, always trying to tell me how to better myself." Sabrina's family knew Mrs. McFarlane and Sabrina's struggles with her teacher to allow her to be herself. Sabrina had regaled her family with how often Mrs. McFarlane had corrected her vernacular speaking.

Carla asked Sabrina to describe Emma.

"She's snotty rich and only knows her own little world of privilege, but she meddles in the life of Harriet, who had none of her advantages."

Carla turned toward Carlo, who shook his head. "My report is totally boring. You don't want to hear about my computer imaging class, and the best thing I did today was thirty push-ups in the backyard. It's crazy that I can't even walk over to Beto's house."

Carla opened her mouth to explain again, but he waved her off. "I know already. It's just driving me nuts."

Sabrina interjected. "We did something fun in one of my classes — name all the countries in the world that have only four letters in their name."

"Cuba." It was Carla, beaming. The rest of them fell silent for a moment or two, before Carlo named Iran and Iraq. Carla's phone rang.

They had a rule at the dinner table: no phones. But Carla glanced at the number and quickly got up and left the room.

It was Marta calling to give her a warning that Arturo worried about M_____ living by himself. He was so scared that Arturo wanted to take him in to shelter him. M_______ had been exposed to the virus by living with S_____. "I think Arturo's going to ask you to take him in." Carla thanked her and they hung up. The two women hardly needed to say anything more. They were the family's early warning system and the lifeline when their men couldn't talk to each other.

By the time she returned to the kitchen, the children had begun to clear the table and load the dishwasher. Sabrina gave her mother a look that assured her they would handle the dishes.

Carla soaked a washcloth in cold water and took it in to Pedro.

— ◦◦◦ —

For two days, Don didn't hear from Janice at all. He Face-Timed each day with Adam, who was surprisingly upbeat about no school and taking his classes by videoconference. He'd been playing hoops outside the garage with a friend every day, but now the friend's parents had told him it wasn't safe to play together anymore.

"Didn't your mother tell you the same thing?"

"No, she just told me to wash my hands when I come back in."

"Is she there now?" Don caught a glimpse of her in the background. A moment later, she joined the call and Adam excused himself, ending the video connection.

"I loved your note." Don ached to ask her to put herself on video but said nothing, waiting for more from her.

"Thank you for taking me back in time. I needed that, needed to remember how close we were, how much I miss you. I really do miss you." He could hear the catch in her throat. "I just don't know how …"

"I miss you too." By the time he had mustered the words, she had launched into another sentence. They were so often out of cadence in their speech.

"… to connect with you these days. You no longer need me to tell you how Adam is doing; he can do that himself. And I don't know what to ask you about yourself, especially since I know it's hard for you to answer."

"Just ask me. I need to talk – especially to you."

"What are your days like now that no one can visit?"

"I'm reading more, right now a biography of George Farmer. I've ordered *The Plague* from our library."

"*That's* cheerful."

He paused. Normally, such a comment would have silenced him with the implied criticism in its sarcasm. "No, of course not. I'm trying to learn from the past. I take some comfort from it; I can't explain."

"I'm glad you can find some comfort. I try to remind myself that Adam is thriving, we have everything we need, and I can still get out to run each morning. But I can't *feel* any comfort anywhere. I just have a vague unease about everything, and I've been having scary dreams."

"Of what?"

She wasn't ready to tell him the one about her becoming homeless when he divorced her. "Of losing things, of not being able to find the car, running up and down the street looking for it when I couldn't find it in the garage...."

"I wish I could hold you." He closed his eyes and paused. "Remember when you were five months' pregnant and worried about losing Adam?"

"Oh, god, yes. You wrapped yourself around me all night to reassure me. And it worked."

He could hear her smile, wanted to ask her to press the Face-Time button but did not want to lose this moment. "If I could do it now, I would."

"It helps me just to hear you say that." She took a deep breath, promising herself to imagine his doing so when she tried to go to sleep tonight. "What can I do to comfort you?"

Don felt the muscles on the left side of his face create a big smile. "Just call me every day – and press the Face-Time button so I can see you."

"I promise."

⸻◦●◦⸻

By the time Arturo called her, Carla had already considered the risks and the logistics of taking in M________, though she hadn't spoken to Pedro about it. Her mind roiled with the logistics. Saying no was out of the question. She couldn't be sure that Pedro had the virus, or if he did, whether time at home would let it run its course. If M________ stayed in the same room as Pedro, M________ could infect Pedro. But if Pedro already had the virus, quarantining them both in the same room made sense. Until five days ago, Carlo had worked closely with M________, which exposed them all. Being close to Carlo might be a comfort to M________, especially since they were close in age. But then where would Carlo study? And to what extent would M________'s presence in the house jeopardize them all? Why not Arturo's home? No one was sick there. Could she tell Arturo he should keep M________? But she was the nurse in the family.

"Manuel is having a tough time," he began. Suddenly he had become Manuel rather than M____. "He told me he wants to give up, he has no money, no friends, nowhere to go. My delivering food and cash to him isn't enough. I worry he's going to do something to himself, or just disappear. He's desperate."

"I know we should take him in," Carla began, using 'we' intentionally to mean the whole family. "But tell me why he should stay here rather than with you." She gained confidence by saying it.

"Here's what I think. We know Pedro is sick and you're keeping him apart from the rest of the family. We don't know yet if Pedro has it. We've all been exposed to S________ one way or another. We don't know when or if any one of us is going to get sick. You're the nurse in the family. But until we know about Pedro I think Marta and I should keep Manuel here. If more of us get sick, we might need to re-arrange ourselves, but for now we'll take Manuel in."

Carla was so relieved she sank into the chair behind her. She thanked Arturo and told him she would provide whatever help she could. Arturo only asked her to take good care of Pedro.

—◦•◦—

Erythea had worked forty-seven days without a single day off. She had so molded herself to her various roles that she could not even conjure what she would do with having a day or two to herself. Work and sleep, repeat. No concerts, no long walks, no yoga class, no long chats with friends. Even finding time to call Elissa had become challenging, especially since Elissa seemed to demand optimism from her. All optimism had drained from her, leaving only a profound exhaustion.

She dialed. It would be seven in the morning for Elissa, perhaps too early, but for Erythea it was ten at night and she needed to go to sleep herself. Elissa picked up on the first ring, saying 'pronto' with a stifled yawn.

"Let me see you, dear heart. Are you any better?"

"Si, si, si, I am so much better, though I probably look like crap." What Erythea glimpsed before tears fogged her vision was her lover in normal waking mode, clear-eyed and plain spoken. Her skin reflected the warm light of morning.

"You look beautiful. Don't even bother to sit up, you fill my heart just as you are." Elissa was trying to prop herself into a sitting position with one hand, while holding her phone in the other. Her little breasts emerged from the covers.

"Oops, I'm not trying to give you a skin shot, I'm just trying to sit up." She explained that her fever had lasted only a day, but the aches kept her in bed a second day and now, apparently, she was well. Anticipating the question, she explained that whatever had bothered Bea also lasted only a day. 'Probably just indigestion,' Elissa lightly dismissed the topic.

"Ryth, what's happening with you? Your eyes are dead, I can tell."

Erythea began to contradict her, but stopped herself mid-sentence. She took a deep hiccupping breath before launching into a dam break of words describing her endless days at work with listless elders. "I've turned into a robot."

"Robots don't cry." Elissa waited, murmuring encouragement as Erythea heaved with tears. Every time Erythea seemed to stop and gather herself, Elissa encouraged her to cry some more. "Let it out, my love, you can cry with me." For many minutes they continued in this rhythm, until Ryth told her she had cried herself out and could now go to bed.

"You'll be better tomorrow," Elissa assured her and signed off.

———◄●►———

We are schizophrenic about isolation. It conjures both the blissfulness of a sunny beach on a tiny island and at the same time the ultimate punishment of banishment from other human beings in a dark cell. This duality is captured eloquently in Benita Eisler's biography of Frederic Chopin, *Chopin's Funeral.* Chopin and his partner George Sand took refuge for four months on the island of Majorca, to restore his health in the sunshine. There he described his first impressions: "I'm surrounded by palm trees, cedar, cactus, lemon, orange, fig and pomegranate trees everywhere…. The sky is turquoise, the sea lapis-lazuli, the mountains emerald and the air smells of heaven. The sun shines all day long." His Impromptu No. 1, Op. 29 echoes this ebullience. Not long after his arrival, though, Chopin needed medical attention and the several physicians he consulted diagnosed tuberculosis. Under a recently passed Spanish law, he was evicted from the home he and Sand had secured, and the cost of burning and replacing all linens and other household effects added to their lodging cost. They found themselves relegated to an abandoned Carthusian monastery at Valldemosa, perched among stark mountain crags. When Chopin's piano arrived in the harbor of Parma and was hauled up five precarious miles of gutted road by a simple cart after weeks of haggling with customs officials, he could at last hear the preludes he had been composing. Sand described Chopin's terrors and phantoms at their retreat. Once, returning from town when she had been delayed by a storm, she found Chopin at the piano "in a kind of frozen despair, playing his wonderful prelude and weeping." Eisler describes Chopin as having suffered "a leper's banishment" in Valdemossa. One of his compositions attributed to that time is Op. 28, No. 2 in A Minor, marked by a darkness not usually associated with Chopin's music. Another, the prelude 14 in E-flat minor, conveys an intense dread.

Chopin's creativity was altered but did not cease in his isolation and weakened health.

⸺•◦•⸺

Erythea traversed the once-public halls of the Evergreen almost alone these days, on her errands to and from the kitchen to help with meals. Each time she passed the galleria of residents' artwork, she thought of visiting Abigail, whom she had not seen at all since the lockdown. Abigail of the beautiful landscapes, she thought, as she passed once again one of her detailed sylvan landscapes.

Abigail spread a large square of plastic under her easel and the simple chair she used for painting in her apartment. With the studio locked down, her choices were to paint from here or not to paint at all, and at the pace she felt her eyesight receding, she knew this was far the better choice. Besides, she even had decent morning light from her apartment window, a distinct advantage over the downstairs studio. This morning offered a warm yellow glow over her tiny universe.

She easily hoisted the painting in progress onto her easel and brought out the palette with yesterday's paints still soft on its surface. Today's light suited her subject, a mountain stream cascading down a rocky slope with trees dappling the light. She set up her tubes of paint on the small table next to her seat. Peering at what she had already done, Abigail moved her head as close as she could to the canvas, then withdrew a foot, two feet, even farther, trying to find what distance worked best with the eyesight she now had. She smiled a small rueful smile at the alteration in her painting style brought on by her retinal disease, the same condition that had affected Degas in his later work. Once highly precise, her images now were impressionistic, unintentionally mimicking Monet, whose cataracts distorted his colors but not his style. "Ah, but I'm still Abigail," she said to herself. "I'm still all here." She would work today on the wet rocks, she decided, and mixed small batches of gray and green for the wet rocks in the small cascade. No sooner had she dipped her brush into the first batch when she heard a knock at her door. Glancing at the large numerals on her watch, she saw it was too early for lunch. "Come in," she called. She smiled broadly when she saw it was Erythea.

"I haven't seen you in the longest time," they each said.

"Have a seat," Abigail invited, looking at her inquiringly, while she put on her mask.

"I'm just paying a visit to residents I haven't seen in a long time, to check how you're doing."

"Actually fine. I find I can paint here in my apartment even better than in the studio; there's better light here."

"I was just admiring the winter landscape of the pond and forest you have on display in the residents' gallery, and I thought I'd come up to say hello. Your painting is now on long-term display with the lockdown."

"You're even better than I am about finding bright spots in this lockdown. Tell me – did you find the geese on the pond in my painting?"

"No," Erythea blushed slightly. "I must not have looked closely enough."

"They're on the far left, almost hidden in the back. Don't worry; it was an intentional trick I created, camouflaging the geese. If I hadn't painted them, I probably couldn't find them myself these days."

"How long ago did you paint it?"

"Seven years, just before I came here. Even then, I knew something like this would happen to my eyes. Funny, that painting is still vivid in my head; I can see every detail."

"May I look?" Abigail nodded. Erythea got up and moved to where she could see the painting in progress.

"Your style has changed, and I like the impressionistic images. I can imagine the water flowing down that little stream, without having to see every detail."

"Thank you. You encourage me."

"Don't you paint from photographs or some other image?"

"No, I can see them clearly in my head. I used to hike along this little stream."

"I read somewhere that Beethoven could still compose even after he lost his hearing," Erythea mused.

"I read the same thing. I imagine he could hear the notes in his head." Abigail picked up her brush and dabbed a few strokes. "I think I'd rather lose my eyesight than my memory."

"I wish I could capture your attitude and spread it all around here," Erythea told Abigail before leaving.

———◦•◦———

Pedro's fever spiked again about nine that evening. At nearly 103, the fever signaled Pedro's urgent need for medical attention. In ordinary times, Carla would take him in to the ER, but all the media broadcast not to come to the hospital unless a person struggled to breathe. Again, Carla told him to lean on her while she took him to sit in a tub of cold water. Groaning, Pedro complained of his broken ribs. When they limped to the door of the bathroom, he signaled he wanted to sit on the toilet, and she turned around to fill the tub with cold water, promising to bring his fever down again. When she turned around again to lift him into the tub, she glanced down into the toilet and saw the pinkish cast to his urine in the water. He cursed when she let him down into the cold water and tried to push her hand away, but she used the washcloth to drain water down his back and over his head. He swatted her arm and yelled at her to stop, she was torturing him. Glancing again at his tainted urine, she decided to take him in to Marin General, where she worked. She didn't know who was on duty at this hour, but they would know and trust her. His kidneys needed attention.

"I'm taking you in," she announced as she eased his body to a sitting position on the bed. He complained about having to lift his arms as she put a shirt and sweatshirt on him, but cooperated in standing up to ease his jeans over his butt. She put socks and shoes on his feet. "Can you sit here while I tell Carlo where we're going?" He nodded, and she hurried into the other room to tell Carlo to watch the children while she took Pedro to the ER. "Let me drive you," he insisted, but she told him he could start the car but needed to keep his distance from his dad. Pedro was barely able to walk himself to the garage and into the passenger seat of the car. As she backed out of the garage, Carla prayed that someone she knew would be on duty at the hospital. The usual half-hour drive took barely fifteen minutes. There were no other vehicles on the road except a Safeway food truck and an ambulance that sped past her. As she approached the parking lot and emergency entrance, she saw the ambulance parked at the entrance and two other tents set up to the left of the entrance. Someone in scrubs, a gown, gloves, mask and transparent face shield directed her to the entrance of one of the tents. As she opened her car window, Carla recognized Gina as the attending nurse and began to describe Pedro's symptoms, including what she suspected was blood in his urine. "I'm bringing him in because I'm worried about his kidneys." Gina nodded.

Quickly, other attendants opened the passenger door, pulled up a gurney and began to lift Pedro onto it. Gina motioned for Carla to drive through. There was another car waiting behind hers. "Where can I park?" Gina just shook her head slowly. "You can't go in. Someone's waiting behind you. I'm sorry."

Carla glimpsed Pedro's gurney rolling into the entrance. Hurriedly, she parked the car and raced to the door to join him. Again she was blocked, again by someone who recognized her but was following new rules to isolate possible coronavirus patients. He will be evaluated, she was told, but we can't let anyone into the waiting room these days. Stunned, Carla wondered how she could have lost contact with Pedro so quickly, with no warning, no words of comfort, nothing. She left her phone number with the attendant. How long will it be? You should go back home, she was told. Stumbling back to the car, Carla wondered how they could even take a history from Pedro, before reminding herself that patients were often admitted from ER unconscious. It was the job of the hospital to find what they could from blood tests. How could she let Pedro go in without her? Pedro needed her. This was beyond anything she had imagined.

Carla sat dazed in her car for some time, absently watching another car pull up to one of the tents and, after some minutes while Gina in her alienating garb leaned over the driver's side, pull away and out of the parking lot with both of its passengers. Carla shuddered, then dissolved in heaving tears. Marooned in the parking lot, she grieved for Pedro. She had abandoned him to cold corridors of strangers in this unrecognizable garb. What should she do? She dialed Pedro on his cell, but was not surprised to get only his terse voice message. She wanted desperately to reassure him. She needed to talk to him. She wanted to tell Arturo what had happened but by now it was nearly eleven. She dialed him.

Arturo answered on the second ring. "What's wrong, Carla?" were his first words. She explained factually what had developed with Pedro since dinnertime, in the voice she recognized as her automatic nurse voice reporting to the physician coming on duty.

"They took him away before I could even talk to him." Again she dissolved into tears.

Arturo assured her she had done the right thing to take him to the hospital. "Do you want me to pick you up and take you home?"

His offer gave her strength. "No, I can drive myself."

"Call me when you know something. Whatever the time."

Arturo was in their living room talking to Carlo when Carla got home. He got up and wordlessly held her for some moments. Her body gradually loosened its tense grip and collapsed against him. He led her to a chair and poured her into it.

She started to explain to her son, but Carlo just lifted his hand to tell her Arturo had already explained. "Wake me if you hear anything from the hospital." He kissed her forehead and went up to bed.

"I feel terrible for leaving him."

"There was nothing you could do. It's how I felt when I saw the ambulance take S_____ away."

"At least the hospital has my number. I can call them if they don't call me. With S_____, he really was dropped off a cliff."

"He'll find us when he recovers."

"*If* he recovers...." She changed the subject. "How's Manuel doing?"

"Better. He just needed to be around people who care."

"And you know how to do that. Thanks for coming tonight."

Arturo got up, hugged her and left.

⸺⸳◆⸳⸺

"I seem to be the only one around here who doesn't have to wear a mask," Don joked as he saw Erythea come in masked and wearing gloves. "What's with the gloves?"

"Our new rules when visiting with any residents."

"Everyone? Not just the crips like me?"

"Don't call yourself that — ever." But Don could see she was smiling. She described having to wear gloves when visiting residents and when delivering meals.

"You have to deliver meals too?"

"All the staff are doing extra duty. You may be the only one whose life hasn't changed by the lockdown."

"Don't rub it in." They smiled at each other, each happy to see the other. "Actually, something big has changed for me," Don admitted. "I think I've got my wife back."

Her face lit like a child's expecting a story. He described his exchange of emails with Janice.

"You must be a good writer."

"You look much better than the last time I saw you. Has something changed for you too?" Don probed.

Erythea resisted the temptation to tell him her personal story. "I think I finally caught up on my sleep."

"What happened to my Camus book?"

"Would you believe the library is quarantined? I have to set it aside for a few days before I can give it to you. Besides, you have better things to do. Why not write your wife another letter, now that you know what works?"

She left to check in with other residents, buoyed by Don's new state of mind.

She set out to visit some of the memory care residents, playing fifties music with Harold on an iPod while he listened and his feet moved as if dancing, and reading old romances aloud to Sharon, who told her she had had such adventures herself, in her day. She saved for the end her visit with Marvin, whose only conversation consisted of some rendition of his physical ailments. After delivering dinner meals in labeled bags to the independent residents, she returned home and, for the first time in some days, had enough energy to do yoga for half an hour, then to meditate, which enabled her to postpone thinking about how much longer her life would function in this suspension.

⸻ ⬦ ⸻

The ring of her phone woke Carla before eight the next morning. She reached for it automatically without looking at the number calling her. Dr. Gelman, with whom she had worked directly a few years back, told her she had made the right move to bring Pedro in as soon as she had noticed his hematuria. "We have him on dialysis right now. He seems to be one of the COVID patients whose symptoms involve the kidneys before they develop breathing problems." With luck, he explained, the dialysis would be short-lived and he would return to full functioning.

"Can I talk to him? He was taken away so fast last night that I wasn't able to tell him what was happening."

"You can, but not now. His extension is 1416. He doesn't have his cell." Dr. Gelman explained that Pedro was sleeping now and exhausted from all the hospital intervention. He was on oxygen but didn't need a ventilator, his fever was down, but he was profoundly exhausted.

"Can I get tested? And our children too?" She had the presence of mind to ask.

"You'd think…. But that doesn't necessarily mean you get one. Let me work on it and let you know." With that, he signed off.

Carla immediately phoned Arturo to thank him and spread the news from Dr. Gelman. She asked about the other members of the family. "Beto's been coughing and has a runny nose, but I'm hoping it's just a cold. We should all get tested, but that's easy to say, difficult to get." He'd already checked with Dr. Gutierrez, who was pessimistic. After they rang off, Carla dressed and went to the kitchen to prepare breakfast and brief her two younger children. It was Pascua morning, ordinarily the most joyous day on the religious calendar. But Carla could not even think of Easter this year.

⸺◆●◆⸺

Gianlucca had the sweet notion of taking Lili out on his bicycle to ride along the *Navigli* early on Easter Monday, before many people would even be out of bed. Lili had awakened cheerful and eager, insisting on wearing again her flowered Easter dress from yesterday in church. Glancing over at the still water of the canal, he reflected on how much cleaner it looked than usual, even beautiful. In the shadows of the building fronts, he could see green fronds undulating in the clear water. Perhaps there were even fish these days. As a boy, he had caught small fish in the canal with his dad, which they used for live bait in the lakes nearby. Lili chirped happily at the doves drifting among the building tops and down toward the lane where they rode. All was quiet. Gianlucca recalled how his mother used to make a round *pane di Pasqua* for Easter morning. He and his sister would help her dye the eggs for it the day before. He always wanted to dye them green but his mother allowed only pink and blue. If only a bakery were open, or even a grocery store. He would find one and break off pieces to share with Lili. His happy memory was interrupted by the sound of a police *moto*. It soon pulled abreast of him, and the officer told him to pull aside.

Gianlucca braced the bicycle against the wall alongside the water and lifted Lili to the ground. She fluffed her dress, as if expecting the stranger to admire her in it.

"*Papieri,*" the officer demanded, without even looking at Lili. Gianlucca handed over his documents that permitted him to be out to exchange Lili between his and her mother's apartment, but the days were off and he was in a different section of the city and the grocery stores were closed. The officer read the permit document and shook his head. "No excuse." Gianlucca shrugged apologetically, saying only that he wanted to have Lili be out on Easter Monday. "You should keep her home safe," the officer told him bluntly, writing out a ticket for 300 Euros.

Gianlucca pedaled home in a foul mood.

———•••———

On Tuesday morning after Easter, Dr. Gelman telephoned Carla a second time. She could tell from the somber tone of his voice that his message was bad.

"Tell me."

"Pedro died a little after one this morning. His heart stopped. He'd been on dialysis and oxygen, very feverish late in the day and then suddenly he gave out. We're going to do an autopsy if you permit it, to learn more. It was just so sudden...."

Carla slumped into the nearest chair. She'd been pushing away this possibility from the moment she'd left him at the door of the hospital. She had no words within her. Her last contact with him would always be his batting away her arm in the icy bath she'd tried to give him to take down his fever. She vaguely heard Dr. Gelman repeating how sorry he was, but his voice came from another realm.

"Do the autopsy," she instructed in her nurse's voice, "and let me see all the details." She hung up.

As the designated breakfast helper in the family, Sabrina dressed quickly and went down the stairs to the kitchen to help her mother, expecting the aroma of coffee to radiate from the kitchen and the sound of her mother bustling inside. But the kitchen was silent. Before going back upstairs to see if her mother had overslept, which she could not remember ever happening, Sabrina glanced into the living room, where her mother was slumped in a chair, her head hanging at an awkward angle. "Please, God," she whispered to herself and rushed to her mother. "Mama?" The figure did not stir. Sabrina touched her mother's forehead, which was thankfully warm, and moved her mother's head to an upright position. "Mama!" she cried loudly. Still no movement. Sabrina ran to the foot of the stairs and yelled Carlo's name. When she turned around, Sabrina saw her mother start to shake her head, as if waking from a bad dream. Sabrina ran to her and threw her arms around her mother, who embraced her tightly. Not letting go, Carla whispered into Sabrina's ear, "Cara, your father is gone."

When Carlo came pounding down the stairs, he found his sister and mother intertwined, weeping uncontrollably. He knew. Carlo sank to the floor, embracing his mother's knees. After some time, Luis came sleepily down the stairs, wondering why his sister and brother clung to their mother. Carla moved to unseat Sabrina, took Luis' hand and brought him to her lap, where he too learned of his father's death. At some point Carlo got up and phoned his uncle Arturo from the other room.

Within an hour, the whole family was gathered, taking turns at embracing Carla in the chair. At some point, Marta half-lifted Carla from the chair and took her upstairs. By unspoken agreement Marta remained with Carla and her children all that first day, comforting and dressing Carla, cooking for the three children and assuring them that their family would survive together.

———◦●●◦———

May
~ Cracking Open

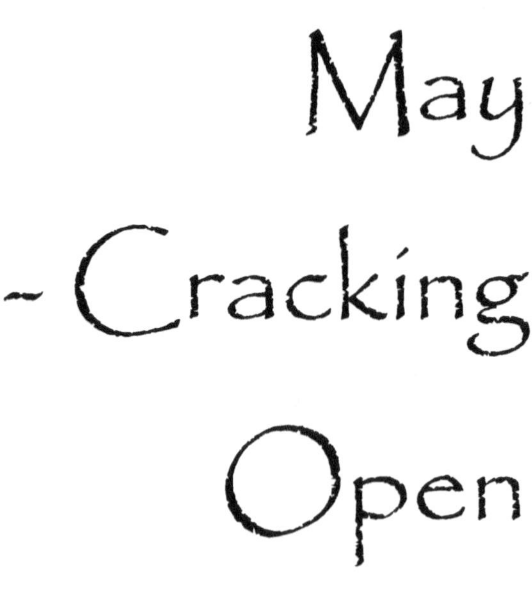

Don read the residents' newsletter on May 1 and asked himself how it could be May already. The first two months of lockdown, or what California had euphemistically termed 'sheltering in place', had vanished like clouds across a windy sky. For that matter, the past three years had blurred in a not dissimilar fashion. When Janice had him moved here, he was able to accept that she could not move with him, because of Adam, but he had had no concept of what it meant to spend the rest of his life in this place. Now it was quite plain that the four walls of this room constituted his last home, and that – except when someone rolled him in a wheelchair to concerts in the auditorium or outside to the terrace – these walls were the stark perimeter of his existence.

He had never before framed the thought of his last home. He would die here, surely, in this small room, and there was no other place for him to go. When he had purchased the home, he had thought of it as a place for the three of them, a family home, but not with any end point attached to the concept. To know that he would die in this bed, in this small room, on some unknown day in the future made him look around with new eyes. The two windows of his room framed a view out toward Mount Tamalpais, and he could watch it cloaked in fog, or with mists drifting across its slopes, or sometimes fully revealed, and the unpredictable cycle became some kind of omen for his days, the variety itself something to discover each day. On the walls of his room some volunteer had hung a mountain landscape, probably in Alaska, judging by the steepness of the mountains and the rusty brilliance of the ground cover. On the table next to his bed were framed photos of Janice, grinning with accomplishment at the end of a footrace, and of Adam in his cross-country uniform, hands on his narrow hips. He stored many more photos on his phone, and he had managed to both hold it and maneuver the photos with his left thumb to expand his visual memory. Don tried not to be limited by his physical perimeters. So long as he had his memory, his eyesight and his mental capacity, he would continue to learn, to remember and to appreciate being alive. He was determined to control his circumstances by his state of mind.

Just within the last week, Erythea had told him he could go to the garden terrace for an hour each morning, and he had gladly accepted the assistance of an aide to roll him out into the sunlight and park him near the blooming rosebushes. That first day provided a kind of surprised vividness -- he marveled that such a world still existed outside his perimeter. Now that he visited the garden every day – he'd asked the aide to roll him to the same spot – he noticed how each rose bush advanced, how the red buds became new blooms of pale yellow tinged with red at the edges and then how the petals faded and fell as the bloom expanded to its full reach. One of the independent residents trimmed the bushes with assiduous care, studying the tilt of each stem before she cut it. He asked her what she was studying, and she laughed shyly, admitting she'd been trained by the rose expert but wasn't certain she had caught the correct angle. What's the correct angle, he asked. She explained that the goal was to have each stem face outward. "So you want them all to be extroverts," he quipped, and she laughed spontaneously, putting one gloved hand to her masked mouth. "I never thought of it that way," she admitted, and they talked for a while, while she made sure to keep six feet away from him. Afterward, he reflected on how long ago it had been since he had made someone laugh, or had even spoken to someone other than Erythea or the person who delivered his meals. Now he looked for the rose tender each day and had even asked his aide, but he was told that independent residents were not allowed on the terrace during the hour reserved for residents in assisted living. After that, he noticed a pair of married residents, the woman in the wheelchair who lived a few rooms away from him, and her husband on the other side of the glass wall, making some attempt at communicating. With both of them masked, they could not even read the whole of the other's facial expression. At least when he spoke to Janice, he could see her full face, since she was inside their home and unmasked. But no one could touch each other. Before the lockdown, Don wondered, did this other couple at the window embrace in her room? He remembered embracing as if it had belonged to another lifetime, like high school track races, or sex. Certainly it had happened, and often, but in an unrecoverable region of his universe.

Don speculated on how long this lockdown would last. It had been nearly two months. The news regurgitated statistics of COVID occurrence, hospitalizations and deaths, but without the grizzly inevitability of gruesome death for each occurrence. Most of the states were relaxing their restrictions, some very cautiously, like California, and even more cautiously some counties like his own, while other states were re-opening fully. People could go to restaurants and to the beach, and they would be expected to return to work even in factories where the closed air and physical closeness rendered them breeding grounds for the next outbreak.

He had by now obtained and re-read Camus' *The Plague*. Erythea had retrieved it from the library for him and quarantined the physical book for a week before giving it to him. He knew that epidemics came to some sort of provisional end, often inexplicably, but with the specter of recurrence. This pandemic had thus far killed nearly five million people worldwide, a magnitude larger than any in his lifetime. But what percentage of the population was this? In the Middle Ages, the numbers of people killed by the plague were in the hundreds of thousands, but huge segments of the populations of different cities were obliterated.

Don was curious to see what would become of the world, even though he occupied only a tiny cell within it. Would the skies stay this blue? Would this country be relieved of its tyrannical president? Don's curiosity sustained him psychologically, even though he knew he could do so little to influence anything. Of course he would vote, but that act, though cultivated as an ingrained necessity, was infinitesimal in the larger universe. More immediately, he wondered whether Oberlin would be open for Adam in the fall. And what would Adam make of his education? Would Janice return?

What mattered most these days was when he could actually see and touch his wife and son again. If the time line was months, he could wait, he had learned to wait, he had developed a patience he never knew existed within himself. His recent exchange with Janice gave him hope, a lifeline to the time ahead.

⸻ ⁌•⁍ ⸻

Simon paced the perimeter of the terrace every morning, before the hour it was reserved for residents in assisted living, counting his rounds as if they were circuits of a prison yard, increasing the number each day. His irritation grew at the same rate, and he bristled as he had to alter his route to make room for other residents getting the same repetitious exercise. One morning he nearly tripped over the extended swollen legs of another resident who was sitting on a bench facing the outer world. He swore, hoping she hadn't heard him. Her sarcastic *"Excuse me"* trailed after him, and he gave her a wide berth on his next circuit. Another bloated one, he told himself, one of the many residents who had grown rounder in their enforced idleness and isolation. They tended to find a seat in the early sunlight and close their eyes, like so many zombies, he thought. How could he get out of here?

⸻ ⁌•⁍ ⸻

Janice helped Adam hoist his cello into the back seat of the car. She had arranged the details of this performance with Naomi, Leah's mother, so that Leah would sit alone in the dining room window facing Adam in the garden and Naomi would sit upstairs where she could not watch the two young people. Janice herself would park in the driveway, out of sight herself. She couldn't resist asking him what he was going to play. He looked back at her from the opposite side of the car.

"You've been hearing me practice it lately; you just don't know what it is."

"No, I don't." She looked at him quizzically; did he not want her to know?

"Part of Gluck's *Orfeo ed Euridice.*"

"You're right; I don't know it, but you've got the right motif. "

She blew him a kiss.

She sat in the car, window down, listening to the plaintive melody and wishing Adam would play it also for his father, who would both appreciate the music and the ability of his son to play it.

Adam was silent when he returned to the car. He hoisted the cello into the back seat by himself and looked down at his hands during the short ride. Janice did not interrupt his thoughts, whatever they were, and he disappeared to his room for the rest of the afternoon. The cello remained silent until dinner.

⸻ ⬥ ⸻

A week after Pedro died, Carla told Ann, her supervisor, that she would be ready to come back to work after the two-week quarantine. "Are you sure?" Ann asked. "You can take compassionate leave, with pay. We're not even crowded now."

"I want to come back. I need to work, and it's not all about money," she'd told her, almost fiercely, and Ann backed down. Arturo had offered her money, Carlo had offered to donate his unemployment benefits when and if they came through, Marta had told her to stay with the children, but Carla insisted. No one had been able to dissuade her, and they had all tried, except for Sabrina, who seemed to understand without words that she simply needed to go back to help people and work for her family. It went to a deep, unspoken place within her.

In the first week of May, Carla put on her clean nurse's uniform for the first time in almost a month and drove to work. She was interviewed at length about the exposure to COVID-19 in her family and answered truthfully that no one in her family had got sick except Pedro. She had tested negative a few days earlier, as had her three children. She had not had to answer about S______ because he was not actually part of her family. She did not in fact know what had become of him, did not even know if she would encounter him in the hospital. She was assigned to surgical recovery and was surprised to find how few beds were occupied. On her first shift, she attended only four patients: a teenaged boy who had broken two ribs and his femur in a bike accident; a Guatemalan man her age who had had an emergency appendectomy; a seventy-year-old obese woman who had had her gall bladder removed; and an eighty-year-old man who had had a stent inserted into his aortic artery. The teenager was the least willing among them to talk; he seemed embarrassed to have fallen off his bike and wanted as little attention as possible paid to him. Carla had given each of them a sponge bath and administered meds to each of them during her shift. Both of the older patients were consumed by fear of the coronavirus. Although Carla wore a mask, face shield, gloves and PPE gown and she assured each of them that she worked only in this wing -- which had no coronavirus patients -- they shrank from her touch. Carla felt relieved when the older woman fell asleep and stopped talking. By contrast, the Guatemalan man – who greeted her in Spanish as soon as she entered the room – relaxed under her touch. She could feel his tension subside as she swabbed his arms with the warm sponge. Even as she changed his dressing, he carried on a conversation as if unafraid of her infecting him. Like her, Roberto had three children. His wife had been in to visit just before Carla's shift had begun. He explained his wife had driven him to the hospital late at night as his gut pain became unbearable, and that she had stayed through the surgery and his immediate recovery. His mother, who lived with them, had stayed with their children overnight. Carla told him he was lucky to have had her with him, and he clasped her hand and nodded as he agreed. "Will I see you tomorrow?" Roberto asked plaintively as she came in at the end of her shift. She assured him she would.

Ann asked Carla at the beginning of her shift each day that first week if she felt okay returning to work. Each day Carla assured her that this was where she wanted to be. The attention required of her distracted her from the unspeakable wrenching of seeing Pedro being swallowed into the gullet of the emergency room.

Carla returned home each day just before dinner. Usually Carlo and Sabrina combined efforts to put a simple dinner together, and the four of them sat down together as if four were the whole number of their family. Luis had the least pretense of normalcy, the least reserve among them.

"Tell me again how Papa left," he said more often than any of them could bear, and one of them each time explained that their dad had died from his sickness. "He is with God," Sabrina told him, as if that would make it any better. "Why?" Why with God and not with them? Carla cradled her youngest, trying to explain that death is hard to understand but that none of them would see their father again.

On the Saturday before Mother's Day, Sabrina assured her that she should sleep in and that the children would take charge of breakfast for her. Over the years this had become a ritual, with Pedro and Carla sleeping in and Sabrina making them pancakes for a late, sweet morning meal. The announcement earned Sabrina a wan smile before Carla went upstairs to bed.

Carla awoke sprawled across the center of the bed, surprised that she had slept deeply. Her right arm lay across Pedro's place in the bed. From the lemony light in the room, she guessed that she had slept in, and a glance at the clock – 8:13 – confirmed her sense. By this time, she would ordinarily be well into her shift at the hospital, taking notes after her first round. Because she could, because she was conscious of creating a new normal (that much-overused phrase these days of re-opening after the peak of the COVID shutdown), she rolled out of bed on Pedro's side because it was closer to the shower. And she lingered under the warmth of the water much longer than she would have with Pedro waiting for it. She dressed consciously in cheerful color for the children, pulling on an embroidered Mexican blouse Pedro had once bought for her on a trip home. She combed her thick long hair and braided it from the back, surprised at her ease. She hadn't worn a braid in what seemed like years.

As she padded down the stairs, she could hear Sabrina and Carlo's voices through the closed door. But when she swung the door open, she was amazed to see Marta at work with Sabrina and Carlo, and Arturo seated at the table with Beto, Bettina, Tomas and Luis. They called out 'Happy Mother's Day' nearly in unison. After hugging each one of them, Carla admired the yellow tulips on the table. Marta thrust a glass of her homemade watermelon *agua fresca* into her hand. Carlo hauled a large plate of pancakes from the warming oven, and the family devoured the sweet treat with real Mexican coffee that Arturo had flavored with cinnamon. Carla ate little but kept basking in the warmth of her big family around her. They hadn't all eaten together since their picnic on Arturo's birthday two months earlier.

When they had all finished eating, Carlo and Beto insisted on clearing and washing the dishes. "No mothers work today," they announced.

Arturo proposed they all go to the lagoon park in San Rafael today. "Isn't it closed?" Marta reminded them. Beto quickly consulted his phone. "Walking only. We can't park there due to shelter in place orders.

"But first, we want to show you something." Beto and Carlo each took one of Carla's arms and led her into the living room. Nestled beside the bookcase was a new construction, a three-tiered *ofrenda* for Pedro, painted in bright orange, Pedro's favorite color. Carla gasped. At the back of the top shelf was a collage of photos of Pedro – smiling in his chef's hat and apron, behind sunglasses in a small fishing boat, his arm around Carla and their children at Carlo's high school graduation, relaxing at the beach, in each one of them Pedro beaming his broad smile. On the second shelf was a small vase filled with large crepe paper poppies and a large candle in a glass with a Madonna depicted on the outside. Placed on the bottom shelf were a bowl full of oranges and a tiny plate of one of this morning's pancakes, dusted with powdered sugar in the letter 'P'. Carla knelt and crossed herself, blinking back her tears.

"I have the best family," she murmured. "I can't thank you enough."

———•••———

Janice proudly told Don about Adam's playing his cello at Leah's window. She intentionally omitted how obsessed he had seemed with his playing, only partly because she knew Adam was waiting for her signal to play for his dad. She added Adam to her FaceTime call with Don and was pleased to hear that Adam had chosen a happier selection of music than the Bach suite. She watched Don's face intently as Adam played, noting every expression that flitted across the left side of his face, the limpness of the other side, and the vivid interest in both of Don's eyes. She heard Adam make a small error and noted a flicker in the muscles under Don's left eye; would he be the acerbic critic he used to be while at home? Adam was hypersensitive to his dad's smallest reaction. As he reached the crescendo at the end of this piece, Adam displayed a small flourish of his bow. He looked down momentarily and then glanced eagerly at his dad.

"Adam, I lost track of how well you play. Your music made my day. " Don placed his left hand on his heart. "Will you play for me again?"

Adam grinned. "Sure, Dad." Janice exhaled a tiny sigh of relief.

———•••———

Arturo watched Carla with quiet amazement over the weeks since Pedro's sudden death. She had the spine and determination to return to work, yet at the same time she kept her heart open. He privately thought she was the strongest among them. He felt consumed by worry. Who else in their family or group of employees would fall ill? Manuel had been quarantined in their home for two weeks at Carla's direction and now had returned to the tiny apartment that he used to share with S____. No one had heard a word from S_____, and Arturo assumed he had also died of the virus. One of his other employees had stopped showing up for his pay because he too had a 'flu' bad enough to stay away from others. Beto had recovered from his cold, but Arturo did not trust in his recovery; every day he watched for new symptoms. Some but not all of his employees had begun to receive unemployment, and his own small business recovery relief remained tied up in a bureaucratic loop he could not penetrate. His own money was holding up fairly well. The only spending he or Marta did was for food. Marta asked him if she could follow in Carla's footsteps and return to work, but he continued to ask her to wait. His reasons sounded feeble even to himself. He knew he was simply afraid of losing her.

Yet all around them the world seemed to be re-opening, at least in the news and even a bit in their neighborhood. Families began to grill outside and sit on their porches in the warm evenings. In the cul-de-sac where he lived, three teenagers positioned their vans to make a triangle of the rear bumpers, and then opened the rear doors to let down and sit on the bottom and share beers and loud music with each other. Some of his neighbors sat together about ten feet apart and caught up with each others' lives. On the news he watched videos of crowds at Florida beaches, no one masked. Arturo did not recognize his world, and he walked around in a daze of wondering what reality he inhabited: critical danger or normalcy.

——◦●◦——

Erythea felt a parallel malaise. She continued to FaceTime with Elissa every day. Elissa was pervasively weak, sometimes achy, and she lay in bed many hours of the day. That Liss, who prided herself on her energy, would lie around watching TV when she wasn't dozing and admit to it was proof that she was truly ill. "I can't believe this is me, Rhyth." Their daily conversations no longer focused on getting a flight home, or even on painting or Italy.

"I worry about my practice, my patients and about running out of money." Erythea offered to contact all of Liss' patients and to help with money, but what Elissa needed most was her ear, something Erythea the professional should have known.

"Just listen, Ryth. Only you know the details of my life."

Erythea nodded and apologized. Elissa missed being the person who could relieve another's aches and pains. She missed the strength and intuition of her hands. She missed being in charge of her life. Her enchantment with Italy had twisted into frustration with unfamiliar details, logistics of getting a flight, the complication of her being ill but not ill enough to see a doctor.

"I spend hours each day imagining myself inside our apartment and the daily patterns our life together, but then I interrupt myself with the reality that I'm sick and I would be endangering you and your work. I go around this mental treadmill much of the day, and there are no answers anywhere. I don't have enough energy to paint or read a book and I don't know enough Italian to follow the soap operas that glaze over me on the television. It's just the pits."

"When we get to the other side of this – and we will – you and I will luxuriate in the simple pleasures of our lives. I can only look forward to that."

"Ryth, that's music to my ears. It's just what I need to hear from you."

Just days later, after five or six such daily conversations with each of them comforting the other, Erythea called Elissa at midmorning, expecting more of the same.

"Did you see what just happened in Minneapolis! Did you see that cop literally suffocate a man with his knee? Did you see the cold look on his face as he held his knee down while the man cried 'I can't breathe'?" Liss practically shouted her fury. "White cop, black man dead."

Erythea had worked late again, had not seen or heard the news. For months there had seemingly been no news about anything other than COVID-19. She listened carefully to Liss, confessed her ignorance. "You gotta watch it. Go track the news and call me back."

Glancing at her watch as she tuned in, Erythea had no trouble finding the video. She watched, mesmerized, even though she knew she would be late for work. For nearly nine minutes, Derek Chauvin, the stony-faced white cop, held his knee on the neck of his handcuffed prisoner, squashing the life out of him. She heard George Floyd, prone and still, pleading he could not breathe. The look on Chauvin's face was coldly intentional, as if showing anyone watching 'this is how we do it.' Bystanders objected, other cops stood blocking both access and view of the doomed man. Stunned, Erythea turned off the set. She had never before witnessed one man intentionally kill another, defenseless and still beneath him. The look on Chauvin's face chilled her. She couldn't talk. She texted Liss that she would call back later.

She got dazedly into her car, wondering what strange world she had stepped into.

Carlo disappeared before lunch wearing a bandana across his face. His mother watched him leave, noting the anger and determination in his stride. Two nights ago, she too had watched the white cop smother George Floyd with his knee. Since then she watched as flames erupted in Minneapolis and other cities. She watched as a black Hispanic reporter was arrested for failing to leave the site of a demonstration, watched as the President summoned the National Guard and fired tear gas into a peaceful crowd in front of the White House, just so he could walk across the street to wave a Bible in front of the cameras. Disgust momentarily replaced her grief. She had no doubt but that Carlo was leaving to join some demonstration. If she were his age, she would join him. Yes, she worried about his contracting the virus in a crowd, she worried about how the police might treat him, but she admired him more than she worried. She had no doubt but that Beto would be at his side, wherever they were demonstrating.

At lunch, only Luis asked where Carlo was. Sabrina and Carla exchanged glances. Carla told him his brother had gone for a walk.

"Why didn't you go too?" Carla asked Sabrina abruptly.

"He made me promise to stay home with you and Luis."

Carla just nodded and passed around a bowl of salad. "The pot is boiling over." Sabrina nodded while Luis looked around the kitchen, wondering what pot they were talking about.

When Carla got to work, she sought out Ann to request a more demanding assignment than post-surgical. "Put me in the COVID section." Ann just shook her head. "There are only two patients in there and we have it covered." Carla gave her a searching look, and Ann reassured her that post-op would likely become more active.

By the end of May, the number of COVID-19 deaths in the United States had exceeded 100,000. The incidence varied immensely from one state to another, one sector within a state to another. The numbers of unemployed reached 14 million, disproportionately among lower-paying jobs and people of color – people who drove busses, stocked the shelves in stores, waited tables in restaurants, served the coffee at Starbucks, rendered the meat in slaughterhouses, plucked the chickens in the chicken-processing plants, baked the bread in industrial bakeries, delivered packages, and manicured people's gardens.

The wearing of masks became political; in some red states those who wore masks were shunned or ridiculed. The unmasked President proclaimed the crisis over and demanded that businesses re-open to refuel the economy, without regard for risk to workers' lives.

When demonstrators massed peaceably in the streets around the White House, he called up the National Guard to create a protective barrier for himself, and his troops tear-gassed the demonstrators to create a path for him to walk across the street to a church where he waved a Bible while flanked by uniformed officers from the several armed forces.

His tweets continued to provoke, while for the first time Twitter inserted notations as to their accuracy and cautions about his incitement to violence.

June

~ Rapunzel

Janice and Zoe happened upon one of the demonstrations in their tiny peaceful community as they neared the end of one of their daily walks. Zoe spontaneously joined. Janice automatically followed her into the small crowd, all of them observing a six-foot social distance, or at least trying to. Some carried pre-printed signs that read "BLACK LIVES MATTER." A few carried hand-painted signs that read "I Can't Breathe." Janice noted the irony: her upscale white suburban community epitomized all the people who could readily breathe. While most of the people here were white, many of them Don's age or older, most were college-age and many of them Hispanic or Asian or mixtures Janice couldn't even try to guess, especially with their masks covering most of their faces. The speakers were young African-Americans who vowed this time they would not let the country forget. They promised demonstrations would continue across the country until police practices changed.

Zoe and Janice wove their way out of the crowd after listening to only a few minutes of the jargonized speeches. She told Janice she had marched across the Golden Gate Bridge with more demonstrators from San Francisco a few days earlier.

They spoke about reactivating their walking group, and Janice volunteered to call Naomi, Susan and Gina to see if they would venture out again. Janice thought it would be futile to invite Naomi but the call would provide an opening to talk about Leah and Adam.

She phoned Susan and Gina that same afternoon, saving Naomi for last. Susan had got over her flu but did not want to venture out, and Gina told her she was still out for the duration – this disease was just too serious to take any risk. Janice broached the subject with Naomi cautiously, as if certain Naomi would not want to rejoin them.

"I'm so glad you called. I've been missing you," Naomi began. "Would you be willing to walk just with me one of these days? We'd have to stay away from everyone else, and I promised Saul and Leah that I would shower and change my clothes when I come back home."

Janice leapt at the invitation, and they arranged to hike the next morning in their neighborhood. Janice would take a day off from walking with Zoe. She neglected to mention having attended the demonstration.

<hr>

They were survivors, all of them, the 142 graduating seniors of Paradise High School. In November 2018 they had fled the firestorm that devoured their tiny town, some of them coming perilously close to death themselves. From temporary shelters they had finished their junior year in the high school of an adjacent town. Then in spring 2020 COVID had closed their school again. But they were determined to celebrate their graduation with a ceremony. Their parents and school superintendent wrote Governor Newsom to help find a way to conduct a live graduation on the high school's football field. What they were told was that only a drive-in service would be permitted – no procession, no live audience, no handling of diplomas or handshakes from the principal. But they made it happen. From double rows of five cars parked facing each other across the 50-yard line of the football field, students emerged, two at a time from cars parked opposite each other, allowing for special friends to choose their graduation partner, each graduate giving the other a socially-distanced high-five as they approached the table for their graduation photograph in their green and yellow graduation gown and retrieval of their symbolic diploma. Performed in half-hour segments of ten cars each, the entire graduation ceremony took two days to complete. But they accomplished a live high school graduation under the most challenging circumstances. If one had to select a cadre of soldiers to find their way out of a dangerous predicament, one might well begin with the 2020 graduates of Paradise High School.

Adam threw down the newspaper article next to his mother.

"You'd think my own fancy suburban high school could come up with a live graduation? Not!" He stalked out of the room.

⬤

Erythea connected to her Zoom meeting with Simon at ten-thirty on the second Monday of June. He was relatively unknown to her, a retired philosophy professor from Berkeley, widowed two years earlier, who had moved into the Evergreen almost a year ago. At eighty-five, he was only slightly older than the average age of Evergreen residents. By his profile, she would have pegged him as among the least likely of the residents to reach out to her for counseling. But she was about to learn. At precisely ten-thirty, his face appeared on the screen. Though clean-shaven, he had unruly, almost kinky hair that leapt out from every angle of his head, and eyebrow hairs that curled like small vines from around the thin rims of his glasses. He had penetrating dark eyes and an open smile.

"We've never met, but I wanted to reassure you that I don't usually look like a wild man." They both laughed and rued the unavailability of barbers and hairdressers during the quarantine. Without any prompt from her, he launched.

"I don't know if you can do anything about my existential question," he began, as Erythea probed her memory for what he meant by existential. "But when I consider my unknowable time left on this planet, I find it nearly unbearable to be totally pent up inside. I'm as close to being depressed as I've ever been in my life, and I want to assure you I've never been a depressive. I came here partly to enjoy a community during my last years, but not to lose the community I have outside. I can't talk my way rationally out of this."

"I don't think any one of us has ever lived through anything like this," Erythea temporized, "and you've been alive longer than I. We're exposed to a lethal, invisible risk and the Evergreen is regulated by the County Public Health Office as well as by the state."

"I feel like I'm in prison, and it doesn't bring out the best in me."

"Have you made any friends here?" She knew he played chess with Don, but that wasn't available to either of them now.

"A few, but I've never been in the habit of just calling people to chat."

"What are your favorite ways of connecting with people?"

"Having dinner with friends at a restaurant, a bottle of wine and talking until late in the night about politics, ideas, books, theater...."

"Have you connected with them like we're doing now?"

"Yeah, but Zoom has its limits. And, I'd just like the freedom to take an aimless walk. That's usually how I have resolved anything that has troubled me in the past. It drives me crazy that I can't go out the front door. I wasn't *sentenced* to this place!"

"What do you think would help you the most?"

"Just being able to share a glass of wine and conversation with friends on the terrace, and to wander at will outside."

Erythea almost interrupted him to say that he could sit and talk with friends on the terrace, provided they are masked and at a designated distance marked by the X'es on the ground. But she had no answer for him about going outside. They continued for a while longer in this general vein, with her even suggesting he set up a Zoom discussion group for political issues, but she could see she made no headway.

Finally, he erupted. "I can tell I'm wasting your time and my own. *Sorry.*" The 'sorry' cast anger, not apology. He hung up before she could say anything further, not that she had anything useful in mind.

As she disconnected herself, she reflected on the difference between her freedoms and his. She took real solace from her walks alongside the Bay in Mill Valley, and now she could even walk out to the ocean and sit meditating to the sound of the waves. She could share a bottle of wine with friends outside. She could take long drives along the ocean or wherever she liked. She could think of nothing to give him a sense of physical freedom without actually opening the doors where he lived.

Simon had pressed the red button to end the meeting as soon as he realized he was about to rail at her that this was not a Victor Frankl moment. She didn't deserve his fury. He was not ready to adapt himself to intolerable circumstances; he was still trying to change them.

⚊⚫⚊

When Naomi emerged from her home, Janice suddenly realized how long it had been – three months – since they had last walked together. Over her blue mask, Naomi's honey-brown eyes smiled. During this time, Janice was learning to read facial expressions from eyes only. "How I've missed you!" they each blurted almost at the same time. By habit, they followed what had been their usual morning route. Not half a block from her home, Naomi exclaimed at how beautifully a large willow tree had leafed out. She crossed the street to stand underneath its umbrella and wave her hands gently through the cascading branches. To Janice, this tree had just been one of the landmarks along the path, but now she saw it with Naomi's new eyes. "Have you not been out of the house at all?"

"Practically not. We order all our groceries in. My own business had almost ground to a halt. I can't show houses except electronically, but I've learned how to sell homes via computer and phone. Saul conducts services and meetings via Zoom, and he's on the computer or telephone hours each day. We've all learned new skills."

Janice asked about Leah. Naomi described how Leah had learned to assemble the high school yearbook electronically, from photos taken before March.

"But not having a graduation has affected us all. We'd wanted to watch her march to Pomp and Circumstance, with the gold braid on her shoulder. And she misses standing up with her class and with Adam specially." Naomi glanced at Janice as a fellow proud parent, but then she shrugged. "Leah has adapted. She's arranged to take an online summer course in biology since she was homebound in any event. And Pomona will conduct all of its fall classes electronically."

They were silent a few minutes while Janice digested this announcement. Adam's own disgruntlement about no graduation ceremony paled against his missing contact with Leah. The ceremony meant nothing by itself to either Janice or to Adam. If he could trade the graduation event for an hour alone with Leah, his choice would be instantaneous. What struck Janice was Naomi's casting doubt on college as usual for the fall. She and Adam were operating on the assumption that Oberlin would open as usual, perhaps with more distance between students in classes. It had not even occurred to her that colleges might not open. She confessed as much to Naomi.

"This is going to last longer than you think."

Janice abruptly changed the subject. No, no, no blasted through her head.

Janice asked if Leah was seeing any of her friends. "She has a weekly Zoom session with four girls, and she talks to Sara, her best friend, and Adam every day."

Janice bluntly asked if Naomi would consider allowing Adam to see Leah in person. "He's not been exposed to anyone but me for all this time. Well, he used to throw hoops with Jason but his parents stopped that a month ago."

"We can't take that chance. She has asthma, she's high risk by definition." Naomi looked at Janice before adding, "we really like Adam but we won't take that risk."

Adam bounded downstairs as soon as Janice opened the front door. "Nu?" She didn't even have time to shower before having to explain to him that Leah's parents would not relent, probably for the whole summer. "That makes no sense!" All she could tell him was that everyone had to gauge their own sense of risk, and that Leah's parents loved her too much to allow her to see anyone. He stormed back upstairs. When Janice emerged from her shower, she could hear Adam playing the Bach suite again.

— ◦●◦ —

On June 2, the President announced to the governor of North Carolina that he would remove the August 24 Republican Convention from Charlotte to another state if the governor insisted on scaling down the size of the space, attendees wearing masks and observing social distancing.

The President taunted the governor with the loss of dollars and jobs the convention would bring. When the governor refused the President's requests for health reasons, the President removed the convention to Jacksonville, Florida, where its Republican administration accommodated his requests for 'business as usual'. The President continued to flout wearing a mask or encouraging others to do so or to keep a safe distance from each other. Republicans coming to the Convention would have to place loyalty over all other considerations in attending.

———•••———

When Carlo burst in and flung off his bandana, Carla looked up at him inquiringly. Each day he had disappeared with Beto to demonstrate in different locations, each day regaling her with details of the peaceable crowds. Today they had driven to Oakland, to a demonstration of 'Brown Folx 4 for Black Lives'. "There were thousands of us!" He flung his arms wide. She looked down to hide her pride. "Did you keep your distance?"

"Yes, Ma." He hugged her.

Now Sabrina wanted to go with him. Carla felt a jolt within herself. Sabrina was younger but at thirteen still old enough to go with her older brother. Carla bent her head, overcome by tears.

"I can't let you go." Sabrina put her arms around her mother. "It's okay, Mama. I'll stay here with you and Luis."

Marta continued to phone Carla every day, replacing their daily meetings at hospital break time with an evening call after dinner. Tonight Carla confessed she had refused Sabrina's request to join the demonstrations even though she thought the demonstrations were important. "I just can't bear the thought of losing her too."

"You acted from your heart. Don't ever feel bad about that."

"It's not that I love Carlo any less."

"Of course not. He's been more exposed, and he has more years of judgment." With that bit of advice, the ache in Carla's chest subsided. She was able to listen to Marta's frustration about not returning to work.

"They're shorthanded at the Evergreen, and they call me every week."

"Maybe Arturo feels about you the way I feel about Sabrina, but he just can't say it."

"Maybe." This had not occurred to her.

Arturo was getting ready to re-open the restaurant again, limited to take-out orders. He'd reached all of his workers except for S______, and each of them was healthy and eager to return. Beto and Carlo wanted to work again, though they each said they wanted time to continue demonstrating. "Until when?" Arturo asked. They each shrugged their shoulders. "Until things change…." No one could say how long anything would last these days. Marta asked to join him at the restaurant. They had worked together in the kitchen ever since Pedro died, and their coordination was automatic, sinuous, even better than his with Pedro. Her being home with him had been a bigger gift than he could have imagined, and he feared life would become more disjointed when she went back to work. But going back to work with him? That was different. He would give it a try. He preferred her working with him to returning to the retirement home or the hospital, where she couldn't stay safe.

⬤◆⬤

Janice had resumed her daily calls with Don, and now somehow she found ways to connect with him. Today she told him about her walk with Naomi and the likelihood that all Leah's classes would be electronic. She confessed she had assumed Adam would attend class in person in the fall. "It never even occurred to me that he couldn't."

"Adam and I have been talking about that." Janice blinked, amazed Adam and his father had had more important conversation than she with either one of them. "He was most worried about his cello classes, but they seem to be going well one-on-one with his present instructor on Zoom. He's prepared to live with it."

"Did he talk to you about Leah?"

"Only glancingly. He told me her parents were strict about her not seeing anyone besides them, and that he had played cello for her from outside her window."

"I think he's heartbroken."

"I do too. He won't talk to me about it."

Janice wondered after the call what she would do if she were Leah's mother. Would Leah's asthma make her so cautious that no one else could have personal contact with her? Easy to second guess someone else, she thought, when the responsibility is not my own. Much more difficult to imagine living as Leah, wondering what her own boundaries would be if she had the chance to set them herself. How might Leah be affected by this year? Janice had no prediction.

—◆◆◆—

For Erythea, the encounter with Simon left her reeling with images of Elissa's profound lassitude, other residents' anxiety about even opening their apartment doors, and the flickering terror in Joseph's eyes when he learned that his nephew Ramon had tested positive for the virus. Joseph headed a family of eight who lived with him in the canal district of San Rafael. He had worked in the Evergreen for nineteen years, now as head of maintenance. Over time, various members of his extended family had also found work in the Evergreen with his help, Ramon among them. Joseph drove Ramon to work most days, although they lived in separate households. Ramon helped clean the kitchen. Joseph occasionally helped with meal delivery, and yesterday he had been teamed with her at lunchtime. Now he and Ramon were each quarantined for two weeks. George informed her she too would need to be re-tested due to her recent contact with Joseph. Irritated, she asked herself if Simon had any clue what it took just to keep this community functioning. Likely not.

She submitted to the nasal test for the third time that afternoon just before leaving for home. Fantasizing about Elissa's return home, Erythea realized that her return would impose a two-week quarantine for herself. She could not conjure a happier scenario. When she phoned Elissa that evening, she visualized Elissa feeling stronger, readier to return home if they could find a flight. Elissa's answer to the FaceTime call revealed Elissa standing before her canvas, with Genoa in morning light behind her. Seeing Erythea's grin, Elissa beamed. "Yup, I'm better. I can stand and paint for an hour or so. I'm feeling more myself every day."

"Should I call the airlines and book a flight?"

"Give me a few more days. I want to be sure I'm getting stronger, and not just going through the next blip."

When Liss asked her how she was doing, she found herself describing her useless encounter with Simon. "He doesn't know how good he has it" was all Liss would say. "He didn't deserve your time."

"He did, though. He was just wrestling in his own way with circumstances he can't control." Liss shook her head, her lower lip turned out. Her dismissal had the perverse effect of summoning Erythea to defend him, arousing an empathy Erythea wanted to hear from her own partner.

On Father's Day morning, Marta managed to slip out of the bed without waking Arturo. Since the closing of the restaurant, he had begun to sleep in a little later, and Marta welcomed his being close as she awakened. In a way she had never consciously recognized before, she savored being able to hold him, hold her children and also Carla. Most mornings he would fold himself around her and gently stroke her belly. The virus had taken her brother-in-law but given her gratitude. She shook her head thinking of such contradictions. 'Focus on breakfast', she told herself.

Shaving the rough skin off a pineapple, she remembered her grandfather doing the same task much more quickly with his machete, marveling at his skill and watching with a kind of frightened suspense as to whether he would cut himself with his sharp strokes. He had rough fingers. When he gently stroked her cheeks, his hands felt like bark. It took her much longer, but she did not cut herself. Washing the sticky juice off her fingers, she was glad to have soft hands.

Marta fried up two rashers of bacon before Beto, Bettina and Tomas showed up. "Where's Dad?" they all asked. "Shhh, before he comes down, would you all sign this?" She shoved a big Father's Day card toward them. They all grinned. "We have our own," and they held it up. They had constructed and decorated it themselves. It was her turn to grin. She had not expected this. Beto insisted on preparing the eggs this morning, and Tomas and Bettina set the table.

Arturo opened the door to a five-way embrace from his family.

At breakfast they reviewed the details of his re-opening the restaurant for take-out. Beto knew immediately how to reactivate the take-out menu and to broadcast to their contacts that Arturo's was pleased to re-open. Arturo took in his family's enthusiasm, which reminded him of that day in March, his birthday, when the whole family had hiked and enjoyed a picnic together, planning for the first re-opening of the restaurant for take-out. Looking around the table, Arturo observed the buoyant energy of his family. But in that hundred days, he had lost his brother and one of his workers. His world had become a far more dangerous place.

Don awoke to the deep-voiced aide Russell asking him to help sit up.

"Special breakfast this morning, sir," he announced, and Don tried to help with his left hand as Russell hoisted him from under his right shoulder into a sitting position and swiveled the tray in front of him. Russell took the cover off a plate of scrambled eggs with spinach, ground beef and mushrooms. "Need any help cutting?" Don said no, thank you, and Russell left the room after raising the shades. Before lifting his fork, Don picked up the card from Janice that had arrived in yesterday's mail. For years they had virtually ignored this day. He had scoffed at it as a commercially created holiday, and Janice had seemed relieved of one less wifely chore. The card felt different now, and he savored just looking at it, without needing to reread it. He remembered every word.

Janice phoned just as he was finishing his breakfast, a tedious process that took all his attention. Pleased to hear her voice, he mustered a joke. "Where shall we go today?" They used to take Sunday drives together, even after his stroke. Falling right into his rhythm, she proposed Point Reyes, or Healdsburg, or even Carmel. "We could drive there and back in a day if we start early." They laughed together spontaneously. When, he thought, was the last time they had managed to laugh together?

She reminded him of the Father's Day they had driven to the wine country when Adam was only a year old, how spontaneous and hilarious it had felt, until they realized she had forgotten to bring diapers and a change of clothing. With the stink of Adam's dirty diaper thick in the air of the car, they had instead toured grocery and children's stores instead of wineries. By the time they had changed his diapers and clothes, the wineries had closed. Again, they laughed together. "It seemed like such a big disaster at the time," she recalled.

Adam called him separately on his own phone after Janice and he finished speaking. Don imagined that Janice and he had worked out their own coordination of calls to him. "Want to hear some more music?" Of course, he told Adam, and once again Adam regaled him on FaceTime with his considerable skill on the cello.

"I'm so proud of you, son." Adam seemed to wince momentarily before showing his dad a big smile. "Good to hear," was all he said before abruptly signing off.

Adam had welled up. He cut the connection before he could blurt, "why didn't you ever tell me that before?"

— • • —

Father's Day was a workday for Erythea, a welcome distraction. Her own father had died while she was still in high school. When she thought of him at all, it was still with a bit of fear at his explosive anger. Even her mother had seemed relieved when his heart had suddenly burst and freed them from the lurking unease that pervaded the small household. He'd had a life insurance policy sufficient to keep her and her mother in their home, and her mother continued as a primary school teacher until she retired at sixty-five. Not long after, Erythea watched her mother gradually fade into dementia. She had found a nursing home for her mother shortly after getting her masters in social work. Her mother died eight years ago, freeing her of any remaining familial responsibility.

Today she could choose whom to see; she had no meal duties and most of the executive staff was off duty. There were two residents she knew she had to see; the nurse had reported to her that they showed signs of clinical depression. Erythea was also tempted to call on Simon, to challenge him to do something for his fellow residents. She had not yet thought that through; the idea popped up as she drove in to work this morning. She telephoned Bertha first. Bertha answered cautiously on the second ring; she must have been sitting close to her telephone. Erythea identified herself and asked if they could visit later today via Zoom. Bertha sounded confused, asked what was Zoom. Likely Bertha, who was ninety, did not have a computer or know how to use one, let alone how to do a Zoom call. Erythea asked if she could come to Bertha's apartment to visit today. "Sure," Bertha told her, "whenever you like. I can make you some tea." They arranged a visit for eleven that morning, giving Erythea enough time to make an appointment with another resident and to check in with the health care office, where she learned that Bertha had last seen her physician four months earlier, just before the Evergreen closed down. At that visit, Bertha had presented as stable. Although she had crippling arthritis, Bertha used almost no pain medication, taking ibuprofen when her back or hands particularly bothered her. That history brought back a visual image to Erythea. Bertha's body had a profile like a question mark, her head peering up from a roundly curving back, from which her thin legs seemed to dangle. Penetrating blue eyes beamed upward at the person facing her.

Erythea found Bertha's door ajar when she arrived at eleven. Still she knocked and heard a faint voice inviting her in. Bertha sat submerged in a large blue recliner, her tiny feet enveloped in bulging slippers and her lap hidden under a plaid blanket. On a side table beside her was a hot plate with a steaming teakettle and a tidy tray stacked full of tea packets. Bertha's eyes now receded behind long tendrils of white hair and her hands curved like a bird's feet around a thin branch.

"Tea?" Bertha offered, trying to swipe her hair from her eyes.

"You have my favorite – mint," Erythea said, "but may I ice it?"

"Of course. You know where the ice chest is." *Ice chest,* Erythea noted, a phrase she had last heard from her own grandmother many years earlier. Erythea offered Bertha ice for her own tea but was assured that she was always cold and needed hers warm. For a few moments each sat quietly drinking her tea.

"It's been a very long time since I've had a visitor. Sunday was the day my son always came, bringing my two grandchildren. Now they have children of their own, but I've never even seen my youngest great grandchild." Before Erythea could ask the age and sex of the youngest, Bertha volunteered, "and at this rate I likely never will. I can't stand it." Bertha rubbed the gnarled fingers of one hand over the other, repeatedly, in what Erythea suspected was a continuous habit.

With gentle questions, Erythea learned that Bertha's son Harry lived locally, as did his own two daughters, one of whom was the mother of the youngest great-grandchild, a six-month-old boy. They telephoned regularly, on the apartment landline, but Bertha had not seen any of them in four months.

"Do you have a cell phone?" Bertha shook her head. "At this age, it seems like a waste of money. I could die any day now."

Erythea lifted her electronic tablet out of her shoulder pack. "Have you ever seen one of these?" Bertha nodded. "It's like an oversized cell phone."

Now Erythea nodded also. "Do you know your granddaughter's telephone number?" Bertha handed her the small phone directory next to her telephone. "Name is Birgit Ostnes, with an 'O'."

"Do you mind if I call her?" Bertha gently shook her head, patiently disbelieving that this exercise would yield anything. But Birgit answered on the second ring. Erythea explained who she was and that she was sitting with her grandmother before asking if Birgit minded speaking on FaceTime. "Of course not, but let me get Tor first." In a moment, Bertha was holding the tablet and looking at her great-grandson and granddaughter. After just shaking her head silently for some moments as Tor gurgled with his fist in his mouth, Bertha whispered, "it's a miracle."

"Should I leave you three alone for a bit and come back?" Bertha shook her head. "I wouldn't know what to do if anything goes wrong."

Bertha's eyes remained transfixed on the screen, filled with wonder and love. "It's magical," she reported at the end of the call. Erythea explained that she could come back with her tablet and repeat the experience, with any members of Bertha's family. "It's part of what I do."

Bertha hooked one of her hands, now warm from the tea, around Erythea's. "You have made this a very good day."

Erythea practically floated down the hall from Bertha's room. Seldom was her task so rewarding. Glancing at a note, she headed up two floors to see Viola, her other referral from the health services office. Viola had been an Evergreen resident for fourteen years, the first thirteen with her husband, who had died a year ago of pneumonia. Years earlier – long before Erythea's arrival – Viola and her husband had been active residents. He had served as an officer on the resident board, and she had reportedly been an informal social chair for the resident community. But within the last year, Viola had cut off most outside contact and was rarely seen outside her apartment. She had missed her last scheduled annual medical in early March, just before the Shelter-in-Place rule went into effect. Of the periodic calls made by the health department to check in on her, Viola had often not answered the telephone. She did answer Erythea's call and agreed to meet her in person this afternoon. The photograph of Viola in the resident directory, taken at her arrival more than a decade earlier, revealed an elegant woman with silver hair looped over the top of her head, eyebrows with a high arch carefully drawn, and friendly eyes surrounded by sparkling eyeglass frames. The woman who answered the door was almost a foot shorter than Erythea and looked up at her warily through thick bifocals. Her thin straight silver hair draped around her neck and down her left shoulder almost to her waist. An elderly Rapunzel, Erythea thought, as she introduced herself and reminded Viola of their appointment. Viola invited her inside with an elegant sweep of her right hand, and they sat in stiff upright velvet chairs. Glancing around, Erythea noted an almost sterile neatness to all of the surfaces – no books, no magazines or newspapers, no cups or glasses. The only sign of life was music emanating from the internal TV channel on the widescreen television in the bedroom, and wrinkles in the bedspread in front of a large pillow with hand rests. Evidently, that seat in bed was where Viola spent part of her days.

"Are you here because I missed my medical checkup?"

"No, I just wanted to check in with you to see how you are. Many folks are finding it difficult to shelter in place, and I'm here partly to see if there is anything I can arrange for you to make it easier."

Viola sniffed. "I didn't expect to see the end of my days sealed in my apartment with no outside contact. I feel like I'm in a large crypt. If you really wanted to make it easier, you would give me something to end my days here and now. I don't want to just drift in place.

"All my friends have died," she proclaimed bitterly. "Or nearly all. I couldn't even get to see Hilde before she died a few months ago." Erythea remembered only too well the rules against visiting Hilde in her last days.

"Who remains of your friends here?"

"There was a couple, Eddie and Teresa, that I was getting to know. But now with my Frank gone, it's awkward – with three people, I'm the odd one. We saw them as a foursome; I never got to know Teresa separately."

"Do you like to go outside? You could arrange to sit with them outside in the sunshine one of these nice warm days."

"My doctor told me I need to stay out of the sun. I can't do that."

"Sit in the shade, perhaps?"

"No, I don't want to do that."

"What about family?"

"I have a niece who lives in San Francisco, but since we've shut down she can't come to see me anymore. She used to call, but that's stopped now too."

"Do you want to try to call her?"

"What for?"

Erythea changed the subject, exploring whether Viola took any of the exercise classes on the internal TV station or walked outside on the terrace. Viola resisted those suggestions also.

"Can I get you any books from the library?"

"No. And you can stop being such a busybody and leave me alone."

Erythea got up and left. Walking down the hall, she tried to fathom what could possibly turn a corner for Viola. She resolved at least to call Viola's niece, if she was listed as one of Viola's contacts, and see if her niece might revive some connection.

⟢ ⸻ •••• ⸻ ⟣

Janice caught a glimpse of Naomi's eyes before she put on her large sunglasses and visored hat. She suspected Naomi had shed tears within the last hour but waited hesitantly to sense Naomi's mood from her voice rather than from her brief glance.

"I'm worried about Leah."

"Tell me why."

"She looks pale. She hardly talks at meals, and she doesn't eat much. She mopes even in the way she walks." Naomi paused.

Ever practical, Janice asked, "Does she get any exercise? You could take her out for a walk."

"I worry even about the air we breathe. We don't know enough about this virus."

"I'm starting to conduct my own yoga classes. She could join one of them. They're all virtual, but at least it's good exercise. I'm always more upbeat afterward."

"Maybe she and I could both join your new classes. I barely remember feeling upbeat."

"I can't tell you how much I rely on just getting out to walk like this, usually by myself. But it's even better with you. I miss seeing the expressions in your face. I haven't seen a real smile since March except on TV or on Zoom."

That same afternoon, Naomi opened the link to Janice's yoga class and showed it to Leah on her portable computer. When she suggested Leah join her for a class the following morning, Leah glanced at her balefully. "As if," was all she said.

"As if, what?"

"As if that would make any difference." Leah turned away from her mother's inquiring gaze.

— ⋅•⋅ —

Liss was coming home. She texted Erythea from inside the plane before it took off, reporting that no one occupied the seats on either side of her. They'd already worked out the logistics, with Erythea to pick her up at the airport this evening without entering the terminal. Erythea arranged for the mandatory two-week quarantine for herself once Liss arrived home. While she could arrange Zoom meetings with staff and residents, she could not physically step inside the Evergreen until after fourteen days had passed and she tested negative. She had shopped enough groceries for the two of them for two weeks and had filled the vases in both their bedroom and living room with flowers – tall yellow gladiolas on the coffee table in the center of their living room and yellow tea roses in the vase next to Liss' side of the bed. Tonight was the homecoming Erythea had held onto as a lifeline for so many weeks. She glanced around their apartment that she had cleaned so energetically. She had made the bed this morning with their favorite yellow sheets and flung open all the windows to catch as much fresh air as possible. A bottle of prosecco chilled in the refrigerator. She clasped her arms around herself, appraising the sunny apartment and wondering how she had made it through these two difficult months. Now they were down to only ten hours before seeing each other again. Erythea had taken the whole day off, a luxury she had not known since early March, before Liss had left for Italy. She decided to drive to Stinson Beach and just walk that long, peaceful expanse, literally to pace herself until this evening. She brought with her a bottle of mint iced tea and a beach hat with a wide brim, the one she had imagined wearing at the beach in Camogli. The drive was satisfying in itself, a winding meander up Mt. Tamalpais and down the other side with the blue ocean in view. But she had not counted on difficulty in parking. After winding patiently up and down the aisles of the parking lot, she finally found a place, took off her sandals and walked up the dune toward the beach. As she looked out at the sunny expanse of sun and gentle curl of waves, she shook her head at what seemed like hordes of people all along the beach, unmasked and basking in the sun. She shook her head at her own myopia at not reading the message from the crowded parking lot. She paused, evaluating the situation. If she walked just at the edge of the water, she would not encounter most of the people basking on the sand, and she could walk around the several people who were themselves walking the edge of the water or running in and out of it. She had not driven this far just to drive back home, so she raised her mask, donned her big sunglasses and wove her way to the shore. The wet sand, cold water and rhythmic wash of the waves soon wiped away her reservations, and she paced the entire length of the big beach, gathering an occasional sand dollar along the way.

From the air, Elissa gazed out the window at the cloud pillows below the aircraft. Never had she felt so grateful to return home. Genoa would now forever be associated for her with the pandemic and her own illness. At the moment, she didn't care if she never returned to Europe. She wanted to sleep with Ryth in their own bed, to paint in her own backyard, to return to work and to reclaim her sense of home space. Bea had been generous, but they had ultimately worn on each other's nerves, and it didn't enhance her sense of Bea's generosity to be presented with a bill for groceries and other household goods on the last night, which, humiliatingly, she could only repay after she got home. She wanted to hear the English language every day, not strain to understand the talk around her. Because she had no seatmates, she was able to raise the two armrests and slouch over the expanse of the three seats, listening to Eva Cassidy and glancing out the window at the clouds. Homeward bound, she found comfort even in the cramped seat.

Erythea ate a quick supper before heading south to the airport. Along the way, she mused at how long it had been since she had met someone at the airport. Ah yes, it was her old girlfriend Sally, six years ago, coming back from visiting her parents. Given the attitudes of Sally's parents, they had decided it was better for Sally to make the trip by herself, but the return invoked conflicts she didn't know they had and they had broken up weeks later. Erythea shook her head abruptly, as if to fling away such memories. She distracted herself by listening to Helen Reddy and watching an orange sunset with plumes of purple clouds. At the arrival to the airport, she parked at the lot for people awaiting texts from arriving passengers. She expected a text from Liss when she emerged from customs. She waited for upwards of an hour before receiving the message "I'm home!" with a heart-shaped emoji.

As she rolled toward the designated arrivals gate number, Erythea found herself astonished at the maze of cars, all edging toward the same small area. And there were Liss' footsteps – funny that the rhythm of her step was the first recognizable feature. Erythea nosed in aggressively, then leapt out and flung open the trunk before she threw herself at Liss. At the same moment, Liss bent over to grab her suitcase, rendering their first touch an awkward head butt. They both laughed and quickly got into the car, where they embraced hurriedly before a cop knocked loudly on the hood of the car and yelled at them to move on.

"Oh my God, how I missed you!" Liss immediately reached for Erythea's hair, untangling its end curls. "It's grown," she murmured appreciatively, taking a hank and bringing it to her nose. "I missed even the smell of you," she sighed. The ride home was quick; traffic had vanished and they raced into the apartment arm in arm. Erythea popped the bottle of prosecco, poured two glasses and brought them into the bedroom, where Liss had already flung back the covers and removed her clothes. They spent that first night just as each had imagined, wrapped around each other sumptuously.

The next day began with Erythea's accustomed alarm at 6:30, her only-too-familiar reality, but the hand across her chest was the welcome new detail. Glancing over at Liss' sleeping face, Erythea grinned. Liss' full lips were slightly open, tempting. Resisting the temptation to wake her, Erythea rolled out from her side of the bed, showered and dressed. Liss remained asleep even as Erythea grabbed her car keys to leave. She was on quarantine from the Evergreen but would do her work remotely from a motel room the Evergreen would rent for her for the requisite fourteen days. Again, she was tempted but decided to let Liss sleep.

Elissa awakened gradually, hazily aware of new sounds, the raucous chorus of geese descending splashily onto the water in the adjacent canal. She didn't hear these sounds in Genoa. She turned to appreciate the greenery just outside their window, tall pampas grass and cattails. Grounded again, not suspended on the tenth floor apartment in Genoa. Elissa threw on a robe and ventured outside the sliding glass door. A red-winged blackbird swayed on a nearby cattail. Home. Elissa smiled and returned inside to brew herself some tea. She smiled again at the vast array she and Erythea had stashed into a special tea drawer, picking up a bold Assam almost at random. She had dressed before the kettle steamed and began its whistle, pouring her tea and awakening to the day's possibilities. Home alone. How long had it been since she had occupied her own space by herself? A luxury all its own. In Bea's apartment in Genoa, they had worked out a kind of audial privacy by each using earbuds. Elissa had tucked them away in their case as her flight home was landing, intending not to need them for a long time to come.

She would begin by drafting a new email to all her clients that she was finally back home and ready to do her chiropractic again, finding the relief in a client's muscle and sympathetic nerves and basking in her clients' calling it her magic. She had fended them off again and again while in Genoa, describing how she had become stranded by the pandemic and then by her own illness. No sooner had she sent her 'home again' announcement than she decided to call two of her favorite clients.

Marge didn't answer, but Elissa listened appreciatively to her cheery voice message and left her own. Terry answered right away, having already read her email. "When can I see you?" he broke into her first sentence. "Tomorrow? My back has been complaining ever since you left." They laughed together comfortably. Elissa explained that she needed to check if her car would even start, having been abandoned all this time. "I'll send one for you if I need to." He might be serious; he was a successful tech engineer for whom money was no problem. They made an appointment for ten the following morning at his home in Tiburon, agreed that each would need to wear a mask, and she promised to call if her car would not start. Marge called back soon after she finished her call with Terry, and they arranged to meet at Marge's home the following afternoon.

As she was walking out to check on her car, Erythea called to tell her she would need to take a nasal test as soon as she could because it affected her own ability to work. They immediately agreed it was a good idea, and Ryth told her where she could be tested and find her result quickly. As a condition to getting on the plane home, Elissa had had a nasal test a few days before, which had been negative. Whether or not what she had had was COVID, she had recovered sufficiently to test negative, so now her only risk derived from the people with whom she had flown.

Elissa found her car coated with dust. As she took her seat, she tried to recall how long it had been since she had driven it – since March, she thought. Sitting still in the driver's seat, she reflected on the small privilege of just being able to take her own car someplace, to move on her own. Almost holding her breath, she pressed the starter and was relieved to find the engine working. She revved it and it growled without even coughing. Then she pressed the windshield wipers to open a line of vision out front. It took three cycles before she was satisfied, and then only the arc was clean. She reminded herself to get a rag and window cleaner and come back to clean the whole windshield. She returned to the apartment to get her driver's license and wallet and the window cleaner, then locked it so she could do her assigned chore of getting the nasal test in the parking lot of the local hospital.

By the time Ryth came home from work, Elissa had got her negative test results, got her whole car washed, napped and put a chicken in the oven to roast. Feeling proud of herself, she threw her arms around Ryth, removed her mask and kissed her. Ryth jolted automatically and pulled away.

"I don't know what we should do" were her first words.

"We have a new employee outbreak, someone in maintenance whom I don't see, but still…. I don't know what precautions we should take."

"I tested negative," Elissa beamed hopefully.

"That's good on our end, but I'm a potential source of exposure to you and vice versa. I don't know if we should sleep separately and keep our own distance. I haven't thought this through."

Elissa gaped at her. Ryth walked into the other room to change her clothes, without commenting on the aroma of the chicken or the set table. When she re-emerged, still looking pre-occupied, Elissa asked her how sick the employee was. Ryth didn't know, but the employee was at home, not in the hospital. Ryth poured herself a glass of wine without asking Elissa if she wanted any, and sat herself outside on their deck, still looking troubled.

Determined not to react, Elissa poured herself a glass of wine and sat herself across from Ryth on the deck. "Is there something else that's bothering you?" she summoned with determined calm.

"I just don't know what to do." Ryth looked genuinely stymied.

"Well, I have an idea. I've been preparing a good dinner. Let's just enjoy it together and leave problem-solving for another time."

Ryth didn't even look up.

Couldn't she even smell the rosemary roasting chicken? "I'll sit six feet away from you if that will make it easier." Elissa could hear her own sarcasm. She disappeared into the kitchen to trim the asparagus and toss a green salad with fresh dill. When she carried the salad to the table, Ryth had seated herself at her place but was still looking downward. Elissa retreated to the kitchen and began carving the chicken furiously while she steamed the asparagus. She plated the chicken, giving Ryth her favorite piece, a breast. She took care not to slam the plate onto the table. She brought out the asparagus, noting Ryth's expression had not changed, then brought in her own plate and sat down, carefully framing words in her own head.

"Is there something else that happened today? What's bothering you?"

Ryth looked up plaintively. "I was so full of joy at your coming home. I don't think I thought it all through."

'Thanks for asking, Ryth. I had such happy day, emailing my clients and setting up my first appointments tomorrow. I enjoyed preparing a good dinner for you." Sarcasm dripped from the first sentence.

"You're meeting with clients? Tomorrow! What are you thinking?"

"What the hell are *you* thinking – that you're the only one entitled to work around here?" Elissa glared at Ryth.

"Can't you see the risks? You don't know where your clients have been."

"You interact with hundreds of people a day and I can't work with two people? What planet are you living on?"

"The 'hundreds of people' I interact with have been sealed off from the world for the past three months, and we staff are supposed to curtail as much as possible our contact with others outside our family."

"And I'm not family?" Elissa slammed down her glass so hard that wine spilled over the edge of the glass.

"I didn't finish. And now I'm on a two-week quarantine because of your return from Italy. I worked from a motel room today."

"A motel room? Why didn't you tell me?"

"Last night wasn't the moment to tell you, obviously."

"So you worked all day today from a motel room?"

Ryth nodded. "I was hoping you wouldn't return to work for awhile," Ryth admitted.

"Just so you could? Are you the only one around here who counts?" Elissa slammed down her fork and left the table, grabbing her car keys and license as she slammed out the door.

"I can't believe this!" Ryth did nothing to halt her exit.

Erythea sat dazed at the empty table, her chicken half eaten, salad untouched. This is not how she had imagined Liss' homecoming. She blamed herself for not thinking it through in advance. She had assumed she and Liss would revel in her quarantine together, leisurely nestling back into their lives. She'd been daydreaming instead of thinking. So now she faced the prospect of an angry, alienated partner, with her living in her drab motel room for two weeks while Liss lunged into the rhythm of her work life from their apartment. Her elbows on the table, she rubbed the sides of her head with both hands, ignoring dinner altogether. After silently bemoaning her plight for some minutes, Erythea began to wonder where Liss had gone. She got up, grabbed her own house keys mask and went outside, determined to see if she could even find Liss and then figure out how to make things right again.

She found Liss still at the driver's wheel of her parked car, but Erythea heard the click of the lock as she approached. Liss' face still fumed.

She knocked on the window. "Can we talk?"

"Only if you listen first," Liss' words spat through the closed window.

"Okay. Do you want me to stand here or should we find a better place?"

Liss pulled down the window. "Let's walk and talk." Erythea nodded as Liss raised the window, got out of the car and locked it, and then put on her own mask. "It's filthy," she complained, wiping her hands. Erythea nodded again, not wanting to take any chances of irritating her partner further. They headed out their accustomed path along the canal.

"First, you didn't even wake me or tell me you were leaving this morning, but I assumed you were at work and didn't want to disturb me. Then when you came home you completely ignored me. I tried to create a special dinner for us. You were outraged that I made plans to go back to work. You knew I couldn't wait to get back to my work. You acted like you're the only one who counts around here. That's not the person I fell in love with."

"You're right. I acted badly. I was hit yesterday with being put on quarantine for another staff person having the virus. I blindly thought we would quarantine together as a kind of vacation before you returned to work, but the fact is – and I still can't get my arms around it – that we may need to quarantine *from* each other. After all this time apart. I can't stand it. I hadn't digested it by the time I got home. When it hit me in the face I was just dumbstruck that I hadn't thought this through. I'm sorry. I so miss you. In a way it feels worse that you are here and we can't be together."

"Why do we need to quarantine *from* each other? I don't get it."

"Your work exposes you to people on the outside, not people like the residents who've been confined together with no outside contact for four months."

"So you don't feel you can live with me so long as I see clients? Is this something the Evergreen requires?"

"I don't know. I do know I need to quarantine from my work because of the new staff outbreak. I assume also because you just returned from Europe."

"Do you know that or just assume it?"

"It's a question on the form we have to sign each day as we go to work."

"Why don't you ask? It can't be worse than what you assumed."

"I'll ask tomorrow."

"That leaves tonight. Let's be together tonight and figure out the rules tomorrow." Liss turned around and put her arms around Erythea, tightly enough that Erythea could not break away.

⬤◆⬤

By the end of June, the incidence of COVID in the United States had exceeded 2.64 million people, 217,000 of them in California alone, and cases had surged dramatically in the states with the most re-opening. California had experienced a surge of over a thousand cases from the transfer of infected prisoners to the prison at San Quentin. The President continued to flout all COVID prevention guidelines, not wearing a mask himself and conducting a rally in Tulsa, Oklahoma with an audience of nearly ten thousand people in an auditorium. He moved the Republican National Convention from Charlotte, North Carolina to Jacksonville, Florida, to dodge the masking and distancing requirements of North Carolina. Even his top advisors warned him about the divisiveness of his messaging in not wearing a mask.

Despite the continuing Black Lives Matter rallies, the President continued to boost white power.

———•❖•———

July
– The Price of Contact

Simon had been a news addict all his life, getting up before dawn to devour the *New York Times* before Julie's alarm even sounded. Even after his retirement and move to the Evergreen after Julie died, he continued his early morning habit, caffeinated and solitary -- though it was completely unnecessary to get up early to be solitary these days. This morning he read of the surge in COVID cases at San Quentin resulting from a transfer of prisoners from Chino, where hundreds of men had been infected with COVID. None of them had been tested before the transfer, and testing was not being done at San Quentin despite the surge in cases. Was the prison system trying to impose an informal death penalty before the press noticed? He slammed his tablet down on the sofa next to him. And began to pace angrily across the small confines of his room.

For the past several months, he had complained bitterly – in his own head, not to anyone else – of being in solitary confinement, experiencing the COVID lockdown as his own personal imprisonment. This morning's news hit him with his own privilege by comparison to San Quentin. But that recognition did nothing to quell his rage. He couldn't even walk it off.

Rosanne's apartment sat immediately next to Simon's. The walls were well insulated and she could hear nothing from his or any other apartment. Before the lockdown, she barely recognized her neighbors, not by name or even by face, even though she used to navigate her walker to the dining room or garden every day. Now she took her walker only to the bathroom within her apartment. She had worn a wide depression into the cushions of her sofa, like the depression in pine duff that revealed the lair of a deer. Even if the space were empty, one could tell where life had frequented it. On either side lay books that she was trying to read, though her concentration faded these days. On the low table in front of the sofa lay a stack of bills secured by a metal clip, a sheet of postage stamps, three prescription tablet containers, several notepads, a landline telephone, a small potted fern, and a remote for the television on the opposite wall.

Rosanne sighed. The depression in her sofa had widened to accommodate her widening thighs, overlapped by the fold of a belly she didn't think she had four months ago. Her shrinking universe, constricted before by her age-weakened limbs, had shrunk even more with the lockdown. She empathized with prisoners everywhere, for the first time feeling a visceral connection between their constriction and her own. She wished there was something she could do for the men and women in prison. For thirty years she had been a resourceful social worker, creating relief in difficult circumstances. But her mind failed her for what she could do now for the men in San Quentin. She knew there was not much she could do for herself.

⸺•◦•⸺

For months Gianlucca had been hearing the monotonous pads of his footfalls as he jogged past the Palazzo de Brera on his daily run, wondering when it would reopen. Unfooled by its drab exterior, he reimagined the light and arches within its courtyard, where he used to meet Fran when she first came to Milano. On June 23, when it finally re-opened, with new rules adapted to the times, he felt a surge of anticipation. Immediately he made reservations to visit, and July 3 was the earliest he could gain admission. With only 100 visitors allowed at one time, he would be seeing the Pinoteca more intimately than at any other time in his life, even when his uncle first brought him here as a child. Waiting on line, he recovered glimpses from those childhood visits. He headed straight toward his uncle's favorite painting, Caravaggio's *Supper at Emmaus*. With so much of the canvas dark, only the essentials were illuminated -- Jesus' hand blessing the simple bread, his face perfectly bisected by the scarce light, and the attentive faces of the couple serving him. "He gives us only the important details," his uncle would say, bypassing many more colorful paintings of large spectacles. His uncle had died at 89, in his sleep, only months before the onset of the coronavirus, and Gianlucca considered him lucky in his timing. Alone in the room, Gianlucca bathed in the comfort of his recovered memory as much as in the depth of the colors of the actual canvas.

When he left the museum two hours later, Gianlucca noticed the place within the courtyard where he and Fran used to meet, touching one of the pillars as if in greeting and wondering how the re-opening had suddenly engulfed him in his own past. It's a good thing, he reminded himself, that Fran now had permanent residence here in Milano; if she now lived back in California, he would have no ready access to their daughter Lili. As of July 1, residents of the United States were banned entry into Italy and everywhere else within the European Union. Given the rampant outbreaks within the US and the uncoordinated response, who knew when US tourists would return? As resentful as he had sometimes felt during Milano's lockdown, he now felt grateful for his renewed freedom. With a bounce in his step, he realized Lili would be with him this evening.

111

Every evening after dinner Carla visited the *ofrenda* in her living room, stopping to kneel in front of it and ponder what lay in and beyond it. The photos of Pedro remained the same, but she recognized that someone continued to renew the fruit and other edible offerings, and there were tiny new folded paper messages tucked into crevices, which she assumed were private and she did not read. Each time she kneeled she remembered new details about Pedro, a random gesture he sometimes did with his left hand circling in the air to ridicule some idiocy, the way he pursed his lips to taste a new sauce burbling in a pot, the way he often sneaked a quick kiss to the side of her neck when she was not looking…. Sometimes she wept quietly and sometimes she smiled at a newly remembered pleasure. This morning both Carlo and Sabrina came into the room while she was kneeling, he carrying two new oranges and she a sprig of daisies. They hastily apologized and tried to back out of the room, but she welcomed them.

"Join me. I was wondering who renewed this." She kissed the hand of each of them as they approached the *ofrenda* and did their intended tasks. "Come kneel with me and remember your papa." Sabrina crossed herself as she knelt, and they both joined her, hand in hand, as they silently remembered Pedro together.

Tonight Carlo lingered after Sabrina went up to bed and asked how she was doing.

"I'm maintaining," she told him with a determined look. "I'm glad you stayed. There's something I want to ask you."

Carlo cocked his head, wondering.

"I know you want to keep rallying, and to resume working with Arturo, but I have another suggestion for useful work you could do, partly in your dad's memory. I know Marta will join Arturo as they re-open, and you are likely to struggle to find your place in the new organization. Why not train to become a contact tracer? We're in desperate need of such workers, and you will likely be able to fit this work around your student schedule in the fall."

"Is this even happening yet?"

"It has to. Let's find out."

Carlo went online to find work as a contact tracer within hours of hearing his mother's suggestion, and the initial responses from employment resources gave him the impression there were many such positions available. That he was a student seemed to create some additional opportunity for finding part-time work. But he could not find his way to any specific offering for a contact tracer except for one that required medical training. And within hours his email was deluged with ads for warehouse workers, Lyft drivers and grocery delivery people. He finally reached out directly to the county Department of Public Health for guidance and from that source finally located resources for training. It took him three times as long to disconnect the online employment resources as it had taken him to sign up initially. By dinner time, he told his mother that the mandatory six-day training was unpaid and that the hourly wage for a contact tracer was slightly less than he had been earning at his uncle's restaurant.

"It's more important work and probably safer too. We can deal with the money part," she told him. He agreed but needed to hear it from her.

Don had not seen Erythea for three days, which was abnormal. When Russell came to prop him up for breakfast, Don asked him if there was anything wrong. Was Erythea sick? "No, no," Russell assured him but gave no further information. Don wondered if he should email her, knowing he had no specific requests, he just missed seeing her. As he slowly forked his sausage without cutting it and ate his scrambled eggs with a spoon, he literally chewed on the idea of what to say to her. As words became more difficult to summon, he chose them more carefully. Like the character Grand in *The Plague*, which he had just finished, he had 'cut out all of the adjectives'. But he couldn't just write that he missed her. He could write, it just now came to him, that he needed a new library book and ask her to exchange Camus for another. That's what he determined to do; he would ask her for any other Camus books that might be in the library. He had found *The Plague* eerily current. The similarity haunted him but of course provided no succor. COVID would take its unpredictable course; there was now a new, dominant variant of the virus and cases were rising throughout the United States, at the same time that political protests wrought their own unpredictable havoc.

After Russell removed his breakfast tray, Don dialed Erythea's extension. He just wanted to hear her voice, which he did, but only via her voice message. He left word that he wanted a new library book, anything else by Camus. After spending part of the morning with the newspapers online and more time than he cared to count composing a new letter to Janice, he occupied much of the remainder of his day rereading a spy thriller he had long ago downloaded onto his tablet. When dinner arrived via Russell to prop him up again and set his tray before him, Don anticipated his dinner as much for relief from boredom as from appetite. He opened his cardboard boxed meal as Russell waited. Steak and corn and mashed potatoes, but for the first time his steak was pre-cut. Without thinking, Don slammed his fist on the tray. "Who told you to cut my steak!" he demanded. Russell involuntarily flinched. "I told the kitchen it would be easier for you if they cut your food." Don's anger fizzled. "You didn't deserve that. I'm sorry." He didn't want to think that from now on someone would cut his food as if for a toddler. Russell disappeared without comment.

One less thing he could do for himself. Would there come a day when someone would have to feed him? His left arm and hand were fine. He did his left finger exercises, touching his thumb to the tip of each finger in succession. He had developed a remarkable facility with his left hand after losing the use of his dominant right, but one hand is just one hand. He wondered morosely what loss would come next. After this, life would unfold as a succession of losses, ideally gradual ones, but there was no bending the downward curve. What had happened to Erythea? She cast light wherever she went.

Taking a chance, he dialed Janice, and she answered on the second ring. Her hello was guarded, and he heard television news in the background. "Should I call back later?"

"No, I'm glad to hear from you," she lied. She had just listened to the President denouncing Dr. Fauci as misinformed about the 'Chinese virus', and she could barely utter a civil word. "Did you hear him trash Fauci?" she bit out.

"I did. It makes me wonder what world we have sunk into."

"I want to give you some good news, but I honestly can't think of any right now. Even Adam is downhearted. He's got no prospect of seeing Leah this summer, and his classes in fall will likely all be online."

"What are you reading?" He knew Janice was more a doer than a reader, but he wondered.

"I've taken up yoga, and I'm reading a book by my teacher. I guess it's taken the place of tennis in my exercise routine these days. Even the yoga class is online."

"If I could, I would join you." The words were out before he could retract them, but she received them cheerfully, remembering out loud the one time he had consented to go to a yoga class with her years ago. They had both hated it, and for some time one or the other of them would fold their hands in front of their chests piously and they would both burst into laughter. The gesture had blocked many incipient arguments. Janice laughed gently now, and he joined her.

"I didn't think anyone or anything could make me laugh today," he confessed. "I was in a dark place."

"It's easy to imagine why. Is there anything I can do for you?"

"Actually, yes. Can you go into my library and check on some books for me?"

"Sure." Janice walked into his library, a full room of bookshelves, and he directed her to show the camera on her phone onto certain shelves where he had alphabetized his books. They readily worked out which books she would bring to the Evergreen and leave at the front door for him, a couple of LeCarre thrillers and a biography of Stalin. She seemed glad to do him this favor. "It's the least I can do."

⬤

Carlo's first week of training as a contact tracer included hours of practice in trying to gain the trust of people he would have to call and inform that they had been exposed to COVID-19 and would need to be quarantined for 14 days. The instructors posed as recipients of the calls, skeptical of a sham or fearful of an ICE raid, or just dreading the time out of circulation. When he spoke Spanish, he lowered their resistance immediately. But proving his affiliation with the Public Health Department was a double-edged sword. Either a recipient did not believe him, or, if he was believed, he instilled fear of loss of liberty. Either way, people did not want to hear from him. He learned to explain how one could be perfectly healthy and still capable of spreading the virus to others.

One day, questioned harshly in Spanish by one of his instructors posing as a single breadwinner of a family, he told her that his own father had died of the virus and how his family had learned to carry on. How his mother had sheltered his father from the rest of the family and likely saved them became part of his 'story'. He had not known this was a lesson until he told it to another. After that, he became eager to get out of training to talk with real people. He was chosen for a 'people contact' team rather than a 'record-keeping' team. Each day the DPH would send him telephone contact information for people who had had some contact with a person who had fallen ill or tested positive for COVID-19 without showing symptoms. Once he told people they would have to self-quarantine, he also explained how they could order food online and obtain other services. He was reminded of how well his uncle Arturo had attended to his workers after S____ had fallen ill and how he had taken Manuel into his own home. Not many would have followed Arturo's example.

On his first day of work with real people, his list included a girl from his high school class in Novato, Celia, who had tested positive yesterday, but had no symptoms. As soon as he finished his formal introduction as a tracer with the DPH, he asked if she remembered him from high school. "Si, si, you still have such long wavy hair?" He laughed. "No, I cut it, but in the last four months it's been coming back."

"I'm not going to die from a positive test, am it?"

"You might be someone who tests positive but never comes down with symptoms. You should be in quarantine now for 14 days so that you don't give it to anyone else. My job is to find out who you've been in close contact with for the last 14 days so that we can warn them and test them, stop other people from getting the virus.

"Oh, Carlo, how much time do you have?"

Celia's list was long. She lived with her sister, who worked at Starbucks. On July 4th, they had had a *pachanga*, a family party with their parents, aunts, uncles and cousins – even her grandmother -- and that night she had joined her boyfriend and a bunch of his friends to set off small fireworks next to the Bay.

"Do you know if any of them have got sick since you saw them?"

"My poppa was already sick, that's why we had the *pachanga*, but I don't think he has the virus. He has a bad heart and diabetes."

"Were you wearing a mask and keeping a distance from each other?"

"No, he's my poppa. I kissed him. I didn't know if I would see him again."

"We'll reach out and get him tested right away."

"*O Dio mio*, I don't want to kill him."

"Celia, maybe you can be the one to save him. We'll reach out to him first."

By the end of the conversation, Carlo had acquired 32 names and their contact information. He shook his head. From his very first contact, while Californians were under 'shelter in place' orders, 32 names. He set to work.

⸻ •◦• ⸻

Erythea left home for her motel room after kissing Liss goodbye and packing a bag with enough clothes for two weeks. That Liss' homecoming would require her to hole up in a virtual cell of a motel room for two weeks was an irony too bitter for her to swallow. As soon as she had unpacked her practical bag, she realized she had brought nothing with her to humanize this closet of a room. There was not even the relief of a window to look out on trees or water. Yes, there was a window but it looked across at the other motel cells that mirrored her own. She kept the shades drawn for the sake of her own privacy, even her sanity.

Before she could even face starting work, talking sympathetically to other people, Erythea needed to meditate. Cross-legged on the thinly carpeted floor, she sat for ten minutes to clear her mind. When she opened her eyes, her first thought was that her own quarantine could perhaps enhance her empathy for the residents. Trying not to think of Liss in their waterside sunny apartment, Erythea opened the first of her 67 emails from the prior day. Don's was close to the top. She sighed as she saw he wanted yet another Camus book, but forwarded his request to the librarian to find what she could and deliver it to Don. Then she paused further, wondering what to say to him. She intuited he wondered where she was, but she was not supposed to tell residents she was in quarantine. She wrote that she would be out for two weeks for some needed R&R, but that she looked forward to seeing him again on her return. Contradicting her R&R story, she also wrote that she would be available for a Zoom conference if he wanted one. Then she emailed George to set up a time to talk by telephone to discuss her own circumstances. Only then did she focus on the other 66 emails, winnowing through to decide to whom she would need to speak today. There were residents in quarantine for the same reason as herself, one of them complaining bitterly. That person – Alison – would be her first call.

Alison thanked Erythea for calling her but launched into her complaints before Erythea could say a word. "I've not seen my own doctor or dentist, I've done all I could to not expose myself to the outside world, and now I'm in quarantine because of a staff member. I wonder where that person went while I was stuck here!" Breaking protocol, Erythea told Alison that she herself was also in quarantine, working offsite and unable to socialize even with her family. Suddenly, Alison shifted focus. "Do you have young children? A husband you had to leave?"

"No, fortunately not." Telling Alison about her partner returning from overseas would be unwise. "But it hurts not to be able to go outside or meet with residents in person. Fortunately, you and I are both well and this will help keep us and the other residents well. But I agree this is hard." She asked Alison if she could arrange for any Zoom meetings with family or books or puzzles from the library, but Alison assured her she could FaceTime with her son and grandchildren. Within a few minutes, Alison was thanking her for reaching out and converting her energy to making do for herself.

By the time George called, Erythea had resurrected her day. She explained that her partner, who had been ill in Italy with what sounded like coronavirus symptoms but had never been diagnosed, had just returned home after recovering. "When was he last ill? And when was he tested?" Ignoring the pronoun, Erythea told him her partner had last been ill about eight days ago and that a nasal test done the day before yesterday was negative.

"You were going to join him in Italy, weren't you?" George was now remembering her thwarted vacation in April. "Why don't you take your vacation now, or at least some days of it? It can't be fun to work from a motel room."

"Fun, it's not." Suddenly all the tension drained from her shoulders. She could be with Liss at home, exactly what she had so longed for all these weeks. "So, even if my partner works, I won't have to quarantine on my return?"

"What's his work?"

Finally she broke the artifice. "She's a chiropractor in private practice. She goes to people's homes to treat them. They wear masks but it's in the nature of her work that they can't maintain six feet of distance."

"Well, it's not ideal, but we'd have no employees here if I tried to control the work of every staff member's family." He reminded her of frequent staff testing. Relieved and buoyed, she told George she would take a vacation starting the next day but would think about whether to take just one week now or two. At lunch time, she repacked her bag of clothes and wondered what it would be like for her to be home while Liss went off to work. And for how long she wanted to be away from residents like Don and Bertha and all the others who made her feel useful.

She beat Liss home, deciding on the way to order takeout food from their favorite local Italian restaurant to be delivered this evening, a seppia fettucine that only Liss liked and a big seafood salad. She changed the water in the yellow vase with yellow roses, hoping to revive them and the initial mood of Liss' homecoming two days earlier. When Liss opened the front door, Erythea was planted in a comfortable chair in plain view, reading a book. She glanced up at Liss' face, watching startle flit to pleasure to caution.

"Why are you home?"

"I'm officially on vacation, free of any restriction." She tried to repress the grin that overtook her face, then gave Liss the embrace she should have given her the day before. "Can we restart?"

Liss took her hand. "Shower with me." Undressing as they made their way to the bathroom, they celebrated Liss' homecoming in a long shower and wet reunion in their bed.

The doorbell woke them from a nap afterward. Erythea slipped on her robe and a mask and took the food she had ordered earlier.

"What was that?"

"A surprise for dinner. Are you hungry?"

"Always."

They ate gluttonously in their robes, hardly bothering to remove the pasta from its plastic container. "You know," Liss mused. "I spent two whole months in Italy and never got to eat this."

"Is it hard to find there?"

"Everything is hard to find when you're locked down or home sick." Liss licked her fork slowly. "You ordered this even though you don't like it."

Erythea nodded. "It's fun to watch you enjoy it." She sorted through her salad for the marinated squid that she liked.

"So how long do you have off?"

"Before we get there, tell me what your work day was like."

"Terrific! I was so glad to see Terry and Marge again. I can literally feel the stress this time has taken on their bodies. To be able to lighten their pain, that jazzes me. I can't tell you how glad I am to be back."

They never got back to Erythea's question of one week or two. She reveled in Liss' pleasure. She knew only too well how good it feels to lighten another's load.

⸻ ◦◉◦ ⸻

Arturo awoke with a sense of weariness, not anticipation, on the day planned for the reopening for takeout only. How many times would he have to reopen, then shut down again? Beside him in the bedroom, Marta bustled with energy, radiating her own eagerness to work beside him in the restaurant. And he was confident that Beto was also eager to return. There would be only three others, all from the old crew, including Manuel. Seeing Manuel well and back at work should be enough to keep me going, Arturo told himself.

As soon as he unlocked the back door, Marta stomped around inspecting the kitchen and tables as they had arranged them for assembly of takeout orders.

"Good thing we arrived early," she pronounced. "There are spider webs under the tables." She grabbed a cloth and busied herself wiping away the webs and dust. Arturo laughed despite himself. Having Marta's energy here would itself rev up the place, he thought.

Manuel showed up early. "Put me to work," he demanded with a grin, before putting on his mask. Beto asked him to help put up the window signs announcing their reopening hours and conditions. He had made a couple of signs with large letters in pen: masks required. He moved a small table in front of the recessed front door, creating a distance between the worker handing out the meal and the customer. Then Beto moved to the table in the corner with his computer, booting it up. "Look at this!" Their reopening announcement had been online only two days, but already there was activity, enough orders for lunch to keep them busy and even a few for dinner tonight.

Arturo installed one worker each at two work stations six feet apart from each other, where they were to begin cutting tomatoes and onions and cilantro. He turned on the large fan that moved outside air from one side of the kitchen to the outside vent at the other side. Manuel was assigned assembly at his own work table, and Beto became the runner of orders and deliverer to customers as they appeared. Marta stood next to Arturo, where he explained what large pots he used for which dishes and how he multi-tasked from the stove. She took it all in quickly and cheerfully. "If you get too bossy, I'll just butt you with my hip, like this," pushing him to the side with her ample hip. Everyone laughed.

As the morning progressed, a kind of muscle memory took over for the workers, and they began to whistle. Arturo remembered to turn on the radio they used to listen to all day long. As traffic began on the sidewalk outside, a regular customer knocked on the window to wave hello and give him a thumbs-up.

They were back in business.

⸻◦⸻

Stifling a yawn, the Evergreen receptionist Barbara watched as the first of the seven a.m. shift workers plodded up the front walkway. In half an hour, she could go home to bed. The first, as usual, was Fiona from the nursing staff, who came early to avoid waiting in line with the others coming on duty. Turning to retrieve the thermometer, Barbara heard a scream from Fiona, now kneeling on the pathway.

"Call 911!" Fiona yelled. Next to Fiona lay another person, unnaturally still. Barbara dialed from the hotline at her desk. Fiona now burst into the reception area. Barbara handed the phone to her. Glancing around to make sure no one else was in the reception area, Fiona tried to keep her voice low, but Barbara heard her tell the 911 operator that there was an elderly woman dead on the front sidewalk. Barbara glanced at the camera monitor and saw the long strands of silver hair and the patch of blood underneath Viola's head. She knew it was Viola because no one else had hair that long. It literally radiated in every direction from Viola's tiny head. Barbara gasped, asked what she should do.

"Check me in." Barbara did as she was told. "Keep everyone away from here." "Do you have a large cloth?" Barbara nodded and handed a tablecloth to Fiona, who ran outside to cover the body just as a small stream of other seven o'clock works began to appear on the walkway.

Sirens and the red rescue vehicle were nothing new at the Evergreen, but a police car was a novelty. Before the two vehicles could pull in, Fiona directed the straggle of workers to keep going and not stop to look. Barbara's hands shook as she took their temperatures and watched them fill out and hand in their daily checklists. Everyone asked. As instructed, Barbara told them nothing. She could see a police officer waiting for her to finish. "It's the seven a.m. shift; it will take a little while," she explained.

"I need to see you when you finish," the officer told her. She nodded.

George arrived in the midst of the melee. Barbara glanced at him and pointed out the front door. George ran outside, lifted the tablecloth and glanced upward. He recognized Viola even as she lay face down. He knew her apartment was on the seventh floor immediately above where she lay. Shaking his head, he approached the first officer, who was talking to Fiona. As the rescue workers approached with a gurney, the first officer told them not to touch the body until she had photographed it. George introduced himself to the police officer and asked if she could take the photographs she needed and allow the rescue workers to remove the body before a crowd gathered. She nodded, told Fiona not to leave, and took at least a dozen photos from different angles before allowing the rescue workers to lift the body onto the gurney. "Turn her over," she ordered them, and then took more photos. "Do you know who this is?" George just nodded. The workers covered the body with their own sheet and quickly rolled the gurney into the rescue vehicle. It left within five minutes of arriving. After photographing the pool of blood, the police officer cast the tablecloth on top of it. Workers continued to file past them, gaping in their curiosity. George asked the officer to move inside to his office, away from the stream of people. He closed the door. The officer questioned Fiona carefully about what she had seen and whether she had touched the body. "Yes, at the neck, to see if there was a pulse. There wasn't. And her skin was cool."

When Fiona was released, George told her to say nothing about what she had seen until further instruction. Barbara was brought in next, asked how long she had been on duty and whether she had seen or heard anything unusual. She told them she had parked in the employee garage and entered from the elevator rather than from the front door at a little before eleven the night before and had neither seen nor heard anything out of the ordinary. "No loud noises?" Barbara shook her head. Barbara volunteered that there was a camera of the front area, but that she did not ordinarily look at it unless she saw or heard anything unusual. The police officer released her. Trembling, Barbara asked George if she could go home. "Yes, drive carefully, and don't talk about this to anyone."

With Barbara out of the room, the police officer asked to look at the camera. George told her he had a duplicate in his office, and they could examine it together in privacy. First, George told Terry, Barbara's seven o'clock replacement, not to touch the camera from last night. Returning to his office, he explained that the camera runs continuously but that they could fast forward it throughout the night.

"When was she last seen?" He told her he could not be sure without checking with other people, but that Viola kept to herself. Under current 'shelter in place' rules, she might not have gone out for some days, and other residents were not allowed into each other's apartments. Her meals were delivered to the outside of her door, as for all other residents. "Lonely existence by definition, don't you think?" George just pursed his lips. He explained that, around eleven each evening a little toggle piece was inserted at the top of each resident's door to verify if the resident opened it the following morning. The officer asked him to send someone up to check the toggle on Viola's door, and he radioed someone to check immediately.

"Let's see what the camera might tell us." George selected the relevant screen, scrolled back to the night before and asked what time they should begin looking. After verifying that eleven was the beginning of the last shift, the officer told him to start at eleven. He scrolled relatively quickly, since the screen revealed no activity for some time. But at 12:17 a.m. there was a flash of a large falling object and then the body on the pavement. "Sound?" No, he told her, it was video only. They scrolled very slowly but no more movement was revealed. The body was still from the moment it hit the pavement.

"I want to see her room." George obliged, taking her up in one of the elevators. On the way, he was told by radio that Viola's door toggle was undisturbed, and they saw it on arrival at her apartment. Here the office donned plastic gloves and asked George not to touch anything. He handed her the master key to unlock the door. The officer looked steadily around the room, intently at the made bed, and then walked to the open door to the small balcony. Just outside the door sat an upholstered chair, which was so wide that the door could not close with the chair on the balcony. The chair faced to one side. "I'm surprised she was strong enough to move the chair." The officer questioned him about her size, age, general weight and condition.

It was evident to them both that even a frail elder could have stood on the seat of the chair and folded herself over the edge of the concrete railing. George got out of the way so that the office could take more photos of the chair at the railing. He stood just inside, shaking his head disconsolately. If someone really wanted to do it, he realized, there was no way he could have prevented it without locking the balcony doors. He could protect the residents only so far.

"Has this ever happened before?" the officer asked on returning inside.

"Not to my knowledge." His head kept shaking, slowly and sadly, even after they locked up Viola's apartment and rode back down the elevator.

"Check back with me once you learn who was the last person to speak to her." He nodded once, then disappeared into his office.

He sat there with his 'do not disturb' message on for over an hour, brooding on this sad death. 'After all I've done to prevent the virus' kept drowning out any other thoughts for much of this time. He wasted another span of time trying to think of ways to prevent anyone else from going over the railing. Finally, he got up and left the building, trying to deafen all his unproductive thoughts. After several times around the block, he finally told himself, "it's not about you." He had to say it aloud three times before his mind opened to the challenge of how he could help the staff and residents cope with this tragedy. The residents could not be told, of course; longstanding rules dictated only a posting of the date of death and a photo of the newly deceased resident. But he would call a staff meeting as soon as possible today. And find out who was the last staff person to have contact with Viola. He predicted it would be Erythea; she had a sixth sense about who was struggling. He would have to call her to alert her to an interview with the police about Viola's condition when she last saw her.

———— •••◄ ————

For Erythea, lying in bed while her partner went off to work was a rich novelty. Liss had even brought her a cup of hot tea before leaving, and Erythea sat up in bed luxuriantly. Glancing around the bedroom, she basked in the clear morning light. By this time, she was usually in full work mode in her cubicle, connecting with her fellow workers or helping deliver the morning meals. She sat still for some time, just wondering what she would choose to do with her day. 'Choose' was the new word; usually the demands of her day dictated her activity.

She picked up her tablet to read the newspaper; that would be its own novelty. The coronavirus pervaded every story, from current statistics of outbreak and death, to the ongoing controversy of whether schools would be required to re-open in the fall, to Trump's belated endorsement of mask wearing 'if one could not keep a safe distance.' She shook her head sadly and turned off her tablet. This was not how she wanted to begin her first day of vacation.

Erythea visualized all the pleasurable activities she could pursue today before Liss returned from seeing her patients. Tea with her friend Sandra? She knew a tea shop in Mill Valley where they could meet outside and texted Sandra to see if she was available. A walk on the beach? That she had tried the day of Liss' return – too crowded. A hike on Mt. Tam? Something to be saved for Liss. Museums and galleries were closed. So too were movie theaters. Shopping had never been one of her amusements. Concerts had long ago been shuttered, converted to Zoom reruns of past performances. A book? She had not been able to concentrate during any of her time off work before now. Should she browse a real bookstore? Sandra replied to her text; she was busy today but could meet tomorrow at eleven, and Erythea readily agreed. They would meet outside the bookstore and café in Mill Valley.

She got up, made the bed, dressed and walked along the canal, her usual 'walking meditation'. She found herself wondering how her favorite residents were facing this day, like Don and Bertha. Strange to think that on a clear, warm day of leisure her thoughts ran to her favorite people at work. What were the things she had wanted to do to learn more about some of the dilemmas at work? They arose in a moment's flash and then vanished as quickly. Now, at leisure, none of them appeared before her. Here she was, midmorning on a beautiful summer day, wondering what to do with her free time. She counted back; it had been more than four months since she had known any leisure, and almost as long since Liss had been away. She decided on her return to the house to pour herself a tall glass of iced tea and call Don. Just one, she told herself.

He answered with a dull hello, clearly not expecting anything to lighten his day. But as soon as he heard her voice, he said 'Hello!' with a new resonance. "Where have you been? I hope you're not sick."

"No, I've been granted a week's vacation. I wanted to reassure you that I haven't abandoned you. How are you doing?"

"Oh, you know, I run a mile every morning before I settle down to the gloomy news."

She laughed. "I forgot. Was there ever a time in your life you began your day that way?"

Now he laughed, feebly. "No, I never got that memo. I got up early and went to work."

"And I bet you stayed late too."

"I suspect you know that drill yourself."

"Hmmph. You nailed me. But I did just return from a beautiful walk."

"Tell me what you saw."

Ah, she thought, he's changing roles on me. Concentrating to recall details, she described a white egret muddling the shallow water in front of it with one foot, intent on finding a fish to stab with its beak. Blackberries beginning to darken on brambles alongside her path. And a kingfisher diving beak first into the canal, retrieving its own small fish and flying off with it to a tree on the opposite bank.

He thanked her for giving color to his day. She promised to come see him in a week when she returned to work.

Only a few minutes later she heard her cell ring with George's identified tone. Apologizing for interrupting her vacation, he warned her bluntly that she would soon get a call from a police officer.

"Why?"

"Viola was found dead on the pavement outside the front entrance, likely a suicide."

Erythea gasped.

For some moments neither of them said anything.

"You probably know I talked with her a few days ago."

"That's what the health care folks told me."

"Viola was very discouraged, but I would never have guessed...." Erythea tried to recall the specifics of her last meeting in Viola's apartment. "She complained of being 'sealed in the crypt' of her apartment and that all her friends had died."

"There was nothing you could have done to prevent this," George tried.

"But still…"

"The police officer will ask you about your last meeting with her."

"Isn't that all confidential? How much do I tell? Will you be on the line?"

George realized that neither he nor Erythea had been down this path before. There were confidentiality issues, and the police were entitled to know the facts. "I don't think they suspect any foul play. Try to describe what you observed without getting into any confidential conversation."

"You know that's not a bright line. Can't you be on the line with me?"

"I'll ask." That abruptly, George ended the call.

Within minutes Erythea found herself in tears. Not about the prospect of talking to the police, but about Viola's horrible death. What could she have done? Viola's despondency was obvious. How could she have prevented this? What could she have said? What was there to offer Viola? Her husband and friends had all died. Under 'shelter in place' rules, she could not visit with her neighbors except electronically. Viola was but one of many residents she no longer knew how to encourage. But she had totally failed to give Viola any comfort.

When she heard Liss' key in the door, Erythea's spirits leapt as if rescued.

"I can't tell you how glad I am to see you!"

"What's wrong? You've been crying." Liss wiped her fingers gently across Erythea's cheek. As Erythea described Viola's dramatic suicide, Liss walked around the back of Erythea's chair and began, slowly and deeply, to massage her partner's neck and shoulders. Erythea leaned in limply. Moment by moment, her guilt eased.

Liss leaned down and kissed Erythea's neck.

"No wonder your clients wanted you back."

By the time the police officer called, Liss had left to tend to another client and Erythea felt prepared. Thankfully, the voice was a woman's. The officer told Erythea she had already spoken with George and several others and that she had seen Viola's apartment.

"Was there anything amiss in the apartment the day you visited?"

"Not at all. In fact, what struck me was how unnaturally neat it was, as if no one lived in it."

"Was there any furniture on the balcony?"

"Not that I know of. I certainly didn't notice anything."

The officer asked her if Viola appeared healthy, and Erythea acknowledged she did not notice any signs of illness. "Her mood?"

"Well, you know I'm a therapist and required to maintain confidentiality in my communications with patients."

The officer asked if Viola was a patient, and Erythea told her that all of her communications with residents were regarded as confidential. Without challenging her, the officer asked about Viola's appearance and again about her mood that day.

"She was neatly dressed. She had very long hair – I remember thinking it looked like Rapunzel, it was so long – and it was hanging over her shoulder. When I had last seen Viola – which wasn't recently – she wore her hair wrapped in a coil over the top of her head, with a decorative comb."

"Was she cheerful, talkative, sad, reflective? How did she present herself?"

"She was very discouraged and noticeably bereft."

The officer let her off with that description. She said she would call back if she needed to ask more questions.

Erythea decided to spend the rest of her day researching signs of suicidal intent. She was relieved somehow that she had not told the officer Viola had dismissed her as a busybody.

⎯⎯•◦•⎯⎯

Carlo's list of 32 names from Celia brought him back in touch with seven more guys he had known from high school, all of them part of the July 4th fireworks party in a local park. They had all been friends with each other in high school and remained friends in the last three years. None of them had worn masks on the evening of that party, and a few of them ridiculed Carlo for raising the topic. Although he spoke to each of them separately, they each seemed to speak with one point of view. Marco in particular became belligerent, challenging Carlo that this disease was 'fake news'. Only old people died of this new flu.

"Maybe you wouldn't say that if you walked in my shoes. My dad died of COVID-19 within the last three months. I can tell you it was worse than any flu."

Marco held his tongue for a moment. Then he asked, in a softer tone of voice, "how old was he?"

"46. He was vigorous. You couldn't call him old. Another man he worked with at our family's restaurant died too. He wasn't more than 22. Both of them died in hospital."

"What happened to your dad?" Marco's tone had changed altogether.

"He had a sore throat for days, tried to hide it. Then he developed a really high fever. My mom is a nurse and she separated him from the rest of us. His fever went up and down, then really high and she noticed his kidneys were damaged. She took him to hospital one night and none of us ever saw him again."

"I'm sorry, man."

"That's why I'm doing this work. I don't want you to get it or to spread it. The smartest thing you can do is to get tested and quarantine yourself the next 14 days, then avoid the kind of parties you had on July 4th.

One more thing – tell your friends this isn't fake news."

Just one of Celia's 32 contacts really gave Carlo a hard time. Tom's response was "that's bullshit." At first Carlo just told him to check with Celia and see if she thought so. "You're just doing this to pull down a paycheck. You don't really believe this crap." Carlo had to fight his rising temper.

"Tom, you know anyone who got sick of COVID-19?"

"Yeah, my great-uncle. But he was 79 and already sick. Nobody our age."

"How's your great-uncle now?"

"He died."

"I used to work with someone at my uncle's restaurant. He was 22, went to the hospital gasping for breath and never came out. Do you want to go like that?"

Tom hung up the phone. Carlo decided after the call he wouldn't waste the memory of his dad on people like Tom.

He assigned himself Celia's family members next, wishing he had contacted them first. Her grandmother at 79 was strong and sensible and completely cooperative with his efforts, as if she knew how unwise the *pachanga* had been but couldn't convince the rest of her family. She lived with one of Celia's four aunts – Tessa – and Tessa's six children, ranging in age from two to fourteen. Tessa also cooperated fully, giving him the numbers of her three sisters, all of whom lived in the same neighborhood and saw each other almost daily. Among them, they had eight children, including Celia and her sister. Carlo felt as if he were reconstructing Celia's family tree, with her grandmother as the head, her aunts as the shoulders, and their children as many limbs. Remarkably, none of them had yet contracted COVID, and all readily agreed to be tested and all but Tessa agreed to quarantine for fourteen days. Among the four aunts, only Tessa was currently married, to Tomas, a bricklayer who had recently returned to work. The other three aunts were all unemployed since the outbreak, and they all had children. Under the protocols of Carlo's employment, he did not receive the test results. The only way he might learn the results of testing in Celia's family is if one of her family members randomly showed up on a daily list of contacts he was provided.

Carlo came home each day both physically exhausted from his many phone contacts with strangers and also oddly stimulated. His mother regularly asked him at dinner about his day. Invariably, the stories tumbled out, along with his sense of wonder at how differently people responded to the threat of COVID.

"You were so right. This is important work," he told his family.

His mother nodded. "You get to them before I do at hospital. You help prevent them from getting to me."

"I had no idea." She just nodded.

He hadn't yet found the words to tell her how this new work helped salve the wound of losing his father.

———•◦•◦•———

Don had finished *The Plague* some weeks earlier, but it had not left him. He had thought it might provide him some sense of balance, some sense of comfort or reality or grounding to his present circumstances. But it didn't. In Camus' book, the plague had devastated but it had also gradually passed; the siege ended. In Don's sense of reality, which he knew was largely vicarious due to his being bedbound, life outside his room, outside the Evergreen, was veiled by an invisible recognition that this siege was not passing. It had not got dramatically worse here in Marin County, though the incidence was magnified by the crowded Hispanic community in the canal district of San Rafael and the outbreaks in San Quentin, resulting predictably from the influx of already-infected prisoners from another part of the state. Was that move just the State's negligence, or a half-intentional wish to execute prisoners at San Quentin by coronavirus? Other parts of the country had seen surges of outbreak, particularly where adherence to medical protocols of closure, masking and distancing had been politicized. Crowded beaches in Florida and Southern California, crowded bars in cities everywhere, parties of young people tired of being pent up indefinitely, political demonstrations against forced closures in Michigan and other states – all had contributed to expansion rather than containment of the infection. The ban by the European Union of travelers from the United States provided a punctuation point. The United States had become a pariah nation rather than an exemplar.

Such were Don's pre-dawn thoughts as he read his newspapers on his tablet. He glanced up at the light from the windows in his room – still a faint gray that barely allowed sight of the outlines of his landscape. Soon the light would take on a faint yellowish cast, as the sun neared the Eastern horizon. This was Don's favorite time of day, cool and quiet as a still life. If he could be rolled out to the terrace at any hour of the day at his choice, it would be now. To think of finding staff to take him out at five in the morning was beyond unrealistic. This summer the heat had exceeded one hundred degrees every day for nearly a week, and no one from the assisted living section was being wheeled outside, even at the regular, designated hour. Don had run hospitals during his professional career and had thought it desirable to have events occur at predictable hours. Now that he was the recipient rather than the deliverer of services, he longed for some departure from routine -- even Russell showing up at this moment to prop him up evenly. Don had developed some skill with his left arm, and he used it now to shift himself more upright and level his tablet, but still he recognized his limitations only too well.

He allowed himself to try to remember the years he had occupied the same bed as Janice, well before his stroke, which had marked her decision that he have his own, adjustable hospital bed in their room. He tried to recall the days before, when he would sometimes awaken curled around her and gently caress the mound of soft flesh below her waist. She was so easily aroused, in his memory. His eyes closed as he lingered on those days.

When he heard someone say, "Good morning, Mr. Goodman," he jolted awake. Glancing at the apparition, he was even more startled. Before him stood not Russell but some alien human clad head-to-foot in pale protective gear, her head encased in clear plastic with a mask underneath it, and blue plastic gloves protruding from the elastic ends of her sleeves.

"What is going on here? Where's Russell?" he blurted in shock.

"Russell is on temporary leave. I'm Dana, and I'll be tending to you in the mornings for the next two weeks. You and the others in this wing have been put in temporary isolation because of possible exposure to someone who tested positive."

"Is Russell okay?"

"So far as I know. I don't get to see him either." She moved closer to the bed. "Can I prop you up? You look a little tilted."

Now Don smiled. He certainly was on tilt. "If you can."

She levered her arm under his right shoulder with surprising strength and adjusted the pillows behind him very efficiently. He thanked her. She was out of the room again before he could generate any more questions.

In her absence, he faced the irony of his potentially procuring COVID from his near isolation in this ward of this very insulated institution. At this moment, it amused him, and he wanted to share it. His cell phone was within reach of his left arm, and he directed Siri to call Janice, who answered.

"It's very early; is something wrong?"

"They put me in isolation." He tried to inject humor into his voice.

"What?" He heard alarm in hers.

"It's not me. Someone who tends to us in assisted living has tested positive. So now anyone who comes in to help me is geared up like the zombies you see on the news. I'm just amused by the irony. Here I lie, unable to go anywhere that might expose me out in the world, and I'm put in isolation. I would laugh if I could."

Janice's mind scrambled as she tried to banish the memory of the nursing home outbreak that had highlighted exposure in this country. She tried to match his tone.

"I can't laugh. I'm not allowed to see you because I'm contaminated by being in the outside world, but a stranger who works there can. And you who are supposedly the most sheltered in place are the most exposed. I can't find any humor here."

"You just made my day. You actually sound like you want to see me."

"Don, I do. This makes me angry, and it scares me too."

"I love you."

"Don, I love you too. What can I do for you?"

"You already did it." He saw the zombie come in again with his breakfast tray and with a stick he knew from TV as a nasal tester for COVID. He signed off with Janice and promised to call back later.

"Please tell me your name again. I was so distracted this morning I forgot."

Dana introduced herself again, with an undecipherable expression on her masked face, and explained how she needed to test him and take his temperature. He tilted his face compliantly. First she scanned his forehead with the thermometer and jotted down the reading. She was quick and gentle with the soft probe that tickled the upper reaches of his nose. When she sealed and withdrew her testing materials, she laid his breakfast tray before him. He noticed that his breakfast sausage had already been sliced. He forgot to ask her his temperature reading.

⸺⸻◦●◦⸻⸺

July was California's worst month of the pandemic so far, with 254,606 new cases, more than the total of all the prior months. More than 3,000 people died in July in the state, despite the rigorous monitoring of Governor Newsom. Cases surged in other states as well, especially where re-opening occurred without limits. Independence Day and beach parties contributed noticeably to the surges.

Instead of becoming a routine precaution, the issue of requiring people to wear masks remained deeply politicized. In Georgia, Governor Brian Kemp banned local officials from ordering people to wear masks and sued the City of Atlanta for its mask ordinance. The President relocated the Republican Convention for the second time when Jacksonville, Florida, required everyone to wear a mask.

The European Union banned visitors from the countries where the coronavirus outbreak was uncontrolled. The United States was one of the banned countries.

⸺⸻◦●◦⸻⸺

August
– Heat

imon learned in mid-August that the Evergreen had relaxed its isolation rules, and he could now walk again outside for the first time in five months. He prepared for it as if for some challenging expedition, at the same time as he ridiculed himself for his preparations. But he could sense the deconditioning of his muscles over this time, even with his daily routine of exercising in place, an excruciatingly boring chore. Even more so, he could sense the deconditioning of his once usual habits, which he now had to reconstruct consciously. So now he girded himself with his mask, gloves, a hat with a brim, sunglasses and a pair of hiking poles, as well as a small water bottle looped over his hip. All this for a walk he used to take daily from the front door when he wasn't doing a more demanding hike. And he would drive himself to the path along the creek where he could walk for five miles on a level wide path.

He knew he had to sign some sort of form as a condition of his exit, but he hadn't anticipated a page full of mostly obvious promises of what he would not do, like go to any store or café or meet with friends who were not residents, or accept food from anyone. Biting his lip so as not to rail at the hapless receptionist, he read and signed the form, then went to the garage, where someone had to open the door on a signal from the front desk that he had signed the form. Just sitting in the driver's seat for the first time, and feeling the car move with the pressure of his foot, were preoccupying novelties that gave him an unexpected sense of pleasure at being under his own power. He readily found parking on the street next to the canal but was embarrassed by the unfamiliarity of parallel parking and having to repeat his effort three times before parking successfully. After locking the car and walking twenty or so paces, he caught sight of a masked man walking toward him and realized he had forgotten his mask and sticks in the car. On his second start, he checked assiduously for all his 'parts' and gave silent thanks that no one was there to see him fumble. A glance in his car mirror at his disguised face gave him a shiver; he was the stereotype of a bank robber.

Once he fell into a walking rhythm, he forgot his foibles and began to look around. He knew this path, the houses along it, the apple tree just outside someone's fence, the house with the chained shepherd that growled at passersby. Today, he felt as if this scene belonged to some time long past, almost in a different life, as if he were revisiting it as a different person or the same person in a different time of life, as if he had traveled back to the neighborhood of his adolescence and was now seeing it again for the first time in those many decades. Yet the scene was more vivid in sound and light and color than when he had last walked here. Rustling trees, distinct bird calls, the toasting warmth of the sun and the scent of the canal infused him with their newness. A fluttering movement low in the sky to his left caught his attention, a small black and white bird hovering in place, wings at high speed but without forward motion, its beak facing downward. Suddenly it dove, a fast clean entry into the surface of the water, and rose again with a band of silver across its beak. The bird traveled to the nearest tree on the opposite bank and dispatched its fish. For some moments Simon waited to see if the tern would loft again but it sat contentedly and almost invisibly among the foliage of its chosen tree. Now Simon consciously searched the water and was rewarded by a school of black cormorants, dipping underneath the surface as if in a wave and others rising around them, a pattern like a corps of dancers following each other. As they rose, most of the cormorants lifted their beaks high and visibly swallowed the lumps in their long throats, part of their own morning catch. Further up the canal, the water narrowed and Simon spotted pairs of mallards dipping for their underwater greens. The further he went, the better and surer of foot he felt. The path led across a street that Simon recalled had a café with good scones just a few paces to the right and a different good coffee roastery to the left. Simon kept to the walking path, eventually encountering a local college campus that was nearly as deserted as the path on which he had come. After an hour, Simon decided not to stretch his good luck and turned around to walk homeward. Reaching his car, he felt a noticeable lift in his spirits at the same time as his fingers ached where he grasped the poles and his calf muscles complained. Simon drove a roundabout ride back home, inspecting a neighborhood that had weathered a full season since he had last seen it. Signing back in, he did not balk at standing in line at the entrance to sign yet more forms and have his temperature taken. That afternoon he discovered more energy to explore a book of theory he had avoided during all of his time inside.

—•••—

Don awoke with the wind slamming the windows to his room, a jolt that almost never happened this time of year. In the next moment, he heard a series of heavy clatters from below, likely the furniture outside on the terrace. He glanced at the clock alit in the dark, 2:32 in the morning. Had there just been an earthquake? Only his windows had rattled; he had felt no movement to the building itself. With the sound of pebbles thrown against the windowpanes, it suddenly began to rain. It never rained in August. He caught a flash of lightning in the distant sky. Perhaps today would be cooler with this storm, he thought, before drifting back into deep sleep.

When he next awoke, the sky was sunlit, a full yellow light, not the pale light of early morning. His skin felt clammy. Had the air conditioner gone out in last night's storm? Zombie Dana appeared before he had fully wakened.

"What happened last night?"

"Oh, we had quite the storm. It blew over some of our tables on the terrace, ruined some of the sun umbrellas, and moved some of the chairs quite a distance. It was a real wind!"

"I heard some of it. Did it take out the air conditioner too? It feels too warm in here."

She gave him a different sort of look, professionally wary. "No, I don't think so." The thermometer came out of her pocket and she focused it on his forehead until it pinged.

"Well?" He demanded. He was not going to be left out of vital information.

"That's odd. It's 99.8. Are you feeling okay?"

"Just warm."

"Then let me adjust your covers and prop you up for breakfast." She removed the light blanket that always covered his legs. His idleness usually rendered him slightly cold. Once upright with his tray in front of him, he removed the cover and saw his favorite breakfast, blueberry pancakes and syrup, with a strip of bacon. He gulped the small glass of orange juice and took his first bite of the pancake, dribbling a bit of syrup down his chest. Dana had already left the room.

His hands were sticky by the time he was ready for the newspaper on his tablet. There was no damp cloth to wipe them. Russell always left him a damp cloth. Before he could summon her, Dana returned with a damp cloth and wiped his fingers herself. Before he could ask why, he saw her pull out and gently clamp onto his finger something he knew was a pulse oximeter.

"And?"

She shrugged noncommittally.

"Please, Dana. Just give me the number." Her glance reflected her annoyance, but she told him, 94.

Adam phoned Don just after Dana left. They exchanged observations about the storm in the middle of the night. At home, their outdoor umbrella had also blown over, and there were tree branches strewn about the yard, but he would clean them up today before it got hot again. He was packing for college. His music was going well. Don asked him to call each night this week to discuss the speeches at the Democratic Convention. Don bathed in Adam's attention.

Janice called later that morning, after her morning walk.

"I'm becoming popular," Don joked.

"You are."

"It's beastly hot outside – and humid, if you can believe it."

"Maybe that's why I'm feeling clammy."

"Could be, even with your air conditioners." She asked if he had watched the first night of the convention (of course he had) and what he thought of it.

"It's more focused without the crowds. Strangely, I find it easier to watch, and more meaningful." They chatted easily for much longer than either of them expected, basking in their shared opinions and relative flow of talk. They promised to talk each morning of convention week.

⬛━●●━⬛

Marta continued to speak with Carla on the phone every day, though now their conversations occurred after dinner for each of them, and each was wearied from her workday, preparation of dinner and management of their children before bed. Often one of them teased the other about trying to stifle a yawn, and they both laughed their comfortable acknowledgement. Everyone in both of their families was pre-occupied with the prospect of their children returning to school, and the family at large had not come to common ground. Sabrina was at peace with continuing her classwork online. She had already lost her father to the virus and she was determined to provide help to her mother. But Bettina, the most extroverted, thrived on contact with her peers and everyone else at school. She was the one who pushed hardest in favor of choosing to attend classes in person. Masks she could live with, they had become her norm, but she had had it with a 'vicarious existence'. Carlo had become paternal – or paternalistic, according to his cousin Bettina – since he had become a contact tracer. "The world is far more contagious than you imagine," he had told her all too often. Tomas was only eight, but he was as gregarious as his older sister, and he also lobbied to go to school. Luis looked around him at the swirl of different opinions, but said nothing. His world was still colored by the loss of his father. What made it all the more difficult was that parents had the option to send their children physically to school or not. Arturo and Marta found themselves moved by the rawness of Pedro's death, Carla's medical expertise, and Carlo's own work experience.

"Why do we have to do what they do?" Bettina demanded of her parents.

"Because we are all the same family, and we don't want to lose any more of us." As soon as these words rolled forcefully out of Arturo's mouth, Bettina and everyone else in both households knew the decision had already been made. School would be by computer until life changed. Still, Bettina sulked. It wasn't her fault that Uncle Pedro had died. COVID struck mostly older people, not teenagers. Sabrina didn't have as many friends as Bettina, she wouldn't know the hardship of not seeing them every day. Bettina felt as if Sabrina had betrayed her; she had never taken an opposite role in the family – or anywhere else – as her.

Beto and Carlo spoke with each other even more often than their mothers did, and they texted throughout most days. Carlo knew the restaurant was humming again. Beto was comfortable with its routines, which he had lived for years, but he was also curious about Carlo's work and wanted to try it. Carlo's supervisors welcomed the prospect of a 'second Carlo'; he'd even heard one of them say it. But for Beto it would mean quitting his work at the family restaurant. His parents gave him the option, and he hesitated for a few days, leaning into the familial routines, but he interviewed and began the training. Carlo's only regret was that he wanted to meet a girl, and his employers had warned him explicitly about dating any of his contacts. Beto had no such constraints at the restaurant, and he flirted with customers all the time, but he had no regular girl. Carlo leaned heavily on his cousin for introductions, but Beto was no help. "I try," he told Carlo, "but no one wants to take a chance during COVID." Carlo forgave but did not believe him.

⸺◆●◆⸺

In the week after the odd lightning storm, fires broke out over much of California and turned the skies the color of sulfur. Fires in Napa, Marin, and near Vacaville rendered the air quality dangerous. At the same time, relentlessly sunny days with temperatures in the high nineties blistered anyone who ventured out. Don watched several luridly red sunsets and joked with Dana – he no longer called her a zombie, even when she was out of earshot – about why she didn't take him out into the smoky air.

He noticed having to breathe harder to inhale enough air and asked Dana whether smoke came in through the air conditioners. "It shouldn't," was all she said. He watched her closely and didn't notice her seeming to breathe harder or faster. Plus he began to complain of the heat. He knew full well it was over a hundred degrees outside. For the first time, he asked Dana to keep the shades on his two windows mostly drawn, except for when he went to sleep. He still savored the pristine early morning hours when no one and nothing moved. Dana took his temperature each time she came into his room and measured his oxygen with the pulse oximeter. His temperature reading was slightly high, the other slightly low. He denied having a cough, but the heat was getting to him, giving him a headache.

For the first time, he took comfort in the Democratic Convention. The presenters felt more genuine, hucksterism was kept to a minimum, and the vows to restore the country constricted his throat with emotion. *If only*, he thought. At seventy-four, having lived this long and through the 2016 election and all that ensued, he almost dared not believe. But Biden, older and stronger than he, with more losses to his history, projected genuine hope as well as determination.

By Friday of Convention week, he begun to ask Dana for Tylenol every few hours for his headache, and in the middle of Friday night he awoke thinking his head would burst open from the pressure. He pushed his emergency button. Someone, a woman not Dana whom he didn't recognize, materialized, zombie-clad, almost immediately, and he moaned about his head. She immediately took his temperature -- it was 104 – and gave him a new nasal test before leaving his room to summon help.

"Take me out," he demanded. "For a drive. I need to climb the mountain. I need to breathe the air outside!" He had begun to wheeze; he knew the air in his room was contaminated and he needed the fresh air outside. The new nurse put a package of frozen peas across his forehead, and a pack of ice behind his neck. "It's melting," he warned. Two other zombies entered his room. One of them, he couldn't even tell if it was a man or woman, began to insert a needle into the back of his wrist, the shunt for intravenous tubing. A gurney was rolled into the room, and he was moved onto it. Four more strangers materialized, he was rolling now, down the hall, down the elevator, out for a few seconds into the real night air before he was swallowed into the cavern of an ambulance. A siren screamed outside. He was mesmerized by the motion, fast rolling motion, faster than anything he had experienced for many months. If his head didn't hurt so much, if the motion did not nauseate him, he might have enjoyed the ride.

For a moment, he knew he was outside again, being rolled out of the ambulance cavern into another cavern with higher ceilings and endless lights. The lights made his head throb worse. "Cover me!" he yelled. "The lights hurt." Someone mercifully put a cool, damp compress over his eyes. He didn't need to see to know he was in a hospital. Just the word "COVID" from someone sent him rolling fast in a direction all his zombies seemed to know. Much subdued talk around him, only a few words emerging, as if he were trying to decipher a conversation in a foreign language.

"Mr. Goodman?" emerged from a zombie standing near him.

"Yes."

"What's bothering you?"

"My head is exploding. It's never hurt this bad."

"We're putting an IV into your other arm. You should feel some relief soon." He felt his blood pressure being taken, his finger clamped into another monitor.

"Are you having any difficulty breathing?"

"Not here. It was bad before I left, though. The air is bad where I live." Someone was prodding his legs and feet. "I have no feeling on my right side – stroke four years ago." He jerked his left foot away. "That really hurts!" Someone said "sorry" gently but continued to press upward along his left leg. At each pressure he grimaced. "Too hard!" Now they were in his groin, prodding gradually upward toward his lungs, pressing hard against his diaphragm. He was relieved when they reverted to a stethoscope and told him to inhale deeply. "Does that hurt?" "No." Pinpricks on the bottom of his left foot next, but they didn't hurt. His head, too, was beginning to feel slightly less bad.

"Mr. Goodman, we're going to keep you here, at least for a day or two. Is there someone we should notify?"

"Yes, my wife. Janice."

"We have her number here, in your records from the Evergreen." She recited the number. "Is that right?"

He tried to nod, but his head still throbbed. "Yes, call her."

Janice reached automatically for her cell when it rang before five in the morning, as if she had already been awake. She knew. The ring was not Don's; it had to be a stranger. "Yes?"

"Are you Janice Goodman?"

Janice sat up and said yes again. This could only be bad. "Who's calling?"

A young doctor identified herself and began to explain that Don had arrived by ambulance in the very early hours of this morning, with a high fever and throbbing headache and pain in his active leg.

"Do you think it's COVID-19?"

"Yes, we suspect it is. We've had him tested and are awaiting the results, but we have him in the COVID-19 isolation area."

"Is there any way I can talk to him?"

"He's sleeping now, making up for lost time last night. If he's able to call you when he wakes up, I'll ask him to do it. If he can't, I'll call you."

Janice leaned back into bed, trying to make sense of what she had just heard. Bargaining, she reminded herself that the more recent round of outbreaks had not always involved hospitalization, and that those in hospital often recovered, not like the early days. But there was no doubting how vulnerable Don was. She got up and showered, determined to carry on. She had somehow to tell Adam, who was to leave for Oberlin in just two days. Mechanically, she made a large pot of strong coffee. When she turned around to set the table, Adam appeared.

"You're up early," they each said at the same time, drawing a wan smile from the other. "What's up with you?" he said. "I know I'm obsessed about packing for school, but what about you?"

Turning around to pour herself a cup and then back to face him, she simply told him. "Your dad is in the hospital and they think it's COVID."

"No!" He turned and swore softly, as if she would not hear. "How bad is it?"

"Terrible headache and aches in his leg, high fever, apparently no trouble breathing."

"Can we talk to him?"

"Maybe. I'm waiting to hear back from the doctor who called me this morning."

They each served and ate their cereal in silence, Adam so slowly that his cereal turned soggy. "Should I even go?"

"Absolutely you should go. You can talk to him just as well from there as here, and he will take heart in hearing what you're doing at Oberlin."

"What about you?"

"I will also take heart in what you are doing. For me, you should definitely go." She gave him a determined smile. "If you want, I'll go with you." Their plan was that he would fly by himself, and she would drive him to the airport.

"No way!"

Now it was her turn to smile at his insistence. It would be unmanly for him to show up with his mother. Besides, he would go immediately into quarantine in his dorm; she could not get past the front door. Today he had his appointment for the nasal test that was required as a condition to entry.

Once he tested negative and passed out of two weeks of quarantine, he would have his lecture classes online but his cello instruction in person. He would even have small live classes with other student musicians.

"You've waited too long for this. Time for you to get out of isolation with your mother and test your wings."

"Besides, you'll escape the smoky air of California." They exchanged ironic smiles.

⬤

From her vantage point of being on vacation at home, Erythea noticed Liss' work habits as never before. It had usually been the two of them bustling every day to tend to others' needs, coming home emotionally and often physically drained but eager to relax with each other. When Liss was in Italy for so long, Erythea slogged it alone, always wanting something elusive from Liss that was not available. Now that she was at home, watching Liss was like watching a mirror of herself at work while Liss was in Italy. Now she was living with a dynamo she recognized as her parallel self. Liss talked each day about the tortured backs and necks of her patients, most of whom carried their tensions physically rather than suffering from any actual injury or deformity. "Some of these folks haven't felt any human touch for weeks or months – can you imagine that?" Liss asked as if the condition were rare. Erythea only nodded, trying to imagine how many years it had been for some of the folks she tended. What was that like, living every day without any physical touch or the hope of any in the future? In bed at night, it was as if Liss' blood flowed faster and warmer than the blood in her own limbs. When they stroked each other in bed, Liss was more vigorous, greedier, Erythea more gently exploratory, languorous and contemplative. Erythea took enormous pleasure in the heat of Liss' presence, but in the middle of the night she awakened and needed to move apart, throw the covers off herself and rest under just a sheet. She wasn't eager to re-inhabit the persona of her partner. For the moment, she relished the calm, the shelter of Liss' heat. She had no immediate desire to resume her own professional caregiving. She longed for nothing beyond her immediate reach. She nestled like a cat alongside Liss.

Early Sunday evening, August 23, in Kenosha, Wisconsin, the video reveals, a young black man walks purposefully alongside the passenger side of his car, with two white police officers a few feet behind him with their guns drawn. He walks around the front of his car, opens the door to the driver's seat, and, as he crouches to seat himself, the two officers open fire repeatedly on him from a range of about two feet. At no point did the officers attempt to physically subdue him, even as he bent over to get into the car.

On Monday, August 24, the news media report the young black man, Jacob Blake, was paralyzed from the waist down from the gunshot wounds inflicted by the police. His three children were in the car at the time of the shooting. The police report that they had been responding to a domestic dispute and that they thought Mr. Blake had a knife. No knife was found on his person or in his car.

The Republican National Convention also opened on Monday, August 24, featuring a white couple from St. Louis, Missouri, Patricia and Mark McCloskey, both attorneys, who described the injustice done to them as they attempted to defend their home from protestors demonstrating on the street beyond the lawn in front of their home. The video of the event shows the couple, he with an assault rifle and she with a pistol aimed toward the protestors marching on the street in front of their white *faux*-Southern mansion. The injustices they describe were that they – not the protestors -- were arrested and charged with a crime – and that one of the demonstrators was a "Marxist, liberal activist" who was shortly thereafter nominated to the U.S. House of Representatives in the Missouri primary.

On Tuesday, August 25, in Kenosha, during the second day of protests over the police shooting of Jacob Blake, two protestors were shot, one of them fatally, by an armed 17-year-old, claiming to protect a gas station as part of a militia.

Janice received the second call from the hospital just before lunch. Don's temperature had reduced somewhat but he still had a fever, his headache persisted, and nasal test results were still pending. Don's lungs were not impaired, but the pain in his leg persisted.

"Can I speak with him?" The doctor said he would try, and in a moment she heard Don say hello uncertainly. "It's me, Janice. I'm here with you in spirit. Adam too."

"I love you. Can't talk. Too much pain."

The physician came on again. "He knows who you are, he can say what he needs. We have to take comfort in that."

Janice agreed. "When will you call again?"

"I'll call again tonight, or if there is any significant change."

Her phone pinged with a text from Zoe, her walking partner, about walking the next day. They had given a rest to their daily walks since the heat wave and smoky air of the past week. Janice just shook her head and fingered the shortest message possible – "no walks this week, explain later." Zoe pinged her again a few moments later; she had decided to go hiking in Tahoe for a few days, to escape the heat. Janice texted just the word "enjoy," relieved she would not have to explain anything for a few days.

Her phone pinged again only a few minutes later. This time it was a news flash warning of a hurricane and 'unsurvivable' storm surge expected on the Texas coast.

She could hear Adam on the cello upstairs, his last lesson before he was to leave for Oberlin. His instructor had given him a new piece, Faure's *Elegy*. Its gentle, sustained notes quieted her. She moved to a chair where she could listen more easily.

When Adam appeared in front of her, she startled.

"Your dad's stable. They let me speak to him." Adam just nodded.

The second physician called back as promised just before seven, as Janice and Adam were finishing an improvised dinner. He reported that Don had tested positive for the coronavirus, as suspected. His headache and fever continued but within 'bearable' limits. She asked to speak with Don but the physician was not in Don's room. "At least you know he's stable," were his concluding words.

When she repeated the gist of the short conversation to Adam, he just nodded. Declining ice cream, he disappeared into his room. As she cleaned the few dishes and table, Janice decided she would call Don again with Adam.

As she entered Adam's room, she could see his packing was nearly complete. Adam was poised with his cello in front of his music stand, his phone propped at the center of the page. He glanced up at her as she walked in, mouthing 'dad' as he inclined his head toward the phone. She began to shake her head slightly, as if to say this is time for talking not music, but Adam ignored her and began to play. The music was new to her, a lighter piece with shorter, more upbeat notes, in a higher register than some of the lugubrious pieces she had heard him play. As Adam paused to turn the page, she heard Don's voice on the speaker.

"It's happy. I can hum it in my head."

"That's just the first one; there are more," Adam told him. "Are you ready for the second?"

"No, play the first one again, and tell me what it is. I'll remember it."

"Tchaikovsky's Rococo Variations." He played the first again.

"You lifted me. When do you leave for Oberlin?"

"The day after tomorrow."

"Play that again for me tomorrow?"

"Sure thing." The connection ended.

September
– The Plague
of Fire

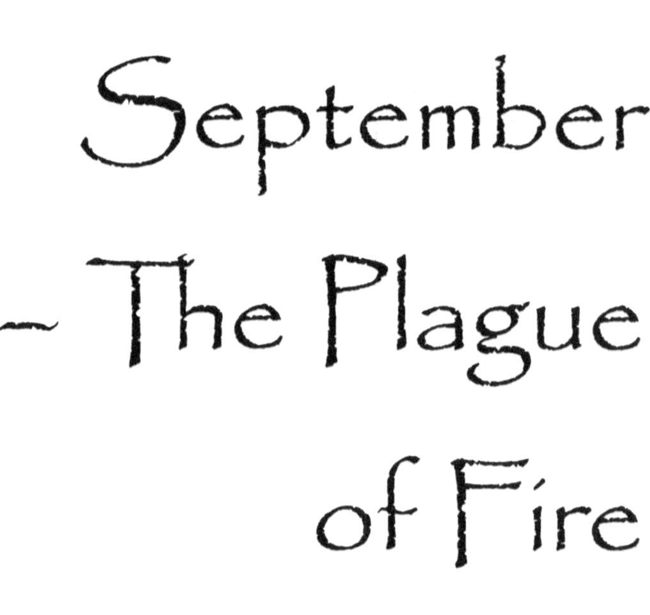

Bettina made dinner for her brothers these days, now that both her parents were busy at the restaurant. Often she just reheated leftovers from the prior day at the restaurant, or eggs, or a pizza and salad, but she and Beto and Tomas ate together every evening and shared what they could of their online classes from the day. It was at best a closeted existence. Tonight, as Arturo and Marta returned, all three children were still at the table, playing cards and laughing together.

"Homework?" Arturo asked skeptically.

"Done!" They all chimed in.

"*Bueno*. Reward." Arturo plunked a gallon container of chocolate ice cream on the table. Bettina fetched a scoop and five bowls and spoons, and they all shared. After they had all finished and Marta and Bettina were cleaning up together, Bettina asked her mother for a favor. Would she read to her each night in Spanish?

"This is a lonely way to be in school," she confessed.

Tired as she was, Marta readily agreed.

"What are you reading?"

"*One Hundred Years of Solitude -- Cien Anos de Soledad.*" Marta interjected a correction to Bettina's pronunciation of 'cien' before she could check herself. Bettina gave her a knowing smile. "See?"

"Have you talked to Sabrina lately?" Marta asked after she had read the first few pages.

"Not since we made the decision about school." Bettina looked down and away from her mother. "She's called me every day."

"And you won't talk to her? *Por que*?"

Bettina shrugged. She still harbored resentment over not being able to go to school in person, and Sabrina was still her target.

"You know as well as I do that Sabrina is probably feeling lonely. She's taking care of her mother and brothers. I know you disagreed with her about going to school physically, but I think she bears a heavier burden than you do. Reach out to your cousin."

Marta continued to read, her Spanish a comforting current of words. Bettina fell asleep after only twenty minutes, as if she were a child again.

Bettina texted Sabrina the next morning. "*Lo siento*. When's a good time for me to call?"

Sabrina texted back within minutes. "Any time between 2 & 5." Bettina promised to call at three, after her last class. When they connected, their words tumbled out in rapid fire, each of them having pent up so much of their reactions for days. Bettina's hard feelings dissolved as soon as she hear her cousin's voice.

⸻ ⬥ ⸻

When Don awoke, he could hear two doctors bantering outside his door. His room was located near a nursing station and someone had left the door open. From the timbre of the voices, a much older doc was talking with one or two residents or much younger docs. The older doc spoke with an Indian accent.

"With cholera it was totally different. When the ambulances came in to the emergency door and opened up, the bodies inside were stacked like so much cordwood, three or four layers of them on the floor, all looking baked and dead. We'd move them inside onto cholera cots, insert an IV tube and fill them with saline solution."

"Cholera cots?" A younger voice asked.

"A cot with a hole about four inches in diameter located just under the patient's anus. We'd put a bucket underneath to catch the diarrhea running out, measure the outflow and make sure we rehydrated with at least as much saline solution. It was amazing; in a few days they'd be plumped up again with liquids and ready to go home." The younger docs laughed quietly.

"Nothing like this." With that, the room outside fell silent, and Don fell asleep again until sometime well after full dark.

Once again, his head was pounding. He groped for the call button and pressed it. "My head," was all he could say to the nurse who responded with one of the interns. "My eyes are bulging out. I can't stand it!" Don implored.

The nurse injected more pain relief into the tube flowing into his arm. "You should feel some relief in just a few minutes. I'll stand here to make sure."

After a very short while, Don could hear her breathing quietly as his pain receded.

"Better?" All he could do was utter a kind of "mmmm."

⸻ ⬥ ⸻

Janice paced her narrow back yard. She had dropped Adam at the airport, where the air itself fed her anxiety. The haze of smoke reduced visibility as much as a thick San Francisco fog, though this air was hot, acrid and dry. She needed her headlights in both directions, even at midday. Back here in Marin the air was better, clearer, though the air still reeked of distant smoke. She wondered about Leah and her asthma in this air, reminding herself to call Naomi later. She should go inside, she told herself, but it was the first time her home would be empty of both Don and Adam. She had the home to herself. There were days when that might have given her a lift -- free to do whatever she wanted, with no one else to care for or attend to. But not today. She felt no direction, no desire. She continued to cross the back yard diagonally, to lengthen each pace on this new course.

She startled when her phone vibrated and pinged in her rear pocket. Adam was to text her as soon as he landed, but it was far too soon to expect word from him. Word about Don could erupt at any moment. As she wrestled the phone from her pants pocket, she dropped it, luckily on the grass rather than on the stones she paced. On retrieving it, she saw the text was from Zoe.

"Unreal! Half the trails at Tahoe are closed because of the bubonic plague. Can you believe it?!"

Janice turned off her phone and put it back into her pocket. Hyperbole aside, Zoe was not someone to make up stories. Janice could not even think of this new element now. Janice began to count her paces, to take her mind off anything else but simple numbers.

⸺•◦•⸺

On Wednesday, September 9, the sky in San Francisco dawned a dull red, as if the earth were somehow in eclipse. But it did not pass in a few minutes, or even an hour. By noon, the sky remained dull orange. Drivers needed their headlights. It was not fog. It was not immediate smoke. It was the tinge of ash borne high aloft, dimming the sun and altering its tone. The air quality was so poor that everyone was warned to stay inside.

Across California, and north to Oregon and Washington, a proliferation of fires erupted across the dry surfaces. In California, some temperatures exceeded 110 degrees. A spate of lightning strikes kindled the hot, dry landscape, sparking more than 7,000 fires that were incinerating several million acres. Not one of the fires was controlled. Vast clouds of smoke were visible in space satellite images.

In April 1815, a volcano named Tambora, on Sumbawa Island in the East Indies, erupted spectacularly for the first time in a thousand years, shooting a gigantic explosion of volcanic ash into the stratosphere and creating a caldera six kilometers in diameter. It was the largest recorded eruption in modern human history. In September of that year, William Turner painted spectacular sunsets in his seascapes – the same orange as the late afternoon light in San Francisco one hundred and five years later.

The Tambora eruption dimmed the immediate region at once but also created three years of apocalyptic disruption across the earth. Its volcanic winter lasted four years. Harvests across Europe perished in unseasonable frosts and floods, causing widespread famine and riots in the United Kingdom and France and a typhus epidemic in Ireland. The European fatalities were estimated at 200,000 people. In June 1816, snow fell in agricultural parts of New York State. Cholera proliferated in floods of India. The political fortunes of many countries shifted, as many people interpreted the climatic catastrophe as punishment for poor administration by their rulers.

In 1783, the Laki volcano in Iceland erupted violently, causing catastrophic famine. Its atmospheric sulphur dioxide poisoned much of the island's livestock. Historians have theorized that its ensuing famine contributed to the French Revolution six years later. Benjamin Franklin hypothesized in 1783 that the unusually cool summer that year was caused by volcanic dust from the Laki eruption.

In ancient times, a volcano caused by the African plate moving toward Eurasia erupted with spectacular violence on the then-circular Minoan island of Akrotini. In preceding months, the volcano had erupted a few times, inducing cautious residents to evacuate. This eruption was so violent that it shot rocks, flames and gases 18 miles above the earth and deposited white pumice stone around it 30 feet deep, reshaping the island now known as Santorini into a ring with a tiny volcanic mound in its center. Buildings of Santorini are constructed with pumice from this eruption. Buried within the deposits of pumice were olive trees on which scientists have performed radiocarbon dating. Current estimates of the date of what is now known as the Thera Cataclysm are 1627-1600 BCE. Like the Tambora eruption many years later, the Thera Cataclysm bears a Volcano Explosivity Index of 7.

Winds from the Thera Cataclysm bore its volcanic ash east to Asia Minor. Thera pumice exists at Tel Ashkelon, the Canaanite seaport in Israel, and Tel al Dab'a in Egypt. The global reach of this eruption has been linked to the collapse of the Xia dynasty in China, accompanied by a yellow fog, frost in July, famine and withering of all the grain crops, all of these phenomena recorded on the ancient Egyptian Tempest Stele of Ahmose I.

The Thera Cataclysm may also have been the source of the ten Biblical plagues described in the Book of Exodus. The blood-red stinking river described in Exodus 7 could have been a kind of red algae that deprives the water of oxygen, killing the fish and rendering the water undrinkable. Environmental stress, including lack of oxygen, can cause an explosion of the frog population and the migration of locusts. Hailstones need solid particles in the air to form -- the longer the particles remain in the air, the larger the hailstones -- and volcanic ash from Thera could have fueled the hail that destroyed the crops in Exodus 9. The ninth Biblical plague, described in Exodus 10:21-23, cast three days of total darkness over Egypt. The parting of the Red Sea that permitted Moses to lead the ancient Israelites to freedom may have been a tsunami caused by the earthquakes accompanying the Thera Cataclysm.

Who can say whether the red sky of San Francisco on September 9, 2020 was just a blip, or part of some larger, longer-lasting phenomenon?

⸻ ◦❖◦ ⸻

Don drifted in and out of a sense of where he was. Now he opened his eyes and was surprised to see a dark-skinned zombie and another at the foot of his bed, with the sheet up over his calf, which they were examining intently. "Glad you noticed that," the dark-skinned zombie told the other. Don recognized the voice with the Indian accent. "Start him on anticoagulants immediately and keep an eye on that swelling."

"What is it?" Don asked. The doctor looked up as though surprised to find him awake.

"Your lower leg is red and swollen. We think you may have a blood clot, and I have ordered anticoagulants to avoid any trouble to your lungs." With that, the doctor quickly recovered Don's lower leg and vanished from the room, as if dodging any further questions.

Don did not connect the idea of anticoagulants with a threat to his lungs, and he was disinclined to try to pursue it. What he wanted was music. He would call Adam and ask him to play for him again. Music was the balm he needed now. A random memory drifted through his thoughts of a makeshift hospital in some war zone, where the doctors played music to ease patients' pain, since they had no anesthetics. Don asked Siri to call

Adam. He could hear the phone ringing but Adam did not answer.

The next time a zombie entered his room Don asked if he could have music. "Absolutely," he was told, and the zombie asked what sort of music he wanted. "Classical," he told her and watched idly while she maneuvered a remote from beside his bed. Soon he was lulled by Chopin.

When he became aware again, the music had stopped but his head was clear. Again he thought about that beleaguered war-zone hospital where music served as the only anesthetic. Did he read of this or was it in a documentary film he had seen? Unbidden, a title emerged in his head, *A Constellation of Vital Phenomena*, a novel he had sometime read of a hospital in war torn Chechnya. Could that be the source? He had been struck at the time by the elaborate title, which was the definition of the heart in Soviet medical texts. It seemed probable from the context of war, but a visual image appeared in his head of a modern cellphone propped against a wall in the improvised operating room. There were no cellphones in the Chechen war. Annoyed by not being able to locate the source of his memory, Don felt the remote near his good hand, and restored the river of lulling music.

⸻ •●• ⸻

Simon had made arrangements with an old friend to meet at a trailhead on Mt. Tamalpais one Thursday, and found himself eager to have a live conversation. But on waking he saw the sky remained nearly as smoky as the day before. Consulting the air quality index, a new tool for these times, he saw a reading of well over 200, a purple symbol of very unhealthy conditions. Soon after, his friend cancelled by text, citing the smoky air. Once again thrown back on himself, Simon debated whether he should exercise his new freedom at the expense of his lungs. He decided to remain inside and read. He could telephone his friend and try to have a discussion with him, but it would not be the same. Something about the rhythm of walking fostered a free range of thought and conversation that he could not expect to reproduce on Zoom or FaceTime or the telephone.

He glanced around his apartment with weary eyes. Comfortable enough, the apartment confined him both mentally and physically. After six months, its contours were unwelcoming, unyielding and completely unenlivening. Would it be different if he were to paint the walls a dramatically different color, like bright yellow? Why even think that way? No painter would be allowed in under current regulations to shelter in place. No, it was not the color. He knew from his very first foray out last week that it was the freedom to enter and leave, to change his surroundings, to see the outdoors, that made the indoors comforting, or even tolerable.

Simon tried to reason his way out of his malaise. It was not as if he were in prison, a prisoner of war camp, or a detention facility, although on dark days he called this a detention facility; he had probably even used this phrase with that nice therapy woman, Erythea, if that was her name. He should probably call her one of these days to apologize for his hanging up on her in disgust. She hadn't deserved his impatience. In prison he would have a fixed term, and he could in essence count his days, months or even years. This was more like being held hostage in an unruly territory where he could not know how long his detention would last, or what combination of circumstances might free him. A vaccine? Before the election, as promised by the President? Ridiculous even to contemplate. Now with the smoke from an unprecedented number of fires across the state, it became difficult even to predict what new catastrophe might befall. He could count himself lucky because he was safe, if he could view life from that perspective.

He could not. That he was adequately fed three times a day, albeit from a paper bag left outside his door, that his apartment was cleaned weekly and that he could shower as often as he liked provided no comfort at all.

Janice phoned Naomi as she had promised herself. From Naomi's halting hello, Janice sensed immediately that something was wrong. The news poured from her friend like letters from an opened mailbox.

"We installed air purifiers in Naomi's room and in the dining room a few weeks ago, but now she won't even leave her room, or even get up out of bed unless I coax her. I've never seen her so depressed. All her friends have gone off to college, and her courses are all virtual. She hasn't been with any other people except us in six months, and she tells me she never will again. Saul tries to talk to her about books, or play chess with her, but she's too listless to engage."

When Naomi paused, Janice commiserated. "And now you can't even invite her out for a walk in the sunshine."

Naomi continued, "we tried doing your yoga classes online for a few days. The first day she told me she was happy to see you again, but then I couldn't get her to continue. She told me she can't do one more thing online. I've thought of therapy, of course, but that would also have to be online, and starting therapy with a stranger online sounds daunting even to me -- though I'm thinking about it for myself."

Janice wracked her mind to think of something to say, something to offer. All she could say was "I wish I could help somehow." Naomi assured her that just listening was some salve. "Any time, just call. When this bad air clears, let's walk again."

As soon as she hung up, Janice wondered whether she should tell Adam. She decided not to. If he wanted to talk to Leah, he would call; if he didn't, she didn't want him to make him feel obligated.

Leah's condition was worse than Naomi described. She refused to move from her bed, which now stank from her unwashed body and urine. Her mother knocked frequently but stopped trying to come in when Leah yelled at her to go away. For more than a day, Leah had eaten nothing and had tried not to move at all. If she could not move like the rest of the world, she would not move at all, not even to lock the door. At some point she ceased having any feeling in her lower legs and feet. Could she accomplish this feat with the rest of her body, her mind? She tried.

⸻ ◦◉◦ ⸻

The French composer Olivier Messaien was captured at Verdun and imprisoned in a prisoner of war camp in 1940 when the Germans overran France. While there, he located a violin, a cello, a clarinet and a piano and the musicians to play them, and he composed the "Quartet for the End of Time," which was first performed in January 1941, under freezing conditions, for an audience of his fellow prisoners and their guards. That melody could be imagined, organized, written and even performed under such circumstances is difficult to contemplate. That this composition summons the angel who announces the end of time and praise for the eternity of Jesus provides some clues as to the comfort he might have taken in this composition. Musicians acknowledge how he altered music's norms of timing, by changing the number of beats per measure. Like atrial fibrillation in the human heart, alarming to those who feel it, unnoticed by others.

"Mom, what's happening with Dad? I got a phone message from him yesterday evening but no answer when I tried to call back." Adam's anxiety bled into his voice.

Janice sighed. "He has a new complication, a blood clot in his calf. They've given him anticoagulants so that the clot might dissolve and not go to his lungs." There was no sense in not telling him.

"And?"

"I don't know anything further; I have to wait for a call from his physician."

"Is he on a ventilator?"

"Not when I last spoke to his doctor yesterday."

"Have you talked to Dad at all?"

"Not since his first day in the hospital. I'm led to believe he's in no condition to talk."

Silence on Adam's end. Janice asked him "how're you doing?" In clipped words, Adam told her he was fine, classes had begun, all okay but he just wanted to know more about Dad. She assured him as best she could that she would follow up and tell him whatever she learned.

Not satisfied, Adam dialed Don again. A glance at his watch told him it might be too early, before eight in the morning, but he guessed that sense of time might be different in the hospital. Don answered with an alert "hello."

"Dad, I'm so glad to hear you. Sorry I missed your call. How are you?"

"Don't know, actually. Called you to play for me. Can you?"

"Of course." Adam scrambled for his cello, and to put the script for the *Rococo Variations* back onto his music stand. "I'll start where we left off the last time."

"No. Please, from the beginning."

Da capo. It took him a few minutes to quiet himself into the music. Then the vibration of the chords began as if straight from his heart to his fingers. Adam knew he had never played before with quite this sensation, and he could immediately hear the difference. He continued in this new vein until he had to turn the page, then paused to check if his dad would say anything. Hearing nothing, he continued, until the next page, and the next, until he had played through the seventh variation and coda.

"Dad?" No answer. The connection had been lost; at what point he did not know. Dialing again, he got no answer.

Adam paced his small room until his next class, only a few minutes away. Too bad it was a lecture. He wondered if he could play like that again, for his dad or at all.

⸻ ⸰ ⸻

Erythea returned to work on September 8, the day before the apocalyptic tinge darkened the whole sky. The temperature was in the nineties, and she comforted herself that at least she would be in an air-conditioned environment, protected both from the temperature and the smoke in the air. Checking in with George, she asked first about Viola and whether there had been any follow-up from the police. "None, and I suspect the police have been satisfied. We just reported her passing here, and I haven't heard any rumors about what happened."

"But," he paused significantly, "we have a resident hospitalized with COVID-19, and his condition is far from stable."

"I'm sorry to hear," she responded automatically. "Who is it?"

"Don Goodman from skilled nursing."

Erythea wondered if her jolt was visible. "Are you in touch with his wife?"

"I spoke with her just once, and she assured me she is in daily contact with hospital. It's up to you whether you want to reach out to her. Probably a good idea."

She resisted the urge to ask if she could speak with Don. Politely, she asked what else was new. A staff member had had the coronavirus and had recovered, but that staff member had ministered to Don and was the likely origin of his infection. Residents were now being allowed brief visits from family and friends, outside, behind plexiglass screens. He was halting all such visits until the air improved, but the new program seemed to lift residents' morale. Residents were being allowed to walk or drive outside the campus, and this also seemed to improve their morale. They were still short-staffed, but robots had been acquired to help clean all the common areas. She would still be asked to help deliver meals on a regular rotation.

On arriving at her own office, she checked her email, which had accumulated to 346, the most recent from Simon, the resident who had been so unpleasant before hanging up on her. She sighed. She was definitely back.

After pouring herself a huge glass of iced tea, she decided to tackle the most difficult tasks first, an act of discipline she had practiced until it was ingrained. She returned Simon's call.

"Simon here." His voice was crisp but not harsh. When she identified herself and said she was returning his call, his tone shifted to warm. "I owe you an apology for how I spoke to you that day. I was frustrated to the max, but it had nothing to do with you. I'm sorry. I know how rude I was and you didn't deserve it."

She felt her shoulders release as she thanked him. "How are you now?"

"Better since I've been able to get out hiking. I'm okay." He laughed, a small grunt. "It doesn't help that smoke now keeps me indoors, but it's certainly not your fault. Thank you for understanding."

Erythea smiled to herself. Tackling the 'worst first' now gave her the energy for whatever followed. She decided to call Don's wife Janice, whom she knew only from Don's efforts to connect with her. Conscious of her impression that Janice cared too little about Don, and professionally wary of relying only on her impressions, she dialed Janice, who answered on the first ring. Erythea identified herself.

"I thought it would be one of Don's doctors. I've been waiting to hear."

"You're probably more up-to-date than I am, but we are all concerned here at The Evergreen. I also wanted also to check on how you are, and whether there's anything we can do to make things easier for you."

Janice paused, audibly taking a deep breath. "The doctors are pretty good about checking in with me every day, bringing me current. Don has the complication of a blood clot in his leg, on top of, or maybe as a result of, COVID. They're giving him anticoagulants to reduce the risk of the clot traveling to his lungs."

"Have you talked to him?" Erythea waited.

"Not enough. I'm never sure when to call. Once when I did he was incoherent, maybe just from my waking him from a nap."

"He took great comfort from your calls when he was here."

"Are you just saying that, or how do you know?"

"Don spoke of it, and I could see his pleasure when you called. It was quite clear." She stopped, fearful of lecturing Janice.

"That's good to hear," Janice said quietly.

Shifting, Erythea asked if there was anything she could do for Janice.

"Oh, you're kind to ask, but I'm coping as well as I can from here."

"Please don't hesitate to call if you want any help." Erythea gave Janice her phone number and ended the call.

Janice sat by the phone for some minutes after this conversation. The therapist with the complicated name – Janice only remembered Thea – had somehow both comforted her and prodded her conscience to call Don more. The old nurse within her remembered clearly how many interruptions patients had at unpredictable hours. But was she using that as an excuse not to reach out to Don more? She knew at some level she feared what she might hear from him directly. She reached for the phone and dialed Don's cell.

His voice jolted her. His hello echoed a remote mind state.

"It's me. Can you talk?"

"Oh, Janice. I thought it would be Adam again. He's been playing music for me – so good."

"Can I get you any more music? I'm glad it's helping."

"No, got plenty on my phone, and the nurses help when I need it." Silence.

"How're you feeling?"

"Tired like never before. I weave in and out of knowing what's going on."

"I love you. I wish I could be there to help."

Don was silent for a few breaths. "Just hearing that helps. We'll get through this. I'm staying with that thought."

"Do. I'll hold onto the same thought. I send you a virtual kiss."

"Too much virtual for one lifetime. I want to hold you."

"Me too."

After the call ended, Janice sat by the phone again. Adam's instincts were better than her own, she thought. She had told Don 'I love you' for the first time in a long time. And meant it.

She stood up, energized to make the most of this day. Checking on Adam's room, she folded and put away various shirts he had apparently decided not to take with him. The bottom drawer, she noticed, contained all his sheets of music, neatly stacked. Just one remained on his stand, the piece from *Orfeo ed Eurydice* he had played for Leah that afternoon. Janice folded it and put it on the stack of music in Adam's bottom drawer.

Too quickly, all sensation becomes memory. In a vivid dream, Don catches the peppery scent under Janice's arm as he cups her infinitely soft, humid breast with his right hand that now lays useless at his side. In the dream, he has just lifted her tee shirt as she returned from a run. She still runs but he sees her only on Face Time on his phone, after she has showered and redressed. She is calm, composed, a video rather than a living being. The music on his phone halts when she calls, resumes in place when the call ends. In his dreams he can have music at the same time as he touches or talks to his wife. He craves these dreams.

As Gianlucca waited for Lili to come out of the school gate, he wondered whether Fran might come to dinner with them. While they spoke nearly every day about Liliana and logistics for her school, they hadn't had a real conversation in months. His apartment has a small, sunlit terrace where he and Lili took their meals when the weather was warm, and today was a brilliant, cloudless day, warm enough for bare shoulders. Unbidden, he remembered a deep purple sundress Fran had worn on one of their holidays, before Liliana was even conceived.

"*Sto impulsivo oggi,*" he texted her, inviting her to dinner this evening.

Fran's cheerful "*perche no*" came back almost immediately, and they readily agreed on a time.

He caught sight of Lili in her orange and pink face mask as soon as she emerged from the school door, bouncing down the few steps with arms akimbo, her orange backpack bouncing over her shoulders. He grinned. How could he not be enlivened by this buoyant little person in his life? She ran toward him and threw her arms around his neck as he bent to lift her. As she prattled about her day, he drew the curls of her fine hair away from her mask and tucked them behind her ear.

His apartment is a short walk from her school, and on the way he stopped at the *mercato* and bought a bottle of vermentino.

"Guess who's coming to dinner," he asked her. "Franco?" She named his best friend. "No." "*Ceci e la sua momma?*" He shook his head. "Who likes this wine?"

"Momma!" He nodded, and they beamed at each other. At his apartment, she practiced her letters and drew pictures with her colored pencils while he marinated chicken he would grill outside for dinner.

"Do you still have the chalks I gave you?" Intent on her letters, she just nodded and pointed to her art basket.

"When you're done, let's draw a picture on the terrace floor."

Her head shot up inquisitively. Ordinarily he did not allow her to chalk the tiles on the terrace. She continued the question with her eyes.

"I think your momma would like it." She hid her knowing smile by dipping her head again and focusing on her own drawing.

By the time Fran buzzed the door, Lili had drawn a rainbow wave across the length of the terrace, he had set the table and turned on the terrace speaker so that they could hear the music he'd been listening to in the kitchen.

Lili hurled herself at her mother as soon as she entered the room. He caught Fran's arm as she stumbled backward from the impact. Fran could barely greet him with a polite kiss on each cheek before Lili led her out to the terrace to show off her rainbow wave. As she bent over the drawing, Gianlucca glimpsed her bare, slim thighs.

"*Che bella – tutto –* the drawing, the table, the music. Is this a special occasion?"

Gianlucca shook his head but opened his arms. "Just a sunny September day."

Fran cocked her head, listening to the music. In the years they were together, they regularly played a guessing game about who and what was playing. There was always music in the small apartments they had shared. She waved a finger in time to the lilt of the music. "Wait, wait, I know I know it."

"*Ancient Airs and Dances*," he prompted.

"Yes, yes, Respighi. We heard this once at an open-air concert on the grass. Long before open-air concerts were shut down."

"They'll come back," he assured her.

Fran shook her head. "You were always the optimist."

They sat companionably on the terrace with their glasses of wine, Lili constantly in motion from one of their laps to the other, chattering nonstop, making any adult conversation impossible. Lili calmed during dinner, intent on cutting her own chicken, popping green beans into her little mouth with her fingers and looking back and forth from mother to father, a rare picture of both parents friendly and occupying the same space. Still she dominated the conversation and both parents indulged her. When Lili finished, Gianlucca excused himself to take her to wash up. Fran moved automatically to clear the dishes from the table and put them into the dishwasher. She had finished by the time Gianlucca returned.

"I should go. I know you'll be reading to Lili and putting her to bed soon."

"Stay." He gently took her left hand. "We can talk while she's in bed."

Fran shook her head slowly. "We can't go back." She reminded herself that he was the one who left, bored with the routine of marriage with a young child. Lili was only sixteen months old at the time. "No."

She kissed him swiftly on each cheek and disappeared.

<hr>

In *The Decameron*, Boccaccio allowed his privileged characters only fifteen days together, after which they returned to plague-ravaged Florence. For ten days of their respite, each of the ten young people told a story, on a theme determined by the chosen leader for the day. The tales ranged from bawdy to highly romantic to cruel to wildly fabulous, and the imaginations of these seven young women and three young men are remarkable. But the telling of tales occupied only a few hours of each day. The young people dined extravagantly, enjoyed wines, strolled the gardens and fruit orchards of their estate, danced and sang together, and took afternoon naps. The three young men, Boccaccio tells us from the outset, are enamored of three of the young women. All of the ten had seemingly endless opportunities to dally with one another privately, to flirt, and to act out their fantasies, yet all behaved with the utmost decorum, which, the author gives us to understand, is part of their elevated status in their culture. The acting out of lust, greed, cruelty, and jealousy stays in the tales, not with the tellers of the tales. It is a marvelous conceit, a fantasy of its own.

October
~Reawakening

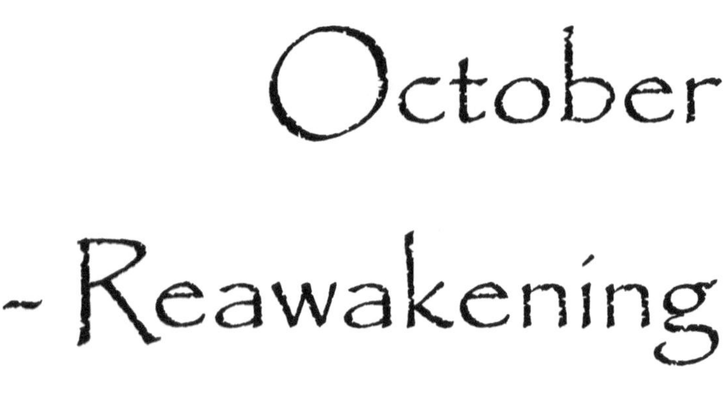

Adam shooshed his feet through the mounds of fallen leaves on the sidewalk as he ambled to class. He had plenty of time, but his cello was heavy, and the sound of the crisp leaves underfoot satisfied him in a way he couldn't explain. Many of the leaves were still red, maple stars on a field of anonymous brown, all of them crunching underneath his feet. A veil of gray fog surrounded him. Soon it would rain and render the path soggy, slippery. He began creating a small rhythm with his feet, alternating his pace at intervals. Soon his classes would need to be moved inside. Impossible to play the cello with gloves, not to mention the fog on his glasses from his mask.

He was the first to arrive at the small covered pavilion where his class of six cello players practiced with an amazing instructor. Six cellists in one class – he couldn't count six cello players he had met in his whole life before now. As he was setting his music on the stand, Ilina took a position next to him, six feet away. He watched her as covertly as he could, fascinated by her every detail. From the first class, when she was positioned opposite him in the circle, he had admired her long fingers pushing tendrils of wavy auburn hair from her intense eyes, and her haunting deep voice. Her sheet music slipped off her stand to his feet, and he grabbed it instinctively. As she too bent down to retrieve it, a tiny gold chain with a Star of David slipped out of her neckline. Handing the music back to her, he grinned and said, "You could have just said hello." She blushed thoroughly. He had clearly said the wrong thing. "Sorry, I'm just glad to see you," he tried. Now she smiled, the blush still visible on her olive skin. "I'm glad to see you too." She blew onto her fingers. "Time for us to move inside, I think." Their instructor had brought two space heaters and set them up in the circle center, one facing Ilina and Adam. "We got lucky."

The instructor started them on a Brahms sonata, ordinarily played with piano. Each of them had practiced since the last class and each was called on separately to play a designated portion. During Ilina's turn, Adam's cell phone rang, earning glares from all around. "I'm so sorry," he told them all as he fumbled to turn it off. It was from his dad. He knew the rule was muted phones in class. But his dad was still in the hospital. When his turn came, he played badly, so embarrassingly so that he went up to the instructor afterwards to apologize and explain. Whatever initiative he might take with Ilina after class was forgotten.

After his classmates had left, he phoned his dad before leaving the pavilion.

No answer. Frantically, he dialed his mom who answered on the first ring.

"Your dad seems better," poured out before either of them said hello. She explained that the swelling and redness on his leg had disappeared and his fever had subsided. He was breathing well, still had some spiking headaches but not as often, but he was very, very tired.

Adam exhaled audibly. "I was worried."

"Tell me about you." Her voice was tentative.

"It's great here!" His words tumbled out about how he was with people again, all of them involved in music, *six* cello players in one class. "I feel more alive than I have in months!"

"I'm relieved for you. Keep trying your father. I'm sure he'll be glad to hear from you."

"Gotta go, Mom. Thanks."

Adam glanced up and saw Ilina at the far edge of the pavilion. He joined her.

"Is something wrong? You okay?" She asked in that haunting voice.

She had waited for him. Adam shook his head slowly, smiling at her. "Good of you to ask. My dad's in the hospital, but he's getting better."

Suddenly there was a flood of words between them, explaining and then planning to get coffee. They shooshed through the path of leaves together.

⟾•◆•⟽

"*Bueno!*" Carla hurled at the car radio, when she heard the President had tested positive for COVID-19. "*Muy merecido.*" Hearing the bitterness in her own words as she drove to the hospital to take care of her own suffering patients, Carla fought back tears. Never had she gone to work with such a foul taste in her mouth. At least no one else had heard her, especially her children. She parked her car as far as she could from the hospital entrance to gather herself before going in to work. She said three 'Our Fathers' and crossed herself. Checking the air quality index on her cell, she donned her mask. The haze she had seen on her drive to work was not benign, it was smoke from the fires not far north.

As soon as she got off the elevator on her floor of the hospital, she entered a different world. Coming off duty, Erika briefed her on the nine patients in their rotating charge. Hazel was so anxious she had hardly slept, Bob presented as calm but his blood pressure was elevated. Had

Dr. Neuhaus made his rounds before she came off duty, she would have asked him about meds for Hazel and Bob. Carla hoped to see at least these two before doctor's morning rounds. But her first task was to change the surgical dressing for Sally, a patient with a wound infection, which involved literally pouring disinfectant over the trough in the patient's lower abdomen. "I can't watch it," Sally had told her yesterday.

"I'm here to do x-rated duty," Carla joked with Sally as she rolled in a curtain to hide from Sally any view of activity below her waist.

"Thank God it's you," Sally told her. "The night nurse just told me to be brave and be quiet. And she wasn't at all gentle."

"There's no reason you need to watch if you don't want to," Carla reassured her as she removed the night dressing carefully and examined the nearly two-inch deep incision into Sally's capacious belly. To Carla, the only disturbing sight was how much of this depth was the layer of fat under Sally's flesh. Everything looked clean. "You're going to feel a cold river now," Carla warned.

"It's almost refreshing when you do it," Sally's voice lofted over the curtain.

Carla repacked the wound with sterile dressing as gently as she could, sealed the wound area, and cleaned up the wet area that pooled between Sally's enormous thighs. By the time she had replaced the sheet and cover over Sally's belly and removed the curtain, Sally was smiling. "Thank you."

Carla gave Sally a reassuring smile. "Your thanks is my reward."

By the time Carla reached anxious Hazel, Dr. Neuhaus had already seen her and noted on her chart that she be given valium, which Carla brought for her in a tiny paper cup. "Do you want to take it yourself, or should I put it on your tongue?" Carla asked her. "I shake too much, dear, can you just put it on my tongue?" Hazel tilted her head backward. When Carla offered Hazel water, she reassured the slight woman that she would be feeling more relaxed soon.

Carla's professional day sped smoothly, a world apart from the day's news. Only when she reached Bob did she get distracted. Glued to his television, he barely glanced at her before pronouncing his views on how many people were being 'polluted' by this virus. "It'll kill us all before long," he muttered. Carla tried not to listen as she attached the nodes to his chest and ankles for his EKG, monitored him and then removed the tiny patches. She could think of no words to comfort him as she noted his reading echo his own agitated state.

By the time she arrived home, Carla was stimulated and fatigued at the same time. From the garage, she could hear all three children chattering in the kitchen, banging pots and plates as they set up for dinner. They fell oddly silent as she came in and kissed each of them. Before she could utter a question, Luis blurted, "will he die?" His young face reflected confusion and curiosity.

"It's too early to know," she said levelly, wondering what her children had already discussed among themselves. On the small television in the kitchen played a scene of the President walking toward the White House helicopter, on his way to the hospital, his hand flashing a thumb's-up. "Usually the President's physician will report to the public on his medical condition."

"But *usually* we can rely on a President's spokesperson." Carlo's sarcasm told Carla all she needed to know of the conversation that had occurred before she entered their home. Carla turned off the television. "Let's talk about us instead this evening. You're the people I care about most."

Carlo recounted details of his day of contact tracing. He had spoken to an old lady who lived in a home for seniors where no one but her had contracted COVID. "She was 85 years old but still really clear," he told them with something akin to astonishment in his voice. Four days earlier she had driven her car to the home of her hair stylist of many years – her salon was closed by county regulations – and had her hair cut and curled in the stylist's garage. It had been so long since she had been allowed out in the world that she had then wandered into the local shopping mall, bought flowers in the grocery store, and met two friends for lunch at a small cafe, where they had shared a large cinnamon roll for dessert. "Can you imagine, cooped up inside her own apartment alone for seven months, and then, the first time she goes out and meets just three people, she gets the virus?"

Carla asked how many people the woman had encountered in the grocery store, and Carlo acknowledged that was the hard part of his work. His supervisors had told him he might be able to locate the grocery clerk but not even to bother trying to find anyone who had stood in line with her. Some other countries, even some other states, were doing contact tracing by the GPS on people's phones, but not here.

Within the week, he reported back to the family that both of the 85-year-old's friends had tested positive for the virus. One of them lived with her three-generational family in which a college student granddaughter had also tested positive. On the same evening as Carlo reported these connections, he and his family watched news on the television of the

COVID infections by some of the senators who had attended, unmasked, the President's large reception on the White House lawn for his Supreme Court nominee. This time it was 13-year-old Sabrina who asked her family, incredulously, why no contact tracing was being done. Over the next few days, they learned that a total of eleven of the attendees at that White House gathering had tested positive for the virus. Yet there was no news of any contact tracing being done. Sabrina and Carlo both railed at the television over this news of the expanded outbreak.

"There's no explanation I can give you for anything this President does," was all she would say, except, "be sure to fill in and mail your ballot." For Carlo, it was his first ballot in a Presidential election, and he wanted to take it personally to the county courthouse. Sabrina looked longingly at Carlo's ballot form, saying she couldn't wait until she too could vote.

———•••———

Open or closed? For Standing Bear of the Blackfeet Nation, the answer had been clear since March: keep it closed. When the reservation's immediate neighbor to the West, Glacier National Park, reopened on June 8, Standing Bear admits that he was among the first to revisit the park. He got up before dawn, drove through the East Entrance and arrived at the trailhead to his favorite trail above Two Medicine Lake by 7:30. He climbed carrying a small covered basket, hoping to harvest huckleberries for his family. Passing through a pocket of lodge pole pines, he noted the tiny firs poking up in their shadow. Already the fireweed was in bloom, and the paintbrush, lupine and poppies created a meadow mosaic above the lake. He was too early for all but a few huckleberries, enough only to half-fill his tiny basket, though he combed the bushes thoroughly. At the pinnacle of his hike, he could see the long snake of cars lining the roadway below to enter the park again, and he knew what he had to do. Within two weeks, he had convinced the Blackfeet Nation to keep the eastern gateway to the fabled park closed until further notice. The eastern park entrance lay on reservation land, and the tiny town of Browning contained the only gas station and coffee shops for miles around. Too many vulnerable people lived within the reservation, and his people had far too much history of disease acquired from its neighbors. Smallpox and measles had decimated his people over years past. Browning had the only hospital in the region, and it was tiny. He would do all he could to prevent COVID from overwhelming his community.

Standing Bear was a student of history, both informally within his extended family, and as an instructor at the Blackfeet Community College in Browning, which had shut down altogether since March. He had considered conducting classes by Zoom, but too few students had computers to make that option viable. He'd already had too much time to ruminate on the ironies of his nation's history. The reservation had begun as an internment camp – he used this term in his classes – and in the early 1900s the children of the reservation had been forced into boarding schools where they were forbidden to speak their own language. From such a place, any free people would want to escape. Many did. Now, many wanted back in, but could only qualify to rejoin the reservation by proof of tribal lineage.

Now, the nation that surrounded his own was making it difficult for his people to vote. There was only one designated polling place within the whole reservation of over a million acres, and voting by mail would be futile, since there were no post offices or U.S. mailboxes in these barren plains. Standing Bear used what he called his 'COVID time off' to convince the Native American Rights Fund, which in turn convinced the ACLU, to sue the federal government to make it easier for his people to vote in the Presidential election. Within days of the filing, the government agreed to open a new polling place in Heart Butte. Standing Bear vowed that he would do all he could to get his people to one of the two polling places, even driving families in his four-wheeler from their homes on remote rough roads. Also, when vaccines became available, he would do all he could to secure them for his people. He was determined to help the Blackfeet would survive as a nation.

⸻ •◦• ⸻

By the time Carla visited the *ofrenda,* as she now did daily, and changed into her nightgown, she could no longer ignore a pain that had begun to plague her ever since the night she had taken Pedro to the hospital. She could often ignore it during her busy days but not as she lay alone in bed. Beginning at her waist, it radiated up and across her left shoulder, delaying her going to sleep. She would lie on one side, then the other, to try to find a pain-free position, but she could not escape it. She picked up the novel next to her bed – Marta had given her a copy of *One Hundred Years of Solitude,* which she was now reading to Bettina in Spanish – but she could not transport herself into that world. As she so often did, she clung to one of the extra pillows and told Pedro about her day. Ultimately, she fell asleep.

Once we were more than one hundred in number, reflected Sister Mary Ann, and now we are only sixty-six. And I, at 75, am one of the youngest remaining. Sister Mary Ann remembered taking her orders at only sixteen, when she, as a middle child among her nine brothers and sisters, was already an experienced caretaker and farm hand as well, in the cherry orchards on her family farm in Wisconsin. By her sixteenth birthday, her youngest siblings were seven and nearly nine, old enough to care for themselves and to take on chores in the family. No longer needed as an underparent, Sister Mary Ann – she was Catherine then – longed to become a teacher and to sing in a choir larger than that of her own family or her community church. Her four older siblings were all brothers, and at least two of them wanted to go to college. If the family had any funds for college fees, there were unlikely to be any left for her by the time of her graduation. Catherine knew then that if she joined the convent, she would not only be able to sing in a large choir but also she would likely be educated to become a teacher. Foregoing having children of her own seemed a small enough sacrifice, having already parented four younger siblings. She did not want to become a farm wife, and she embraced the Church sufficiently to enter the convent with a full heart and full commitment. That was fifty-nine years ago, a decent lifetime measured by the lifespans expected at that time. There were four other teen-aged girls who had taken orders at nearly the same time, two of them from her own high school and one of them a close friend from childhood, Sarah Mae. Sarah Mae became Sister Elizabeth Ann, and the two of them had had to be counseled often during their first year not to maintain any special attachment to each other. They were all to be treated alike, as sisters in service of Christ. Elizabeth Ann and she had learned their lessons well, but their closeness survived as they attended college together and became teachers, Sister Elizabeth Ann in history and herself in music. For forty years they had taught together in the local high school, driving to and from the convent together each day. Two days ago, Sister Elizabeth Ann died of COVID, the youngest of seven sisters who had died in the past three months of the new disease.

It gave her some solace to sing at Sister Elizabeth Ann's memorial service. Her voice was still strong, though now an alto instead of soprano, but the voices were well separated throughout the chapel, and the sisters conducted the service in two separate seatings, so as to keep their distance. "I know that my Redeemer lives, such sweet comfort that sentence gives," a hymn she had sung since childhood.

Sister Mary Ann confessed to herself that Sister Elizabeth Ann's passing had sorrowed her more than any of the others, all of them sisters in their late eighties or nineties who might have died naturally in their time. But the numbers! Eight of them one after the other, filling in rapid succession the small COVID ward the convent had established. Not one of them had survived a trip to the COVID ward at the end of the most distant hallway. Sister Mary Ann's bewilderment was compounded by knowing they had all taken every precaution throughout every month of the outbreak. They ate in isolation, they all wore masks, they had no visits from family, they sacrificed their prayer and discussion groups. Sister Mary Ann had a new grandniece, ten months old, whom she had never seen -- unheard of in her life of regular family visits. Some of her sisters were nurses, volunteering themselves in the ward, dressing in the peculiar new 'habit' of the COVID nurse. Instead of being laundered like their old habits, these COVID paraphernalia were wrapped into large plastic bags and specially discarded, separate from all other garbage.

Sister Mary Ann had become, by default, the administrative head of the convent, handling all of its worldly affairs – ordering food and other materials, managing the convent's finances and reporting to the Mother Superior each week. The Mother Superior was ninety-two and dwindling in her mental capacity, but she was the acknowledged leader on all matters spiritual, and she still conducted services and counseled the dwindling number of sisters. There were no inductees to train and there would not be any in the future.

In the days when Sister Mary Ann still taught high school, a brief part of their American history lesson had covered a Native American man, Ishi, whose Yahi tribe had been decimated by the Indian wars, until he remained the only survivor. He had wandered out of the wilderness of eastern California into the strange culture his people had long tried to avoid. Anthropologists studied Ishi's habits and recorded him as the last man to speak the Yahi language. Sister Mary Ann empathized with Ishi each time she had taught his history. He lofted now, unbidden, in her thoughts. She would likely become the Ishi of her convent.

There would be no new generation of sisters.

———•••———

Arturo dreamt. He was frantically packing his backpack with shoes for a long journey by foot, and he knew that his choices were wrong but he couldn't get it right. One of the running shoes on his feet had reflector bars on them, and he knew he couldn't show himself in the dark. He tore off the shoe with the reflector bar but couldn't readily find the match to the other shoe on his foot. Another pair he pulled from his closet had broken laces, and he couldn't survive a long distance without strong laces. As he frantically searched for the right sturdy pair, he was aware of the floor gradually collapsing underneath him. Next to where he knelt an oval hole was forming in the wooden floor, collapsing like a soaked egg carton as he looked on. Leaning over the hole, he saw the same oval collapsing multiple floors underneath him, to depths he didn't know existed. He had to escape the abyss while he still could.

Arturo awoke. Marta was peacefully asleep beside him. He remembered he had not yet mailed his ballot. As he had been reminded on the television that very evening, only twelve days remained until the election. Sleepless, he was tempted to get up and complete the ballot now. He had watched the last Presidential debate a few hours before going to bed, with Marta huddled next to him, muttering at the President's bluster. They were used to the emphatic, repeated lies, but neither of them would ever forget his utter indifference to the 545 children orphaned at the Southern border, whose parents could not be located months after being forcibly separated from them.

Arturo and Marta had both gone to bed anxious about what would happen in November. Even if this President were ousted -- as it seemed from the polls -- would he leave? Would he have to be dragged out by the Army? Would there be riots from the Proud Boys and other militias across the country? Would they have to leave this country? Their U.S. passports locked into the home safe with the cash stockpiled from years of savings might not protect them from what lay ahead.

Arturo was not given to dreaming, and this one left him puzzled, except for its clear note of anxiety, which was an all-too-familiar undercurrent of his days. When had this begun, he asked himself. Had he always been this way? Unbidden, he thought of Manuel and Stefano, whose fate after being hauled away in the ambulance he would never learn. Manuel was a doggedly faithful worker these days, but they both knew without saying that Stefano remained in both of their thoughts. Knowing he could not return to sleep with such thoughts on his mind, Arturo slipped out of bed as inconspicuously as he could, glancing at the lighted clock as he did so. 3:20 – far too early to get up, without ruining the energy he would need for the restaurant later. He grabbed a blanket from the hall closet and took refuge on the sofa in the den.

Carlo had found online what he thought might be a good remedy for his mother's back pain. He was the only person she had told, and she had sworn him to secrecy. Instead of trying to convince her to order it herself, which he intuited she would not do, he ordered and paid for it himself. The product was an adhesive patch, with a pattern of charged tiny receptors across its surface that was advertised to work within minutes by intercepting pain messages to the brain. The receptors acted as a kind of cellular distraction, or rerouting of messages from the nerves to the brain. It sounded to him either hokey or brilliant, and it offered an affordable experiment that sounded harmless at worst. It was advertised to work on athletes, ordinary people, and even sufferers of fibromyalgia, that vague, generalized pain. Carlo longed to give his mother some relief.

Back in his room, Adam took his cello out of its case and set up the Brahms sonata again, intending to remedy his errors in class. But he found himself just playing single keys, apparently aimlessly, as his mind drifted over the tumble of conversation with Ilina over coffee. Whatever one of them said, the other picked up and took further, until they had a hundred loose strings of ideas, memories, and places swirling around them as they talked. He was somehow mesmerized by the timbre of her voice as much as by what she said. That's what his fingers were groping for just now. An open G came as close as anything he could render on his instrument. In the middle of their conversation he had burst out, "did you ever sing?" And of course she had, in high school chorus as a contralto. "But not well enough to continue. I prefer to play the cello." Which she did very well, better than he, Adam suspected. Which brought him back to his Brahms assignment.

After he had practiced diligently and eaten the bagged dinner he had brought back from the dorm cafeteria, Adam phoned his dad again, this time reaching him on the second ring.

"Adam!" His dad's voice was weak but enthusiastic.

"You sound better," Adam told him.

"I'm so tired of this stupor, waking and sleeping.... I barely know what's going on. Has the election happened yet?"

"No, Dad, the last debates just happened a week ago. People are voting all across the country, but the election isn't until next week." He paused to let that fact sink in.

"And I didn't even get to vote, now when it matters so much."

"It's all right, Dad. California's safe even without your vote. I got to vote in Ohio this year, thanks to the organization on campus."

"Glad to hear." His dad fell silent for a few moments. "Play for me?"

"Of course." Yet again, Adam played the *Rococo Variations*, since his dad always seemed to prefer this music. By the time he came to the end, the connection had ended on his dad's side.

—•●•—

Erythea thought often of Don but did not have his number at the hospital. She wished she had asked Janice for it in their one conversation, but it had not seemed appropriate at the time. She could ask the health center for the number but intuitively hesitated. She wanted to call him privately, without having to report back to anyone.

Back at work, she felt a restored energy, as she usually did after a vacation. Strange that simply staying at home with Elissa could be as replenishing as it was. The residents also seemed more cheerful than they had when she left. They now had more freedom to socialize with each other, and they were planning a costumed Halloween event on the terrace, the first collective celebration since they had been shut down eight months earlier. Even she, as part of the staff, was expected to dress in costume for the event. In prior years, they had had competitions for the best pumpkin carving, but this year not, since carving was a partnered exercise. What might she become for the day?

Elissa had suggested she go as a female Dionysus, a goddess of wine and ecstasy. No, that's just your vision of me, she had told her. Together they decided she would go as a grapevine, and they had fun finding a cheap green shift and hanging plastic grapevines and leaves that she could pin onto her sleeves and drape around her neck and head.

On her second day back at work, Erythea encountered Simon coming back from a hike, looking refreshed, buoyant, and even a little silly with a baseball cap constricting his mop of curly hair that even now escaped around his ears and at the back. When she asked him how he was doing, he regaled her with his hiking nearly every day, finding trails he hadn't even known of before. "It makes all the difference in the world to get out," he told her.

"I can see it on your face."

"Thanks for putting up with me when I was so grumpy."

She nodded and they went in their different directions.

After delivering meals, Erythea dialed Janice and asked how she was doing.

"How nice of you to call back! I'm doing much better now that Don seems to have come over the worst of it." She filled Erythea in on the details of Don's blood clot that seemed to have resolved. "But he's still foggy and very, very tired, and he still has surges of fever that are debilitating."

"Are you able to talk to him?"

"Yes, I call him every day. Sometimes he can talk and sometimes not. There's no obvious time. I have to just keep trying."

Erythea took a breath. "Would it be okay if I tried to call him?"

"Oh, do. I think he would love that. He treasures you." Janice gave her the number, which she clearly had in her memory.

"Thank you. Is there anything I can do for you?"

Janice gave a short, rueful laugh. "Get my son to call me. He's made himself scarce since leaving for college two weeks ago."

—•◦•—

Just mute yourself, Janice, she told herself. A year ago, this phrase was not even in her vocabulary. Now she used it several times a week in the exercise class she led via Zoom, with her friends and a growing community of others who used to go to the gym and now could not. Extraneous noises from phones or dogs or outside trucks crept into the classes unless she kept attendees on mute.

Now she was alone, having just awakened from an erotic dream, the first she'd had in years. In the four years since Don's stroke, she'd had no sex with anyone but herself. Even that had been at the urging of her therapist. She'd been surprised by the suggestion, reluctant at first to introduce masturbation into her adult life. But then it had become part of her life, an almost daily release, done in the solitude of her bedroom with music while Adam was at school. Now he was away all of the time and her life was more private than at any time in her memory. Maybe this privacy gave her unconscious permission to imagine another life. She had no idea who was the partner in her dream, could not remember any details other than that she awakened throbbing.

Just after Don's stroke, when she was still privately feeling a bit sorry for herself, she had told herself to forget about sex. In the two years that she had taken care of his every need, she was too exhausted even to fantasize about sex, and too saddened by the realities of his incapacitated body. Even after Don was moved to the Evergreen, she hadn't much thought about sex, that is, until her therapist had suggested that she do. In her first marriage, long ago, after her husband had hit her the first time, she had lost all interest in sex and actively avoided it. Her reawakening with Don had been one of the many lovely surprises of her life with him.

What to make of this reawakening? Clearly, even if he recovered from COVID, Don was never going to come home again. Her relationship with him would always be asexual. It would survive only through their words while COVID still reigned, and even afterward their touching would be friendly but chaste. At 54, was she going to live the rest of her life singly? This new solitude at home and release from the daily constrictions of motherhood – and now this arousing dream – brought the question to mind. She now had in fact a privacy that would enable her to do whatever she liked, but she had never even fantasized about there being a new man in her life. And now, during the pandemic? A laughable time for the thought even to arise.

Just mute yourself, she imposed again. And yet, and yet, she didn't want to. Her life was not over. She did not want to live alone for the decades ahead. She did not want to live without desire. For the first time, she welcomed it. She even found herself watching a bit more closely one of her Zoom exercise students, a man about her own age with beautiful rounded leg muscles. There was physical pleasure in just watching him move.

―•◦•―

Erythea dialed Don from the privacy of her tiny office, after hours. He answered, recognizing her number.

"I feared you had forgotten me."

"Not at all." She explained that she had been on vacation, had learned of his hospitalization only after she returned.

"Excuses, excuses."

"I'm happy you haven't lost your sense of humor," she told him. "Janice told me you're on the road to recovery."

"What does she know?" Erythea could not interpret what lay below this remark, so she glided past it.

"How are you feeling?"

"I'm still out of it, have no sense of time, forget where I am … still have bad headaches and then they put me in limbo again. But I think I'll live."

"Just your saying that makes my day. I'll keep calling to keep up with you, but now I'm due home."

"Thanks." There was no doubting he meant it.

His warmth infused her drive home.

Liss was already home, cooking with the vigor of banging pots. Erythea caught an earthy scent before she even walked into the kitchen to kiss her partner.

"Smells great – what kind of pasta sauce is it?"

"*Arrabbiata.*" When no explanation followed, Erythea took her cue from Liss' preoccupation and left the kitchen.

At dinner, even after a glass of hearty red wine, Liss was uncharacteristically brusque and still preoccupied.

"What's bothering you?" Ryth asked gently.

"I can't stand not knowing what's going to happen next week. There's endless news of the polls but we know from four years ago that we can't rely on them. That plus the COVID stats has me saturated. I just want to go to sleep and wake up after the election is over. Today one of my patients – he's a stockbroker, if that tells you anything – wanted to keep the sound going on his computer during our session. I told him no, he could send me home, but I wasn't going to do that. He hesitated but then he turned it off, but you can guess how much he was able to relax his muscles."

"Sounds like you could use a massage yourself." Liss gave her a half smile. "If you can tolerate an amateur."

"You're no amateur." Now it was a full smile. "I just can't stop worrying for the whole country if he wins again.

"I'm not sure how I thought of it, but remember how we went to Renee and Jackie's home four years ago to celebrate the returns? And watched as state after state dashed our hopes. The champagne we were going to drink for a woman president was never uncorked."

"I remember only too well. I was thinking today how I wanted to share election night with friends but we can't even do that. I'm just glad you're back here with me, and not stuck in Italy. I don't ever want to be separated like that again." Ryth lifted her glass, and Liss clinked hers with it.

When the doorbell rang, they exchanged quizzical looks. Neither of them had imagined children would be out this year trick-or-treating, but there was a young Robin Hood and a cowboy on their doorstep with their mother. Both of the costumed children were girls. Both were masked and appropriately distanced. While Erythea asked them how they had decided on their costumes, Elissa ran to the kitchen and found two mandarin oranges to give them. "They are who they are," their mother explained, as all three adults grinned behind their masks.

November

~ Counting

S imon spent election night eating and drinking alone in front of his television. Enduring the flash graphics and hurried speech of the newscasters – how could anyone talk that fast? – he reminded himself that this year there would be two waves of results, the first from voters who had voted in person and the second from mailed ballots, which each state would count according to its own rules. He was prepared for the red states to flash on the board, but not for the volume of the red votes. As the numbers began spiraling upward in the President's favor, contradicting the polls even more floridly than in 2016, Simon downed the dregs of his third glass of wine. How could this many people stomach the lies of this President enough to vote for him to serve four more years? Simon screwed the cap back on his wine bottle, turned off the television, and stomped to put his dishes in the kitchen sink. He lacked the energy to wash them tonight.

Sleep came readily but not for long. By three in the morning, he was wide awake, glued to the small TV in his bedroom. Still, it was torture. The early returns in Pennsylvania were red, and Wisconsin was too close for any comfort. As if to make it worse, he tuned into Fox News, where Sean Hannity was verbally bludgeoning a Democratic commentator who stoically refused to accept that a red outcome was inevitable. He turned it off and tossed himself back to a much-delayed sleep, waking with the morning light and switching on the TV again. Mailed ballot counts were coming in, but the map still threatened four more years.

Simon got up, showered and ate a quick breakfast without the distraction of the TV. He determined he would walk as soon as it was light enough outside, walk as far as he could stand and hope that he could burn off his fury. There was a nearby trail of several miles along a canal. Before the lockdown, he used to watch the ducks and other water birds along that canal, and doing so now might give him peace. The sun was rising in a cloudless sky and he was beginning to sweat even before he reached the trail. He tore off his sweatshirt and tied it around his waist, leaving only a white undershirt covering his chest. No matter, the trail was empty. The arresting white of a solitary egret caught his eye as it patiently waggled its foot along the shallow bottom of the water. He stopped to watch, wondering if he could be patient enough to wait until the egret had caught something in its beak. He wasn't. He stomped onward.

A woman was coming toward him on the path, with an even, brisk stride. She wore a brimmed hat, mask and large sunglasses, obscuring her age and identity. He pulled up his own mask. "Good morning," she called out cheerfully.

"It's *not* a good morning," he pronounced. They both paused, facing each other from a safe distance.

"It's tense," she admitted. "But a walk helps," she told him as she resumed her pace. As Simon continued his march, he realized she was right. He reflected on her brisk pace and even gaze, wondering who she was.

On the evening of the second day, the election returns began to shift as more mailed in ballots were counted in the six open states. Wisconsin was called for Biden, and Democratic votes began to rise in Pennsylvania and even in Georgia. On the third day, Simon sat transfixed before his television, which he *never* did, and watched the numbers rise in the remaining states. He remained edgy, preternaturally pessimistic after watching the returns in 2016, but he watched even during his meals and didn't resort to any wine.

On the morning of the fourth day, the media called the election for Biden as conclusive returns came in from Pennsylvania. In Paris, church bells pealed across the city. That evening, after Biden and Harris gave their acceptance speeches before a crowd of onlookers in their cars – or atop their cars – fireworks cascaded across the dark sky -- aerial banners with displays of stars. The brightly-lit names Biden and Harris emblazoned the night sky, via a multitude of invisible tiny drones. By the sixth day, Biden announced the members of the coronavirus task force for the new administration, all of them prominent health care experts, including the former U.S. surgeon general whom the current president had deposed early in his administration.

Simon felt a surge of unfamiliar buoyancy. He wanted to share it. Ebullient texts and emails came in from his various colleagues and friends, but they weren't enough. He wanted to see real people in real time.

⸺•◦•⸺

It had been a gray, overcast morning in Milano as Fran drove to the airport with Liliana. As the plane rose through the layers of clouds, Fran grew increasingly elated. Now, as she looked down on the billowing clouds with the sun gleaming from above, Fran felt nearly weightless, as happy as the first time she had flown in an airplane with her parents, looking down on the same sort of clouds. She still thought of them as piles of cushiony cotton balls, though her father had instructed her they were cumulus – no -- cumulonimbus clouds. As a child, she would find faces or shapes of animals in these clouds. Now, as she glanced over at Lili watching the intro to a Dreamworks video, she realized Lili would always think of such clouds with a little boy sitting atop with a fishing pole. Fran didn't bother to distract her with the real thing.

They were only in the first hour of a twelve-hour flight. Thus far, Lili still had her mask suspended properly across her nose and mouth, but Fran wondered how long each of them would be able continuously to remain masked. A daylight flight – the only relief Fran could imagine for Lili was a few hours' nap. Never mind. Her mother would meet them on the other side and provide some of the relief Fran had craved for all these months. Her gelateria had been shuttered for the first months, then re-opened to the crowds of an overheated summer, then partially closed and re-opened again with strict distancing rules and new plexiglass shields. Now it was likely to be shuttered again, though in November business was normally light. Fran closed her eyes. Her manager Gianni was in charge for the next month, and he knew what to do. Fran could sit in San Francisco with her mother and try to imagine a way forward for herself and Lili. For now she had the comfort of clouds.

⸺ ⸙ ⸺

Ilina waited at the campus bike co-op for Adam just as they had arranged. As he approached, he watched the moisture balloon around her masked face in the November cold. Her head was an intermittent cloud as she blew onto her mittened hands.

"Is that you behind the mist?" he called out, and she laughed, in that low, warbling voice of hers.

"Should we bike or walk?" she asked. "This trail leads all the way to Lake Erie, but we can't walk that far."

"Let's walk. It's better for talking." He looked as far ahead as he could see of the wide trail. "Is it this flat all the way?"

"Welcome to the Midwest. Yes, it's flat all the way."

When he asked her how she knew of the trail, she told him her parents had introduced her to it as a child, which led to where she was from – Cleveland – and what her parents did. Her mother was a journalist and her father a professor, she told him, without elaborating, before she asked him the same question.

"She's a nurse and he's a retired hospital administrator."

"So how did they meet?"

Adam gave her a blank look. He had never asked his parents.

"Weren't you curious?" She looked at him incredulously.

"Apparently not." He was silent for a moment. He had assumed they had met at work, but he had never thought to ask.

"Do you know for your parents?"

She shot him a look that made the answer obvious, before she embarked on her parents' story.

Her father was invited to play before the Cleveland Orchestra – he was a violinist – and her mother was assigned to review his performance. She noticed that he was left-handed and was intrigued by the anomaly. "Imagine," she used to tell me, "one violinist bowing in the opposite direction as all the others in the orchestra." Again, that low laugh. "It's become a family joke." He granted her an interview in which she asked him that question, and he answered that that's why he became a soloist. "As if his talent had nothing to do with it. Apparently many lefties have perfect pitch; I know I don't.

He started me on the violin when I was five. While I loved playing, it became quickly obvious that I would never, ever approach him. I switched to the cello when I was twelve, to try to differentiate myself. He wisely transferred my teaching to others, and that liberated me from his exacting judgment." Adam realized he had not asked Ilina her father's name, or even her own last name, but now was not the moment.

"Do you ever play for him now?" Adam asked. Ilina shook her head.

"It's better that way."

"It's so different for me," Adam began. "My dad doesn't know anything about music, but he was still ultra-critical. Now that he's sick, he loves to hear me play."

Ilina extended her hand slightly, as though to take his, he thought, and then pulled it back.

"How is he now?" she asked softly.

"Much better; my mom says he may come home from the hospital soon."

They walked silently for a few minutes. It had rained, even snowed a bit since their first walk in the dry leaves. Now there was just a quiet crunching of frost that was gradually melting as the pale sun lifted above them.

"Do you play for anyone besides your dad?"

Adam thought instantly of Leah and tried to push the thought aside.

"Just my instructors."

"Me too. It's safer that way. "

An oncoming cyclist caused Adam to slip behind Ilina, and he walked behind her for a short distance, marveling at the odd grace with which she moved. At each step, he thought, she lifted herself slightly on the balls of her feet, so that her movement forward contained an up and down rhythm. He was so pre-occupied with her that he neglected to ask her any further questions about her father.

A gust of wind created a slanting drift of oak leaves from a tree in front of them, some of them still golden in the backlight of the sun. Ilina stopped, glanced at her watch and suggested they turn around and go back. For a moment, she stood no more than a foot away, facing him. Her dark eyes glistened. He wanted so much to tear off both of their masks and kiss her. He may have moved ever so slightly toward her. She gave the barest shake of her head, contradicting her eyes. The rules. No, he thought, if it were just the rules, he would break them. But when he thought of his father, he curbed his instinct. No. Not in this time.

Before they parted, Ilina told him she wished she could invite him to her family's home in Cleveland for Thanksgiving. "We always have a small group of students who are not able to go home for the holiday. I asked my parents if I could invite you, but they told me not this year."

Adam told her he was touched that she had even asked.

"My mom makes a killer pumpkin pie. I can bring you a piece at class next Monday."

◦•◦

Don was released from the hospital, fatigued but COVID-free at last. Returned to his bed in Assisted Living at the Evergreen, he felt an ironic gratitude for the slight improvement in his circumstances. He had not needed a ventilator, but for some time he had been fed intravenously. The tubes were now gone from his arm and he was no longer secured to the bed. He could now eat meals again, and he could choose from the menu of offerings. Freedom is relative, he mused. His right hand was as limp as ever but not tied down. His left hand ruled. He lifted it over his head to stretch, he swung it in an arc as if throwing a lasso, he picked up a pen as if to write. His room was familiar, and once again he could look outside. A few of the trees within the frame of his view were tinted a blood-orange, and they virtually leapt out of the sunlit landscape.

His reading support restored to him, he opened his iPad for the first time in several weeks, since before the election. He wanted nothing more than to catch up with the outside world for an hour or so, without interruption. He opened the *New York Times* and began to read. Biden's cabinet appointments, his appointment of a climate envoy, his messages of healing and of combatting the virus as a health concern rather than a political tactic, his admonitions to wear a mask – all of this made him feel like Rip Van Winkle (he couldn't think of a more adult analogy). The current administration was still -- weeks after the election -- challenging the outcome, and blocking Biden's access to transition information, but the pace forward was ineluctable.

When Erythea appeared in his doorway, welcoming him back, he grinned his one-sided smile. "The world has changed since I left – for the better."

"Hasn't it," she beamed. She did not remind him that COVID incidence had worsened throughout the world. "Can I get you anything?"

You already did, he wanted to say, by her showing up in his doorway, but he answered only that he wanted to catch up with the news before any books from the library.

Janice called, not long after Erythea had left, leaving him wondering if Erythea had set it up. She used FaceTime, he clicked to join her visual. "I didn't believe it until I saw you back in your own bed. Welcome back!" He gazed, almost unbelieving, at the vision of her face, grinning back at him. "This is such a relief," she repeated, "just looking at you again. Once I thought not being able to visit you was a deprivation; now I know what deprivation is."

He looked at her with new eyes, appreciating the genuine pleasure in her face. She even wore lipstick and whatever she used to emphasize her eyes and the arch in her brows. Her thick, wavy hair had grown, curling down over the front of her shoulders. "You look beautiful."

"For you." She pushed her hair back to reveal her ears, and the earrings dangling from them. "Remember these?"

"Florence, the Golden Bridge."

"So true. I still love them, and love the occasion." She loved too that he remembered instantly, not something she took for granted. Noting his reading support in front of him, she asked what he was reading.

"The news. I woke into a whole new world."

"You did. Lawsuits are flying and the current president denies he lost, but the media are beginning to acknowledge his delusions. You're going to enjoy this sojourn into the news, and it'll take you awhile. I should leave you to it for a few hours. I'll ask Adam to wait a few hours before he calls." With that, she blew him a kiss and left the call.

Don's phone rang again almost instantly, with Adam on FaceTime. "Welcome back!" he boomed, in what seemed like a newly confident voice. "Are you all back?"

"I think so, whatever all back means." He gave his son a tentative smile.

"Tell me about you, about life on campus, about your whole new world."

Adam raved about the music, about seeing people 'in real life' again, about making new friends and being able to have live discussions in class and outside. Don drank in Adam's enthusiasm, his new wordiness and confidence. Adam offered new music to play, but Don told him to wait, he was more interested in hearing what Adam had to say right now. So Adam continued, conscious of holding back about Ilina but not about anything else, even as Don's lunch was delivered. Adam asked if he should hang up.

"Not if you're willing to watch me eat like a little kid," his dad offered.

"Absolutely," and Adam gushed on as before, noting meanwhile that his dad did indeed drop food as he tried to fork it up from the plate with one hand.

"I'm glad you insisted I come, rather than study here remotely."

"That was your mom. You should tell her."

"Dad, will you tell me sometime how you and Mom met?"

"Of course, but that's a conversation for another time."

When they rang off, Don's food was cold, but he felt warmer than he had in weeks.

⸺◦•◦⸺

Carlo had finally met a girl who interested him, but his experience with her was entirely virtual, with Zoom meetings, telephone calls and email. He reported in to her each day the contacts he had traced, including the names of new people and how they had encountered the person who had tested positive. Sometimes she jokingly made up stories about the connections he had found, and he improvised in return – always after she had recorded the information he provided but before they disconnected. About a young woman whose name came up independently in connection with two separate young men, she said, "I think she's interested in both of them but doesn't want either of them to know about the other." And they riffed about how their tracing duties might interfere with the young woman's tactics.

"No," he joked, "we only tell each of them about her; we don't tell each of them about the other."

He was in a good mood when his mother arrived home from work. No one else was in the room when she told him her news.

"I've been given COVID duty on Thanksgiving and the weekend after. The hospital is short on staff."

He nodded slowly. "Does that mean you won't come to Thanksgiving at Arturo and Marta's?"

"Yes, and I'm going to ask them to have you and Sabrina and Luis for those four days as well. I'll isolate here. I haven't talked to the rest of the family yet."

His head flooded with anxious questions. But he only asked the professional one, from his training. "Shouldn't you isolate for 14 days?" She nodded and launched into how she might isolate at home, with him and Sabrina cooking and leaving a meal at her door, knocking and then walking away.

"You're sure you want to do this?" He asked, though he knew the answer.

"I need to."

Carla decided to email rather than call Arturo, since she knew he would object to her decision as risky. She also knew he wouldn't object to her children staying with him and Marta, but she asked very politely. His reply came by telephone that evening after dinner. From what he said, Carla knew he had spoken to Marta, who would understand.

"We'll miss you at Thanksgiving. I can't remember a year we haven't all celebrated together." He reassured her the children would be welcome for as many days as she would be willing to be without them. In fact, he encouraged her to allow them to stay a full two weeks following her last day in the COVID ward, so as to minimize the risk. They both knew without saying that this would be the first Thanksgiving without Pedro; even with her, it would not be a full family gathering. That fleeting recognition reinforced her decision to spend the holiday weekend in the COVID ward, keeping company as she was unable to do when Pedro was admitted months ago.

When Beto asked him privately why Carla hadn't asked to be relieved of work on Thanksgiving, Arturo told him of the night when Pedro was carted away from her at the hospital, how much Carla had suffered for not being able to tend to him, even to see him before he died. "I think it helps her to do this for others." Beto just nodded. At dinner Arturo gave a special blessing for Pedro and Carla, at the same time as giving thanks for having their children with them. Silently, he also blessed Stefano, who still haunted him.

———•◦•◦•———

Janice read an article at breakfast about all the travel deals being offered by resorts and airlines to lure travelers back after the months of COVID. One of the airlines announced that soon there would be a requirement that every international traveler provide proof of a COVID vaccination before being allowed to fly, and it was preparing an online registry for this purpose. That she even read the travel section word for word surprised her; she hadn't even thought of traveling anywhere for a very long time, well before the pandemic, maybe as far back as Don's stroke. She didn't want to try to remember how long ago or why, she only reveled in the new possibility.

The day before, she had had a long conversation with Adam in the morning, about how good Don looked now that he was back. Although he was going to eat dinner with a few friends in his dorm, Adam sounded remarkably cheerful without saying why. She asked him about his classes, which were all in person except for his European History lectures. He praised the instructor of his small cello class for being both an inspiration and forgiving. She wondered what lay underneath his enthusiasm but refrained from probing.

Last evening, she had shared dinnertime with Don on FaceTime. His turkey had arrived pre-sliced, accompanied by stuffing and gravy, cranberry sauce, and green beans with almonds. She had prepared for herself a salmon filet (aha, for once freed of the obligation of turkey!), with broccoli and a large salad, succumbing only to the tradition of pumpkin pie, which Don had too. It had been almost a year since she had watched Don eat, and she admired how someone had precut his portions to bite size, so that he did not have to labor with his left hand. Without staring, she noted how he pushed portions against other food on his plate, so as to manage with his one hand. Janice also remembered what it took for her to do this for him three times a day before he had gone to live at the Evergreen. She sighed inwardly at all the effort involved for him in just eating, or sitting up, or lodging a book on his reading platform.

After finishing her coffee and the newspaper, Janice put on her running shoes, a fleece and gloves and went for her morning walk. Without any companions, she spontaneously began to jog briskly, breaking into short sprints of running from time to time. Unencumbered, she could set her own pace and her own route. She paused to admire the bright orange persimmons on dark, leafless limbs in someone's yard that she had never noticed before. The dawning sense of her own unrecognized freedom exhilarated her. With Adam away at Oberlin and Don in good care at the Evergreen, she was free as never before in the last twenty years. A vaccine was likely to arrive within the next six months. If she wanted to, she could fly off to Hawaii, or plan a trip to Australia or Venice or even Egypt. Egypt – why had that even occurred to her for the first time in her life? It was mentioned as a destination in the travel section this morning. Why not?

Of course there were a hundred why nots. But that this was even possible lifted her like nothing else in quite some time. For the last block, she raced, testing to see how fast she could run. Panting, she bent over to catch her breath at the gate to her back yard. The fresh November air enlivened every pore of her being.

———•◉•———

Before she left for the hospital, Carla FaceTimed her three children, wishing them a happy celebration with the family. As she drove across the bridge over the canal, she became aware of her own sense of dread. Yes, she had wanted to do this, but she did not underestimate the challenge. After parking, she was directed into the basement of the hospital for fitting of her PPE. Was this where the COVID ward was located, she wondered, hidden from the rest of the community altogether? She didn't know the man who led her into this region. He introduced himself as Salvador, and she had to bite her tongue not to comment on his name. He had a very solemn face, but as he too suited up, she could see only his dark eyes through the mask and shield. She was likewise outfitted, plastic booties first, then the gown and gloves and face coverings. Change it every time you leave the room, he instructed.

There were four large ward rooms, two of them with patients on ventilators and the other two with patients who did not need them. Salvador led her first into a room with four patients on ventilation. The first was Jonah, a man in his fifties who needed sedation to tolerate the large tube in his throat. Salvador showed her the dosages of sedation Jonah required every four hours so that he would not panic. At the moment, Jonah's eyes were closed as if he were asleep, or maybe just trying not to see where he was. Carla could barely hear Salvador over the relentless sucking noises of the four ventilators, each on its own separate rhythm for each patient. Only one of the four patients had her eyes open, and Carla peered at the unwavering gaze of Nyx, an 85-year-old woman whose chart revealed she spoke limited English, her main language being Greek. She does not need sedatives, Salvador informed her, and she is most alert at night. Carla tried to smile at her with her eyes, but Nyx's eyes were like marbles, bright but without expression. On they went, to the second ventilation room and finally to the two rooms where the patients did not need ventilators. All of these patients, Salvador advised, were to be given remdesivir intravenously every 12 hours, once during Carla's duty this night. With almost a physical start, Carla noticed that all of these patients were unmasked, to facilitate their own breathing. Salvador showed her how to reposition these patients, from one side to the other, to their stomachs, also to help their breathing. All of them were too weak to eat, and their nutrition was delivered intravenously, tonight at five-thirty. Someone would bring the meds and nutrition on a cart, and Carla was to deliver the dosages. She asked Salvador if any of them could speak, and he shook his head. "Too weak." Together, she and Salvador repositioned all of the patients, administered meds and nutrition, monitored their oxygen levels and temperatures. Four hours later, Salvador told her it was their evening mealtime, but that COVID nurses were not allowed into the hospital cafeteria. He showed her the makeshift room, with hot tables, plates, utensils, tea and coffee urns. Someone had taped a makeshift turkey on one wall, its pleated paper tail the one bright spot in the plain room. There she and Salvador served themselves. They sat six feet apart on Thanksgiving night. She was too stunned to talk, and he made no effort.

By the time she left at eleven, Carla felt nearly as drained as the night eight months ago when she had abandoned Pedro to this abyss. Before she left, Salvador gave her a sheet of written instructions on how to remove all of her clothes on entering her home, washing them immediately, showering and washing her hair, remasking with a new mask before meeting any other members of her household.

"Do you live with family?" Salvador asked.

"Yes, but they're away for these four days."

"Good," he told her curtly, then left before she could ask him about his own circumstances. "See you tomorrow."

As she walked to her car, Carla glanced at the distant spot in the lot where she had parked on the night she lost Pedro. Every time she parked, she avoided that spot. She practically collapsed into her seat, closing her eyes as she blinked back tears. When she had regained herself sufficiently to start the car, she turned on Mexican music to keep herself awake. She dutifully changed, laundered, and showered, washing her hair twice, before sinking gratefully into bed and falling asleep immediately.

Waking came to her early, long before dawn. She had slept for almost six hours, and she woke from a dream. Pedro had convinced her to hike up a steep hill, too steep for her comfort, and as he reached down to pull her up over a jagged rock, she stumbled, twisting her ankle and scraping her shin on the rock. When he saw that she could not walk on her ankle, he lifted her, hoisting her easily up onto his back with her arms around his shoulders and his arms supporting each of her legs around his waist. She marveled at his strength. It's easy, just hold on, he told her. In the dark of her room, she swung her legs over the edge of the bed and tried to stand up, expecting a disabled ankle. But she was fine, intact if surprised. She went to the bathroom without turning on the lights, then returned to bed, hoping to sleep again. She hadn't known Pedro was that strong.

She toiled through each of the next three days in similar mode, falling into bed exhausted after her sanitizing ritual, then sleeping deeply, but without any more dreams. Marta phoned her on Monday morning to warn her, before bringing back her children. "They've been worried about you, and Sabrina shows it in anger."

As soon as the car pulled up and Carla stepped out, Luis tumbled out of the car, ran up the path and threw himself at her, nearly knocking her over. His head came to just above her waist, and he clung to her like a cat to a tree. She stroked his dark hair gently. His body trembled. Sabrina stalked into the house, giving her a dark look. Only Carlo smiled, hugging her and Luis together. "I'm proud of you," he whispered. He gently untangled Luis from their mother and hoisted him around his waist, just as Pedro had done with her in the dream.

Carla heated frozen pizzas for their lunch. Carlo chopped lettuce for a large green salad while he asked her about the patients she had attended. Luis hovered on a chair listening eagerly to their conversation. Sabrina had not left her room since coming home. When the meal was ready, Carla asked Luis to get his sister for lunch. He bounded up the stairs, returning by himself after a few minutes.

Carla and Carlo both looked at Luis, the question in their faces and shoulders.

"She's coming down."

Sabrina slumped into her chair without a word to anyone, grudgingly taking her brothers' hands as they said the brief mealtime prayer of thanks. She served herself some salad but refused the pizza. "We had home-cooked food at Marta's," she taunted.

"We will too if you help cook tonight," Carla told her levelly. Sabrina crunched on her salad but did not answer. Neither Carlo nor Luis spoke, waiting for whatever would come between Sabrina and their mother.

"Why didn't you tell us in advance about Thanksgiving?" Sabrina shot out.

"I told you as soon as I knew. The hospital was short-handed and asked me to substitute in."

"So you chose to be with strangers who are dying anyway rather than your own children?"

Carla pounded her hand on the table. "Did you hear what you just said? That you don't care about strangers who might die? Is that what you wanted for your dad when he went to the hospital?"

"All the COVID patients die anyway," she sulked.

"Not so!" Carlo leapt in, eager with his statistics. Carla put her hand on his for a moment.

"One of those patients came back home today," Carla reported pointedly to Sabrina. "Do you really think it doesn't help that they get care at the hospital?"

Sabrina looked up for the first time at her mother, her eyes now wet.

"I didn't want to lose you too."

She got up from her seat and put her arms around her mother. Carla embraced her silently.

"I took your dad to the hospital when I realized I couldn't help him enough here." Carla swallowed before continuing. "That was in the early days, before anyone knew how to treat this disease. We can do more now, and I want you all to know that I will continue to substitute in the COVID ward when they need me, whether you like it or not."

"What can we do to help?" Carlo asked. She thanked him with her eyes before explaining that she would need help with meals and housecleaning. She would need to do all her own laundry when she was on COVID duty; don't mix any of your clothes with mine, she warned.

"Will you get the vaccine when it comes?" Sabrina asked.

"Yes, I'll be among those first in line."

Sabrina cleared the table and washed and put away all the lunch dishes.

------◆◦◆◦◆------

Erythea awoke, the sky still gray. Her head pounded when she turned toward the clock and the window. She had not drunk much wine the night before. And she was hot. When she moved her arm to toss aside the top cover, her arm burned as if she had banged it into a wall. "Liss?" Her word came out as a whispered hiss, and Liss was sleeping. "Liss?" she tried harder, but her throat hurt and the voice was still a whisper. Her mind began to race. She knew she had the virus. She flung the sore arm over to wake Liss, who stirred at the blow and leaned up to look at her questioningly. "What's up?"

"I'm sick. I think I have COVID. You should get away from me."

"Too late for that, my love." Liss placed what seemed like a very cool hand on her forehead. "You really are hot. Let me get a thermometer." Liss leapt out of bed and shoved it gently under her tongue. "101, and it's only morning. You have a real fever."

Liss mobilized, fetching a cool wet washcloth for her forehead, asking Ryth to drink water. In a moment she was on her phone, checking what sessions she would need to cancel for herself. "Should I call George? Dr. Frank?"

"I can't think. It hurts even to move." A tear dripped down the side of Ryth's face.

"I'll call them for you. Just stay where you are."

Elissa reached George on the first try, even though it was only a little after seven in the morning. He let out a stifled moan, expressed his sympathy, told her to keep Erythea at home unless she developed difficulty breathing or her own doctor ordered otherwise. He reassured her he would handle matters at the Evergreen, offered his help if she needed anything further. He would send someone today to test Erythea and Elissa. She texted her clients, cancelling all her pending appointments due to illness in the family. She gave Ryth two Tylenol tablets, asking her to sleep if she could. Within twenty minutes, Ryth was again asleep. Only then did Elissa slump into a chair, de-adrenalized and wondering what would become of her wife.

Erythea never got sick. Elissa could not remember a single occasion when Ryth even had a bad cold. Sometimes a headache and fatigue when work overwhelmed her; at those times she would go into another room to meditate until she became herself again. But sick – never. They both prided themselves on their good health. Liss remembered how intolerable it had been for herself to fall ill just as she was trying to get home from Genoa. It would be that much worse for Ryth, she thought. Ryth's whole way of being was to be available to help others. If she couldn't do that, she might crash, Liss worried. Not die, no, Liss was convinced this was not going to happen to Ryth. But she would need to help Ryth ward off depression. As for her own work, Liss shrugged. At this moment, it didn't seem so important. When she had first returned from Italy, she remembered how angry she had been at Ryth for not taking seriously her need to return to her patients. But, in this moment, her priority was clear.

At the Evergreen, George slumped in his chair. Other staff had either tested positive or actually fallen ill with COVID, and he had arranged for their quarantine and return. He had asked others to do second shifts to cover, and staff had amazingly agreed. In that, he had been lucky. But Erythea -- there was no one to substitute for her, no one with anywhere near her skills or knowledge of the residents and their personal needs and failings. Not to mention how much he himself relied on her judgment and empathy. This was the worst blow so far, he felt, and then corrected himself, Viola's suicide was objectively worse. Objectively, but not personally worse. He knew he would need to have one of the Evergreen's health care staff test Erythea and then to instruct the County to do contact tracing. But what to tell the residents? He knew he was required to maintain anonymity in reporting a new staff outbreak. But the residents would readily miss Erythea, and he no longer had the excuse of her being on vacation, since she had so recently returned from one. His sense of resolve flagged. He rubbed his head in his hands.

Liss dozed off while sitting next to Ryth, then awoke with a start. Had she caused this infection? She was somehow convinced she had brought it back with her from Italy a few months ago. Logic did not intrude on her sense of guilt. Please, god, let her sleep this off, she bargained with herself.

When Ryth awoke again midmorning, she moaned about how her whole body hurt. Liss recorded her temperature, now up to 102, and gave her another dose of Tylenol and another cold cloth over her forehead and eyes. Again she fell asleep. Liss had to wake her when the Evergreen employee, fully garbed in PPE, came to test them both. By that time, the morning was nearly gone, and Liss tried to get some food into Ryth. But she had no appetite, would only sip a little water. Her breathing was noticeably shallow. Liss asked if she could breathe okay, and Ryth just nodded, then dozed off again. Liss realized this could be a long vigil.

December

~ Tanabata

Arturo and Marta removed the outdoor tables and chairs, stacking the chairs inside the restaurant. Arturo rolled up the bamboo fence they had used to delineate the outside dining area and stashed it in the storage area. Ironically, the weather was still sunny and warm enough midday to eat outside, but the local health orders had once again decreed takeout orders only. Arturo recognized he had become adept at these modifications, and the restaurant had survived shuttering and then re-opening and now adapting once again to new restrictions. Ever the skeptic, he marveled at how their modest restaurant had survived the crisis, with no more employees stricken and a more-or-less constant flow of orders. Their burritos went not only to the local Hispanic population but also to young white IT types working from home and wanting a quick, simple meal. He had even begun to replenish the cash savings in his home safe, in modest amounts, but still it was a plus.

Marta had been a great partner ever since giving up her other two jobs, but now she had begun to pester him to return to the hospital and to the Evergreen. Both were short on staff, and her former supervisors had been calling to ask if she would return. They had even offered her a modest raise. As far as he could imagine, her COVID risk was likely no more than at the restaurant, maybe even less, since she would be exposed to fewer people and tested regularly. Still, he resisted. He would miss her being at his side throughout the day in more ways than he could express. She seemed to know what he was thinking at any given moment, she had solid ideas and a good, steady way with all the employees. When Beto had been at his side, he also knew what to do, but there was some level of daily friction that they both knew derived from nothing more than Beto being the first son. Arturo knew that Marta would defer to him, but still it was only fair that she make her own decision. He would tell her yes this evening after dinner.

Marta too was prepared for their discussion after dinner. She had spoken to her former supervisor at the Evergreen. She felt reinforced for what she anticipated would be Arturo's resistance.

"You don't need to do this for the money," Arturo began.

"It's not about the money." She saw the old pride in his eyes, pleading with her. She hesitated to tell him she longed for her own work, for contact with all of her co-workers, not his, but this was not her strongest point.

"If I go back to the Evergreen, they don't want me to work at the hospital at the same time. Too much outside risk." Arturo nodded approvingly. "And," she paused for effect, "we are second in line for the vaccine. They expect to get it for all employees and residents within a month."

He swiped his hand over his head, as he always did when he heard important news. She could practically see the tracks of his fingers through his thick hair.

"That's huge," was all he said. They just nodded at each other.

When Arturo came to bed from his shower, Marta ran her own hands gently through his wet hair, admiring its fullness, and nibbled at the bottom of his ear. It was all the invitation he needed.

At breakfast the next morning, he insisted on cooking the eggs and serving her with a small flourish. "So when do you begin?"

"Next Monday." She explained her new work plans to their children and told them about the vaccine coming to the Evergreen.

"When can we get it too?" was all they wanted to know.

❖

Four days had passed between the day Erythea fell ill and the day she and Elissa got their COVID test results. Of course, they were both positive, but Elissa had not developed any symptoms. By this time, Erythea had begun to eat a little, sitting up in bed, but she still remained in bed all day, sleeping many hours during the day. Her fever was down, just a little above normal, and her throat was still tender but not as sore as the first two days. She no longer complained of her body aching, but she was profoundly fatigued. "I've never felt this tired," she confessed.

Elissa patiently encouraged her to just "sleep it off," only forcing her to sit up for meals of oatmeal for breakfast, soup and apple sauce and anything else she did not have to chew. Elissa slept on the sofa so as not to crowd her partner in bed. Sometimes while Erythea slept deeply during the day, she ventured out for a short walk, energizing herself in the brisk air and sunlight. She had never had to take care of anyone before, and she surprised herself with her own patience.

Elissa marked the days on an advent calendar she had brought home before knowing she would have a quarantine countdown. Friday the eleventh was the fourteenth day since Erythea had become ill and they were tested. To her own patients, Elissa neither explained nor provided a date when she would return. She was tending to "an illness in the family." She binge-watched an old thriller she and Ryth had clung to years earlier – "The Kiss of the Spider Woman." She made her own chicken soup, with the remains of a whole chicken and vegetables she had ordered in. For herself, she mainly heated frozen meals.

George phoned every afternoon, gently and without wanting to intrude. Elissa gave him a daily report, emphasizing that symptoms were very gradually subsiding. He asked about her too, expressing relief that she had not developed any symptoms. On the tenth day he sent someone else out for another nasal test of both of them. They waited another three days. This time they were both negative, but Erythea still lacked the energy to return to work. Elissa took her out for a brief walk, which revealed the first smile on Ryth's face, but still she asked to come back after only a few minutes. George encouraged her to take as long as she needed.

<hr>

December 14, 2020 – On this day, the United States marked a total of 300,000 deaths from the coronavirus, and many hospitals across the nation neared or surpassed capacity in their COVID wards. On this same day, the first coronavirus vaccine was administered in this country, to an urgent-care nurse in Queens, New York. The first dose in California went to an ICU physician in Los Angeles.

On the same day, Joe Biden received 306 Electoral College votes, officially ending the long siege of fruitless lawsuits by the current president to challenge his victory.

<hr>

"This is crazy!" Simon yelled at the news. The vaccination distribution plan prioritized residents at retirement homes with nursing care services like his. At the Evergreen, the staff was to be vaccinated within days -- definitely not crazy -- but so too were the residents. "What about teachers, firefighters, bus drivers, grocery clerks, police?" All these workers had daily interaction with people all the time as a necessary component of where they worked. "Not like us, living in a virtual cave." Simon checked himself. Part of the change he'd noted about living in the cave was his tendency to talk aloud to himself. Besides, he thought, putting his voice on silent, shouldn't the younger, productive component of humanity be vaccinated before 85-year-olds like him whose productive years were behind them? Of course the oldest old were the most vulnerable, that was in the natural order of the universe. If we die, we die, he spoke to himself in his provocative old professorial mode. Of course the medical caregivers have first priority, that's a given, went his lecture, but right after them, shouldn't we vaccinate those people whose only choices are to get close to other people every hour of the day, or to quit work to save themselves? He was sufficiently riled that he phoned his former colleague Jake, one of hiking and verbal sparring buddies. Before even asking Jake to meet him for a hike, he asked Jake who he thought should get the vaccine first after health care workers. "It's complicated," was Jake's reply, and Simon growled at him laughingly. "You always dodged taking a stand." They agreed to meet in an hour at an open space near Tiburon to hike alongside the Bay.

Under the new rules at the Evergreen, residents were not supposed to gather anywhere with others outside their household, but Simon knew Jake's solitary habits and level of care. Simon grabbed his car keys and hiking stick, put on his mask and locked his apartment door.

Jake was slouched against his car when Simon pulled into the parking lot. Although he wore his old Cal baseball hat and sunglasses above his black mask, Simon knew from Jake's posture he was grinning at him. If they hadn't had a history of teaching together for seventeen years and a friendship that arose from their mutual eccentricities, Simon might have struggled to read anything from Jake's masked face.

"No sticks, old man?" Simon teased. Twenty years younger, Jake never used hiking sticks and never stopped ribbing Simon about his age. They both knew it kept Simon competitive. Simon confessed he needed to get his sticks from the trunk of his car. And so they took off, Simon determined to walk faster than Jake.

"Who do *you* think should get the first vaccines, after the health care workers?" Simon wouldn't let go of the conversation he'd started earlier.

"If you listen to my students, everyone who has to work with the public should go second, and old people should be 'sheltered in place', where they're less likely to get COVID than the active public."

"Yes, but I asked what Jake thinks. Do you go with the model of who is most vulnerable or who is most useful?"

"That's too binary, Simon. Should our distribution system give the message that old people are expendable?"

"I'm less concerned about messaging than about stopping the spread. Even your students seem to think it should go to whoever is most exposed, and that seems logical to me."

"Then should prisoners get the first doses? That's where the highest outbreak is."

They ragged on at each other in this vein for a couple of miles, until they rounded a curve of land and confronted the brunt of cold wind across the Bay. Simon rolled his wool scarf higher on his neck and leaned into the wind. "Want to keep going?" Jake asked. "Definitely. Haven't had this much fun in a long time." Jake shrugged and kept going but admitted after a short distance that he was definitely cold. They turned back, to Simon's silent relief.

"How do you like where you're living?" Jake changed the subject.

"I thought I'd be part of a community, somehow, but we're so cloistered we could all be monks in a vow of silence. That's not the Evergreen's fault, it's due to COVID and the rules from various agencies to keep us safe. But it's also infantilizing, which of course makes me feel ancient and feeble – or rebellious, depending on the day."

"What about you? How are you managing?" Jake lived in a tiny old house at the top of the Filbert Street steps on Telegraph Hill.

"Well, if it makes you feel any better, COVID has practically ended my relationship with Tana."

"I'm sorry. How?"

"Neither of us wanted to live with the other full time, and she spends too much time around other people for my comfort. I don't mean another man, at least I don't think so, but she spends live time with a lot of friends. I don't even go inside a grocery store; I get my food delivered."

"So you're almost as much a monk as I am," Simon teased, "except you don't have to sign out of your dorm."

"No, I don't have to account for where I go every day."

⚊⚊◄●►⚊⚊

Marta's first day back at work coincided with the day the vaccine arrived at The Evergreen. All the staff lined up outside, warming themselves briefly as they stepped past tall heat lamps. Cheers erupted for the first employee to receive her shot. Even local news media appeared, hoisting cameras at their shoulders.

As she entered residents' apartments to change their sheets and towels, Marta was repeatedly greeted with congratulations on being vaccinated. Her old friends in the laundry room joked in good spirit and welcomed her back. Even though the COVID numbers on the outside were alarming – a surge higher than the incidence from last spring – her co-workers radiated good spirits.

Marta introduced herself to each resident as she knocked and entered the apartment. While most of the residents readily introduced themselves and put on their masks when she came in, some residents failed to mask themselves and some barely spoke to her. Though she had worked before at the Evergreen, she had not met most of the residents since her prior duties had been confined to the laundry room. She found herself surprised now by how very, very old some of them were. She had rarely seen people so old. Some of them leapt up to move out of her way when she vacuumed, but for some of them any movement was an obstacle. One of them was a woman so arthritic that her whole upper body curved into a large letter C and her fingers were as gnarled as the stumps of a pruned sycamore tree. Bertha was both friendly and apologetic. "I'm sorry, dear, you'll have to work around me." Bertha even offered her tea from an ever-warm teapot plugged into the wall next to her chair. Marta asked if she could bring her anything and Bertha asked for the tin of Christmas cookies on her counter, only so that she could offer one to Marta with a cup of tea. Marta accepted her hospitality even as she marveled at Bertha's ability to use her aged fingers. As she changed the sheets on Bertha's bed in the adjacent half-room, Marta learned about Bertha's great-grandson Tor, who would turn one in January. Erythea lets me watch him crawl on a little TV tablet she carries around with her. "I can even talk to him," she marveled. Bertha was not the only resident who craved conversation from their apparent isolation. Marta repeated various snippets of her family story to several of them, each time finding herself warmed by her conversations with new people. Driving home, she tried to count how many months it had been since she had met and talked to new people, other than taking meal orders on the phone.

Phoning Carla after returning home that first day, Marta found her sister-in-law in an opposite frame of mind. Stressed nearly to tears, Carla told her how crowded the ICU had become in just a few weeks. "Almost all the beds are taken, and I can barely keep up with all the patients in my ward. There's no time at all to give them comfort. I might as well be a robot checking their monitors and giving them fluids and meds."

"Why *don't* they use robots?" Marta asked, just to try to lighten Carla's load. "We've got a robot here who cleans the public rooms every day."

"Can you imagine?" they both said at the same time. Carla finished the sentence for them both, "being so dangerously contagious that the hospital only allows a robot near you?" They laughed nervously. "I only hope Pedro had gentle nurses with him at the end."

⸺•❖•⸺

Adam brooded. Not a moody person by nature, he found himself missing Ilina much of the time. She had returned the Monday after Thanksgiving, as promised, and brought a huge slice of pumpkin pie to his dorm room. The pie was delicious, and she watched him devour it. But she wouldn't even enter his room. They had taken a few long walks before exams began. Then they both went into exam hibernation, and she left for Cleveland when her exams ended a day earlier than his. She'd been there ever since, and he remained on campus over the Christmas holiday break.

All the Conservatory students had been given an assignment for the weeks of the break, and Adam disciplined himself to work on his assignment every morning after breakfast. His was to learn the history of his instrument and then to teach himself to play a new piece of music featuring his instrument. For the history assignment he chose to research the evolution of the cello from a five-stringed to a four-stringed instrument. Such a change must have had an impact on the sound and technique of playing. For the new piece of music he selected the Dvorak B Minor Concerto after streaming recordings from the campus library. The Dvorak score from the library arrived the next day at his door, a minor miracle of COVID-based library delivery. The comfort of Dvorak's melodies inspired him to practice relentlessly.

But even more intriguing was the five-stringed Baroque cello, with its E string at the top of the bar. With catgut strings instead of steel, it was quieter but offered a larger dynamic range. Why had it been replaced? He couldn't find an answer in any of his readings. In his isolation, Adam located another student musician on YouTube, Beiliang Zhu, whose rendition of the Bach Cello Suite No. 6 on the Baroque cello mesmerized him. Her words – to stop trying to control the music and submit to its spirit – spoke to him. Try to let it sing, he told himself as he played.

Every day at four, he'd play hoops with two other students who remained in his dorm over the holiday. Nate played piano and Justin the bass. The three of them joked about starting to play together, but Justin thought they needed a violin and Nate was more interested in jazz than classical music, so it remained just talk.

Adam phoned his dad every day at eight and often he played for him. He noticed his dad's improvement in mood after each time he played. He basked in his father's praise. He didn't question what had caused the shift, he just reveled in his dad no longer withholding his praise. For Adam it was a daily balm from his anxiety over how he had done on his exams.

Every few days he phoned his mother, who seemed much less worried about him, less curious about the details of his life, and lighter in her own mood, somehow more carefree.

At the end of each day he wanted badly to talk to Ilina, but he restrained himself from phoning more often than every other day, usually in the evening after playing for his father. She had taken on Brahms' Double Concerto as her assignment, a bold and confident piece. She agreed it was. When he tried to compare notes with her about the history of the cello, she was casually dismissive.

"Oh, I learned that long ago from my dad, when I first switched to the cello."

Her comment prompted Adam to ask more about her father. "Where does he teach?" A long pause ensued, so long that Adam wondered how he had mis-stepped. Finally, she replied.

"He's the dean of the Conservatory."

"Oh, shit! I'm sor—"

She giggled. "Don't apologize. You were bound to find out sooner or later."

"But you don't have his last name," Adam blundered forward.

"I use my mother's name here, for reasons you've just discovered. It's not exactly boyfriend bait."

Now they both laughed, easily and together.

"I was going to ask if I could drive up to Cleveland and visit you, but now I don't think I will." They laughed again.

"No, not a good idea, but not for the reasons you think. My two brothers and an uncle and cousin are here, and my family is strict about not mixing it up with other people. They made my uncle and cousin quarantine for fourteen days before they came to visit. So, that's a very long way of saying no."

"So how about your coming back here sooner?"

"That's a yes. My dorm opens the day after New Year's, and I'll try to come back then. Besides, then I can be on campus when my exam grades come in."

"I see. You're just trying to avoid your family by coming back early."

"You can think that if you want."

After she got off the line with Adam, Ilina prepared for her private lesson, positioning her cello and its stand at the corner of her father's study, where he himself practiced. She ran her fingers over the soft velvet of the dark green walls that absorbed rather than bounced the sound from his violin. Having her lesson in his study was a privilege by itself, reflective of her father's taking her seriously. His study was sacrosanct, forbidden territory to her and the rest of the family except when they were explicitly invited in. Beside the velvet corner where he practiced, the other two walls contained floor-to-ceiling bookshelves, stocked painstakingly with his music references – also forbidden territory – his rosewood desk sheltered in the middle of one library wall. When the family watched her father play, they had to bring in chairs from the dining room.

Her cello instructor of the past two years was Jan Frankowiak, who ranked highly in her father's world and sometimes played chamber concerts with him. She knew it was a sign of her father's taking her seriously that he had arranged for Frankowiak to tutor her. Whether his permission to use his study for her lessons was tribute to her or to Frankowiak didn't matter, she felt privileged.

Frankowiak was waiting in the study when she walked in with her score. She seated herself and began to play the first movement. He stopped her within the first few bars of the Allegro. Demonstrating with his ring finger, he told her she would get more resonating sound if she repositioned her own finger. "Linger there just slightly. " She tried it herself three times and could hear a difference. At the moment of the dramatic single pluck of the cello strings, he stopped her again, asking her to pause for a longer breath after each note to give it more drama.

"I can hear you like this music," he offered, after listening to her play the rest of the first movement. "What do you take from it?"

"Confidence. The cello in this piece is assertive, not mournful." He nodded. "And the second movement? Let's see what you draw from it." She played the tender andante in a much more lyric manner.

"Someday, I want to play this piece with my father."

Frankowiak gazed at her thoughtfully. "That's a tall order."

"I know," she acknowledged with a rueful smile. This was the first time she had voiced her ambition.

"But you will," he reassured her with a hand on her shoulder. "Work hard and you will."

Gianlucca glanced up from the color swatches before him on his computer screen and contemplated how this array of purples would fit the sweater line for autumn of the year to come. Outside everything was a pale gray, all details obscured by a dense fog. He could not even see the building across the canal. On the screen a gorgeous display of cabernet hues, outside, nothing. Yet he was drawn outside. Although confined again by a second lockdown due to the surge in cases, he was drawn to the mystery, the unreachable, the unexpected. His pass allowed him access only to the essentials, the grocery, the pharmacy, and the route to pick up his daughter Lili. He couldn't afford another fine, but he could devise a defensible route among his allowable destinations.

Grabbing his jacket, gloves in its pockets, he practically raced down the steps and out the door. Already in a different universe, he took a deep breath of the damp air. Left or right? It didn't matter in this envelope of fog. He could barely see or be seen. If any *polizia* ventured out in this morass and found him, he could claim to be lost in the fog. *Sono perso nella nebbia*, he rehearsed. Not even the sound of his footsteps would betray him with sneakers on his feet. He turned left by habit. Lili and Fran's apartment lay this way. He could walk there in his sleep, he thought. But he didn't want to get too close and risk a chance encounter and any need to explain why he was there.

What silent streets! So quiet that when a whirring of wings sounded just in front of him he stopped, startled. As he resumed his pace, he imagined he could hear his heart pounding. It set the rhythm for his stride. He continued in a straight line for many blocks, not bothering to count them, just obeying the red and green traffic lights, paled in this shrouded universe.

The pandemic had reduced the frames of his universe, removing the distractions of commuting, of concerts outside, of flirting with women wherever he might ordinarily find them, browsing the shops, visiting with friends and traveling anywhere, whether to bring flowers to his mother on her birthday or to explore any new horizon. He used to inspect silk farms in China and wool sources in Sardegna. He had learned over these many months that the online universe replaced the need for almost all of his business travel, and that color matching could be refined and verified online. He could handle all of his business meetings via Zoom.

But the spark of human encounter – that was missing almost altogether. Whatever chatting he indulged in these days was limited to the checkout clerks at the large grocery. Even the wine merchant was more guarded in his encounters with customers. Other than Lili, there was no one he embraced. Fran's rejection a few months ago had stung. He didn't know at the time how hopeful his overture had been. It had just seemed like a cheerful evening reunion. He realized now he had harbored a deeper hope of reunion with the mother of his only child. Friends had asked, but he'd never had a good explanation even for himself of why or how that relationship had withered. He wished he could revive it.

Glancing around him, Gianlucca realized he had actually lost his bearings. The universe of buildings around him were unrecognizable in the fog, but at the next intersection he looked up at a street sign and oriented himself. A cheerful man, he told himself, *sono securo che trovero' la mia strada*, I will find my way.

•◦•◦•

Don hadn't seen Erythea since the day he returned from the hospital, weeks ago. He had even emailed her to request a book, but she hadn't responded at all. His mind leapt to the possibility that she had COVID, but he knew no one would tell him the truth. Such were the rules of anonymity at the Evergreen. He phoned the front desk and explained that he ordinarily requested books from Erythea but that she hadn't answered his email. The receptionist paused – and of course he read the worst into her pause – before referring him to Tammy, who was handling library requests these days. He asked for Tammy's email, but the receptionist offered to transfer his call directly to her. Tammy answered with a buoyant cheerfulness on the first ring and asked what book she could get him. "A biography of Woodrow Wilson," he explained. "Author?" she asked automatically. He replied he had no particular author in mind. Then she blurted, "what makes you interested in him?"

He heard curiosity in her question and smiled.

"Do you know he was president during a pandemic ?"

"Flu, yes, but I never thought about that." She sounded genuinely interested.

"Do you know he was seriously ill with the flu while he was trying to negotiate terms for the Germans at the end of World War I? He wanted to offer the Germans gentler terms but was talked out of it by Clemenceau and Lloyd George?"

She was silent for a moment. "All I remember about Wilson was his creating the League of Nations. How do you know this?"

He told her he had just read about it in the newspaper and wanted to learn more.

"I'll try to get you the book. Then when you've read it, will you tell me what you learn?"

"I'd love to." He was so engaged by her apparently genuine enthusiasm and curiosity that he forgot to ask her about Erythea.

The world lost between 50 and 100 million people to the 1918 flu pandemic, 675,000 of them in the United States. During that siege, President Wilson provided no leadership or guidance about the pandemic; he did not even report about it. The ostensible reason for his silence – and that of the other nations engaged in World War I and afflicted by it – was that providing the information would weaken the war effort. Only Spain, which was neutral in the war, reported accurately about the scourge, and for that it was dubiously rewarded with the moniker "Spanish flu."

Wilson's silence was reinforced by the 1918 Sedition Act, which made it a crime to say anything that the government perceived as harmful to the country or the war effort. The Sedition Act was nurtured by Wilson's attorney general, A. Mitchell Palmer, and it was deployed against Eugene Debs, the Socialist candidate for U.S. President in several elections, for delivering an anti-war speech in June 2018. Debs was convicted and sentenced to a ten-year term that was upheld by the U.S. Supreme Court.

Elissa interrupted her soup making to peek in on Erythea napping in the bedroom around the corner. This morning they'd been on their longest walk together since Erythea began to heal. She had lasted nearly a mile but then collapsed in bed as soon as they got back. Now she was sitting up and talking on her phone. Even from just one end of the conversation, it was obvious Erythea was talking to George. Elissa paused in the doorway.

"Even if it's just part of a day, I want to connect with them again, before the end of this year." Erythea swung her long hair over her right shoulder, one of her signal gestures of determination.

"I know. I promise I'll go home when I get tired. Can I start Monday?" Another pause. "Yes, yes, thank you. See you Monday."

Elissa slipped out of the doorway before Erythea turned around to see her.

"Lunch is almost ready," she called from the kitchen.

Erythea nearly charged out of the bedroom. "What's cookin'? My appetite's back." She kissed the back of Elissa's neck before reaching for the dishes and tableware.

"White bean and kale stew."

"Smells great. I'm going back to work Monday!"

Only when they sat down did Elissa trust herself to speak. "Why are you so excited? Isn't the company here good enough?" Even Elissa could hear too much vinegar in the words.

Erythea put down her spoon and gave Elissa what she called her 'searchlight stare' before she began to speak. "You've been amazing, Liss. You've cooked great food, you've massaged my sore limbs, made love to me when I couldn't give you any satisfaction back. You talked me through all my fears, reassured me I would get well when I didn't believe it myself. I don't know what I would have done without you. I can't imagine how people get through this on their own." Erythea's eyes now cast in a different direction. "I want to start giving back."

The old refrain. "Give back at work instead of here at home is how that somehow sounds."

"Remember how eager you were to get back to work when you got home from Italy?"

"I do, and I remember our fight just as well. I don't want to have that battle again."

"I don't either. But what do you want?"

Now Elissa's eyes cast about the room before she could focus on an answer. "I want to celebrate your getting well – just you and me – and I don't want you to relapse somehow." Elissa covered her face. "I don't want to be that scared again."

Erythea got up and encircled Elissa with both her arms, kissing her on the side of her neck. "I don't want either of us to be that scared ever again. How should we celebrate?"

Together they drove to Muir Beach with a large blanket, a bottle of zinfandel and two plastic glasses. Wrapped up together, they watched the sun set over the ocean and promised themselves the daylight hours would get longer each day.

On Erythea's first day back at work, she checked in with Don just after reporting in with George. His surprised smile was her first reward, his comment her second.

"You survived," Don breathed. When she asked how he knew, he told her only, "I surmised." They compared notes of their bouts. He was relieved to learn she had not needed to be hospitalized. From Don, she checked in with the health center nurses, who gave her tips on who seemed neediest. Even with masks muddling words, Erythea could hear the warmth in their welcomes.

She visited Bertha, who had again fallen behind on her medical appointments. As Erythea passed what had been Viola's room, she shuddered inwardly, the memory too vivid. Every time Viola came to mind, and it was often just as she was trying to go to sleep, Erythea tried to resist her memory. Bertha called a cheerful "come in" and showed off the new tablet her son Harry had given her for Christmas. "I even have my own Zoom account," she giggled. "I can also read books on it by making the type bigger." Erythea encouraged Bertha to show off all she could do on her new tablet, including showing off photos of her great grandson Tor, who could now walk. "And I watched them open presents under their Christmas tree on Christmas morning. Isn't that amazing?" Bertha's penetrating eyes shone. "Now if only I could visit my friends here."

"But you can. If you wear a mask and stay at least six feet apart, you can visit with a friend in the gathering room."

"I'm too crippled to get down there," Bertha explained, shrugging her shoulders in acceptance of her limitation.

"Do you know I can get someone to wheel you down there?"

"Really?"

"Part of my job. Just tell me when and I'll arrange for someone to come with a wheelchair."

After Bertha, Erythea visited Pernille, one of the residents the nurses had identified as failing. Erythea remembered her as one of the residents who painted, regularly using the art room and once having had her own exhibit in the residents' gallery. Pernille spoke with an accent that Erythea did not recognize. She often wore floor-length skirts instead of pants, and wore her long pale hair in a braid that she sometimes wrapped up around the top of her head. Erythea heard "come in" at her knock. Inside she found Pernille, scarf around her head, sitting at her easel and staring at an unfinished painting with her hands folded in her lap. An almost-black purple wash with starkly uneven edges covered the lower right quarter of the canvas.

"What are you painting?" Erythea asked cheerfully.

Pernille gazed up at Erythea with vacant eyes. "*Ikke taler.*"

"What did you say?" It took Erythea a couple more questions to realize Pernille was answering in another language. She pointed at the painting and asked what it was.

"A painting." Pernille's glance turned expectant rather than blank.

"I remember what beautiful paintings you had on display in the gallery last year. I hope you can display this one when you finish it." Erythea suddenly remembered her encounter months ago with Abigail and wished all over again that she could inject Pernille with some of Abigail's buoyancy. Pernille smiled but said nothing.

"Would you like to take a walk outside? It's a nice sunny day."

Pernille smiled again, now childlike. "Yes."

"You'll need a mask," indicating her own. Pernille shook her head quizzically. Was it possible that some residents still did not have masks? Erythea tried to calculate how many months Pernille must have remained alone in her room. "I have an extra. Here, you put it on like this," Erythea gestured.

Together they walked down to the residents' garden. Pernille paused as they encountered a crow, sipping water from a rain puddle. "Crow," she said, "thirsty crow."

"Thankfully we've had rain for it to drink," Erythea commented.

"When did it rain?" Pernille framed the words after a pause, smiling as she did so.

"Last night. I love the sound of rain at night."

"Me too."

They continued in similar small talk as they circled the garden. As soon as Erythea returned Pernille to her apartment she phoned the health center to report that Pernille needed an aide, every day if possible. She desperately needed stimulation to reawaken all the skills she had lost during the nine months of isolation.

Erythea admitted to herself that one of the reasons she wanted to return before the end of the year was to create a "wishing tree" for New Year's Eve. Tammy helped her create and distribute small strips of paper with ribbons attached, so that residents could write on them their wishes for the New Year and hang them on one of the trees in the Evergreen garden area. She knew that the Japanese custom, *Tanabata*, entailed hanging the wishes on a bamboo tree, but since none was available they selected a tree with branches low enough for ambulatory residents to reach. For those residents like Bertha, she and Tammy offered to hang the wishes for them. Bertha asked specifically to be rolled out to the tree and watch as Erythea hung her message. By evening on the first day of January, the tree they had chosen was fully garlanded with messages from the residents, and Erythea brought home a photograph to show Elissa, who wanted her own message to hang on the tree. Erythea grinned at Elissa's eagerness. "Can it be a secret wish?" Liss asked. "I can tie the paper in a folded position, but no guarantees," was her reply. "So you're going to read mine?" Liss winked.

"If I can't restrain myself."

Ryth tied Liss' message to the tree the next day without reading it. After all, she thought, Liss could not read hers, which read, "Connection -- every day, all my days."

In Japan, the Tanabata festival is ancient, dating back to the Empress Koken in 755, and it is observed on the seventh day of July, based on the annual conjunction of celestial deities. By coincidence, in 2008 the G8 summit meeting coincided with Tanabata. and Prime Minister Yasuo Fukuda invited the G8 leaders to join in the custom. Each leader was asked to write a wish on the piece of paper called *tanzaku*, to hang it on a bamboo tree, and then to take necessary action to change the world for the better. The request caught on with nongovernmental organizations such as Oxfam and CARE International, which set up an online wish petition to coincide with Tanabata.

⋙ ◆ ◗ ◆ ⋘

Don awoke at a jolt to the massive building. His eyes darted open. It was still dark but the lighted clock on the wall read 5:42. At least it would be light soon. As if bolted to the bed, he lay inert, in suspense. Would there be aftershocks? Was this the prelude to a larger quake? Would he be pancaked if the building collapsed in a large earthquake? Would he be left behind if the building had to be evacuated? Of all the matters that had troubled him this year, he never imagined an earthquake would strike on the morning of the last day of the year. He lay there for some time pondering this new way his life might end. Like most people, he had avoided thinking about the specifics of his life ending or the number of days, weeks, or years left within it.

He waited until seven before phoning Janice. By then she would normally be up and alert. Adrenaline still coursing through his body, he used the voice dial mechanism on his phone, which was propped on a stand next to him.

"Did you feel it?"

"What do you mean? Did you have a dream that I was supposed to share?" They both chortled. Occasionally, years ago they would have similar dreams, usually after good lovemaking.

"I'm afraid that was too long ago," he was still laughing quietly at the shared memory. "No, I mean the earthquake we had just before six this morning."

"Now you *are* teasing me." She paused, still thinking he was joking.

"No. Isn't that the perfect coda to this year?"

At that moment, Russell appeared in the doorway with his breakfast. He put the tray on the cart adjacent to the bed and seamlessly hoisted Don's body to the perfect sitting position. Don gave him a long look of appreciation. "I was just wondering if I would be left lying here in a big earthquake."

"No, Mr. Goodman, that would never happen," Russell promised solemnly. "We have carts, but I would carry you if I had to."

After half of his coffee and his eggs and bacon, Don felt relaxed for the first time this morning. He gazed out the window toward the mountain, deep green in the full sunlight. Unbidden, he recalled a weekend he and Janice had spent years ago to celebrate her birthday at an inn halfway up the mountain. They had enjoyed a vigorous hike early in the morning, returned to a luxurious brunch at the inn with champagne and orange juice, and tumbled into uninhibited sex in their room afterward. "Shhh," he kept warning her, "people can hear us."

That memory belonged to another lifetime, he reminded himself. Yet Janice was still – or again – with him, after all these years. Gratitude washed through him. In this useless body of his, gratitude and memory would have to be enough.

Don reflected, perhaps for the first time, what this must like for Janice. Her body was far from useless. She was still muscled, lean and active. She should be able to use her body while she still could, he mused in a burst of generous empathy. She deserves a lover. But as soon as he formed that notion, his rational mind took over. She wasn't likely to enjoy sex without forming an attachment to another man. With the privacy and freedom she now had, no matter how discreetly she might conduct herself, he would inevitably lose her if she took another man. He could not imagine her enjoying sex like a tennis match or a climb up a mountain or an exciting dance performance. No, she could not have a lover in his imagination -- that was far too dangerous.

⸻ ●●● ⸻

January 2021

~ Janus

On New Year's Day, Adam received an email from Leah, the first words from her in months. He hesitated several hours before even opening it, not welcoming this reminder of having left her behind. Instinctively, he knew that whatever she wrote would be difficult to answer. She had written a few times earlier in the fall, plaintively mourning her isolation even as she began college from her bedroom. Without even opening her email, he knew he would have no ready answer for her. He didn't know whether her parents would relent their protection even when her college would open its campus. He barely knew what to write. To tell her of his enthusiasm for his new life seemed almost cruel. He didn't want to inflict anything on her. He knew he would not tell her anything about Ilina; that much was clear. Selfishly, he wished he did not have to reply. But he knew he would; he must, he was not mean and he did not want to feel guilty. He told himself he would read it and respond after lunch. During lunch he watched and listened to Carl Nielsen's Symphony No. 4 on YouTube, which cheered him.

When he finally opened and read Leah's letter, he practically gasped. She was much worse than he had imagined. She hadn't left her room in over a month, refusing to join her family for the holidays. Mostly she had stayed in bed. "It stinks, just like my life," she wrote. She had 'attended' all of her classes from bed, read all that was assigned to her, but nothing 'spoke to her'. She was indifferent to the outcome of her exams; "college is not life." She went on in that vein for nearly a page.

He answered as soon as he finished reading it, mustering all the encouragement he could, assuring her that her world would re-open and seem all the brighter for the period of absence, that her parents could help her if she let them. He encouraged her to listen to music; it was his balm. After he ran out of words, he reread his note, paused and pressed 'send'.

Not more than twenty minutes later, he received her reply. "Too late," was all she wrote.

He stared at her note for a long moment, before texting his mother: Leah emailed me and I'm worried about her. Can you ask Naomi to check on her right now? After staring at it, he phoned his mother and read her the email. She read it as urgently as he had.

"I'll call you back when I know something," she told him.

Janice dialed Naomi immediately, and she answered. Without preface, she said, "Adam has received a disturbing email from Leah. Can you check on her and make sure she's all right?" Janice heard Naomi drop the phone.

After leaving the line open for some minutes, Janice ended the call and made herself a sandwich.

Naomi did not call back until the next morning. Halting at first, she admitted she had not told Janice before how bad it was with Leah. "I can't thank you enough for your call. Leah had just swallowed a bottle of aspirin – praise God she didn't have anything more lethal. We called 911, EMTs took her to Marin General, where they pumped her stomach. She now has a psychiatrist sitting with her in person."

Janice texted Adam before she even called Naomi back. "You did the right thing."

Carl Nielsen wrote his Symphony No. 4, "The Inextinguishable," in his native Denmark in 1914, just before the First World War began. In a letter written four years later he described it:

> It is meant to express the appearance of the most elementary forces among men, animals, and even plants. We can say: In case all the world was devastated through fire, flood, volcanoes, etc., and all things were destroyed and dead, then nature would still begin to breed new life again, begin to push forward again with all the fine and strong forces inherent in matter. Soon the plants would begin to multiply, the breeding and screaming of birds be seen and heard, man's aspiration and yearning would be felt. These forces, which are "inextinguishable," are what I have tried to present.

Ilina returned to campus on January 2 but told no one. Since there was hardly anyone else in her dorm, she had the privacy she craved. First, she retrieved her grades – a relief instead of the agony she feared. Still, the relief did not relax her. She set up her cello and the Brahms Double Concerto score, wishing she had a partner for the violin part. She would ask her instructor as soon as classes resumed. She could hear the violin in her head as she practiced. Asking her father was out of the question, he would not deign to practice with her -- not at this stage. Someday, she hoped, but not now.

He had always pegged her as 'such a diligent girl'. Of course she was, she could not become a musician without being diligent. She wanted to be fearless.

She worked on capturing the suspense of the plucked strings. That moment, in the first two minutes of the concerto, enthralled her, and Frankowiak had helped with his instruction. Over the holiday break she had watched and listened to Yo-Yo Ma, Rostropovich and Maisky each play these chords in their own quite different ways. Intrigued by plucking rather than bowing, she played through the first two minutes seven or eight times, each time in a different way, finally arriving at how she wanted the notes to sound, before continuing through the rest of the movement.

By lunchtime, Ilina realized she had made an error in not telling anyone of her arrival. Instead of the lunch bag arriving at her dorm door, she would need to go to the cafeteria and see what food she could find. She bundled up for the cold, pulling her purple stocking cap over her head and wrapping the matching scarf around her neck. At the cafeteria she grabbed an apple and a steaming cup of chicken noodle soup, put a lid on it and began to walk back to her room.

A light snow had just begun to fall, drifting peacefully onto her coat. No wind disturbed the gentle drift. Crunching through the deep snow already on the ground, she veered suddenly from the path to her room and headed toward Adam's dorm. He must see this beautiful day. What did he know of snow from where he lived? She walked faster.

Standing outside his door she could hear deep sad notes emanating from his room. She placed her lunch on the floor beside his door, took off her mittens, and knocked. She watched him in her imagination, as she heard him stir and walk to the door.

His door swung open before she could see him.

"It's you! Come in, come in."

Ilina bent over to retrieve her soup and apple before walking in. Adam gestured toward the table just inside. She put her mittens and food onto the table and began to unwrap her scarf. Adam spontaneously took off her cap and leaned in to kiss her, pausing only as she tore off her mask. He kissed her once, lightly, on her mouth. She searched his eyes, asking if that was all. He unwound her long scarf, taking what she thought was forever, wrapped his hands gently around her ears and gave her a searching kiss. He tasted like berries. She wrapped her arms around him and tasted him fully.

"I've been wanting to do that forever," he confessed.

"Me too." She kissed him again, then pulled back gently. "Did you have blueberries for lunch?"

He laughed. "Are my teeth blue?"

"No," she laughed too. "I could taste them. You must have just eaten them."

"I did." As she took off her jacket, he tossed it onto his bed and brought her a spoon, savoring her every movement as she uncapped her still-steaming bowl of soup. She ate quickly. "I want to take you outside into the snow. It's the kind of snowfall where you can look at each flake and see how different it is from the next."

"Didn't you do that as a kid?" she asked him before realizing he grew up in California.

"No, we went to the snow at Tahoe, but only to snowboard. No one slowed down enough to look at snowflakes."

"You deprived child. Let's do it today."

As soon as she finished eating, she rose from the table and moved toward his bed. Adam watched transfixed, imagining her taking off her sweater, but she grabbed her jacket instead. "Come on," she urged. "There's more to do in the snow than snowboard."

He dressed quickly, donning the hooded parka and gloves he used to need only for Tahoe trips but wore now as a daily armor from the cold. Outside, the snow continued, and they treaded a cushiony path where no one else had laid tracks. Pointing to a slight rise, Ilina walked ahead of him in the virgin snow. She turned around suddenly to face him, her face blank. All at once she fell back, stiff as a statue, before he could reach out to stop her. He gasped. Giggling, she swept her arms and legs back and forth.

"I'm making a snow angel. Now it's your turn," she taunted.

Adam glanced down at her and at the untouched snow beside her wings. He imagined himself falling and hurting his cello hands. He knew he could not do it. He shook his head.

"Yours is perfect. I can't improve on that." She shot him a skeptical glance.

"Let me help you up." He extended his arm, bracing his feet at hers. She took his hand and levered herself up easily. He began to brush the snow off the back of her jacket. "Don't bother, I like it." He heard the edge in her voice.

The snow continued to fall gently as they plodded along silently. Adam knew he had broken her spontaneous mood and wondered how he could fix it. She stopped again and held her hands out in front of her, facing away from him. Again, he just watched. She was collecting snowflakes on the backs of her mittens, peering at them intently. "How many different patterns can you see?"

He was more interested in the snow collecting on the exposed strands of her brilliant hair. Coming closer, he touched her hair with his gloved hands. "Here I can find millions," he teased, bending to kiss her again.

She stepped away. "But I can't see those."

Unable to recapture the moment inside his room, he offered cocoa, but she shook her head and told him she would see him later. He watched her walk away, wondering if he would ever catch up with her.

Ilina could still taste Adam, even as she stomped away from where he stood. If she had been fearless, she would have followed him – led him – back to his room and explored how the rest of him tasted. But in these days of COVID, that could be suicidal. An overstatement, she told herself. But she had watched her father quarantine his immediate family. Adam was tempting but no one knew what was safe to touch or taste.

⸺◦●◦⸺

Carla continued to work each day in the COVID ward because she wanted to serve -- there remained a deep hole within her that she wanted desperately to fill – but it seemed the hole grew deeper each day at the hospital. When she arrived early each morning and left each afternoon, she saw the cars and ambulances being turned away by attendants who assessed at the door whether someone's condition was serious enough to warrant admission. Sometimes an ambulance waited just beyond the door, because there would soon be a bed. Carla knew from her work inside that the person awaiting a bed would more likely take the place of one who died rather than one who had been released to go home. One of her few sources of relief was knowing that some patients did recover sufficiently to return home. In the beginning, that didn't happen. Once inside the doors of the ICU, Carla quickly assessed who remained in the beds in the hall, who had been moved to a room, who was missing from the day before. When she began in this ward, she was assigned to just six beds. Now she had twelve to fifteen, including the second room and the beds in the hall. Patients had become beds in the frantic vocabulary and pace within the ward. Instead of having a second person regularly with her, she needed to summon help to turn a heavy patient, one to pull the sheet from below while she pulled on the legs and shoulders. Her tasks had become mechanical. She caught herself speaking at rather than to the intubated patients who could not respond. She no longer had time just to swab a patient's forehead for comfort. Such swabbing as she could do now was part of a hurried, inadequate bath. Feeding patients consisted of injections into a tube, except, today, for one patient who was soon to return home. Carla wished she had time to sit with this survivor, to congratulate him and wish him a good recovery at home. All she had time for was a smile behind her double mask and a gloved thumb's up. Had patients learned to read the smile in just the eyes of those attending them?

When she paused to glance at the room and see who needed help, she sometimes wondered how each patient could emotionally survive this atmosphere. Paced by the slow but noisy mechanical rhythm of his own ventilator, each patient had to contend with the relentless noise of the others around him. There was no pace of change, just the relentless breathing by machine, the crude intrusion of turning from side to side several times each day, the emptying of the containers of waste from the catheters between the legs. Carla found herself going to the bathroom less – each trip entailed an entire change of clothing – and she learned to pace herself while at work and to drink less before leaving for work in the dark. All her movements felt mechanical, from the moment she got up in the morning to her return home -- hyper-efficient and mechanical. Not even dinners with the children gave her solace. She watched how they too had become efficient, a well-coordinated team, but a joyless one. Luis set the table and served chips and salsa, Sabrina made the salads and often braised vegetables, Carlo prepared the main dish.

Dinnertime conversation had become listless. The family held hands for the prayer, then passed the dishes and fell into the food. Even Carla's questions to the children about school had become rote; none of them had anything interesting to relate. Carlo no longer reported on his work; it was too depressing. Carla knew from their occasional private conversation that he could not keep up with tracing. Increased testing in Marin had only increased his caseload, and the county had not hired more tracers to keep up. Carla caught his eyes as she glanced around the table. "Mom," he began in a cautious, adult voice that she recognized as the beginning of some advice.

Just then Luis' milk glass tipped and fell to the floor. Instinctively, Carla grabbed her napkin. As she swung her arm to mop up the spill on the table, Luis flinched as if she were going to hit him. Tears welled in his eyes.

"Oh, my baby, don't cry." She wrapped her arms around his shoulders. "I wasn't going to hurt you. It could have happened to any one of us." She rocked him as if he were three instead of seven. She began to cry herself, at first just gentle tears, but, without being able to staunch them, her tears turned to sobs, great wracking sobs that she couldn't stop. She heard the chairs being moved and then felt the warmth of Sabrina's and Carlo's arms around her shoulders, felt Sabrina's tears on her arm. Only Luis, embraced close to her chest, stopped crying; the others sobbed with their mother. "It's too much, it's all too much."

After they had all finished eating -- none of them ate all the food on their plate – and Sabrina had taken Luis upstairs to bathe before bed, Carlo cornered his mother.

"What I was going to say, before all that happened, was that you look dead tired. We can all see it, and I think Luis felt awful that his spilling caused you more work. I want to see you get some rest."

"I'm not helping the people I care about most."

"I hate to say it, but it's true. And I want you to help yourself. Take some time off." His eyes pleaded with her.

Carla just nodded.

Carla awoke to her alarm as usual and leaned over to turn it off. Then she leaned back onto her pillow and drifted back to sleep. She had already notified the hospital the night before that she was taking a sick day.

By the time she awakened again, the sun was high in the sky, another day of false spring. She sat up, well rested and idle. By now her children would have prepared and eaten their breakfasts and were likely in class at their desks. There was nothing she needed to do for any of them. So new was this feeling that she just sat in place for a few moments, appreciating the warmth and comfort of her bed, the morning sun, the colors in her room, which she barely remembered seeing in the morning sunlight. She dwelled for only a moment on the wine-red recliner that had been Pedro's favorite chair. It still bore his imprint on the back and seat, or so she imagined. She never sat there, only looked at it from time to time as if expecting him to appear in it.

It occurred to her she could watch morning TV, a soap opera as she had occasionally glimpsed from a patient's room, or late morning news. Infused with this sense of novelty while still in bed, she reached for the remote and turned on the television. What she saw she could not place in any reality she knew. Was this some drama that belonged on nighttime TV? Quickly, she changed the channel, only to find the same ruckus on more than one channel. She turned to the all-news channel, still not believing what she saw. Crowds of belligerent men, some helmeted and armed with automatic rifles over their shoulders, hurled themselves at overwhelmed policemen in front of the Capitol building in Washington. Hordes of people, some bearing signs that read "Stop the Steal," broke through barricades and literally chased the Capitol police, who retreated more than once to form a new line of impotent defense. When the camera shifted to the building interior, she saw members of Congress pushing to escape the main chamber and take refuge. Riveted and still not quite believing, she watched the President address a more peaceful version of this same crowd from earlier the same morning, up the street from the Capitol, where he urged them to fight for what was right and retake the election by force. The cameras switched back to the Capitol, where the horde smashed windows and forced their way into the building, invading the now-vacated House chamber. Carla almost stopped breathing. Was this really happening?

Beyond the fray, she heard loud knocks on her own door. She called out "come in," and watched all three of her children race in, each of them as distressed as she was. They tumbled onto her bed around her, Sabrina and Luis clinging to her. Only Carlo sat rigid at the foot of the bed, shaking his head and mumbling.

"What are you saying?" Carla asked him.

"I was worried something like this would happen," he said, turning to his family. "He couldn't accept reality. They're going to have to haul him out of there on Inauguration Day."

Luis began to cry. "Mama, what's happening? Are we safe?"

"I'm sorry you have to see this, Luis. It's a riot. It's not happening here, and yes, we are all going to be safe," she recited in her best mother's voice, not believing herself. She cradled him, and Sabrina rubbed his little back with one hand while holding her mother's shoulders tightly with the other.

Carla reached for the remote and turned off the television. "We're going to restart our day. We can watch again later. Meanwhile, you go back to school. I'm going to get up, get myself dressed and bring you each a cup of hot chocolate. We've got better things to do than watch this riot." Carlo caught her eye skeptically even as he heard the bravado in her voice. He knew she would not mind if he continued to watch for the remainder of the day.

As soon as her children left the room, Carla got up and dressed with the same grim purpose as she did on each workday. She combed her hair without looking at her face, put on her work shoes without thinking and marched down the stairs as if she were off to work. She poured milk into a pan and turned on the heat while measuring the cocoa for three cups from directions on the box. Come off automatic, she told herself, needing almost to mouth the words. She poured another cup of milk into the pot and enough cocoa for another cup for herself. Foraging in the back of a cabinet, she even located tiny marshmallows, colored for last Easter but still soft. After delivering a cup to each of her children, she sat with her own at her kitchen table in the unfamiliar sunlight, just staring and sipping until the cocoa was gone. She made herself a second cup, sat and stared out the window, trying to recover some sense of herself.

I can't do this anymore. I can't. By the end of the morning, Carla had nearly decided to stop working as a COVID nurse. Nearly, but not fully. She told no one. In mid-afternoon, after Carlo's classes ended, he joined his mother in the kitchen, where she still sat staring out the window.

"Have you thought of returning to your regular work?" he asked gently, one hand on her shoulder.

She startled, a smile sneaking from the corner of her lips. "Have you been reading my mind?"

"You've done more than anyone thought you could. It's time to give yourself some slack." She nodded wearily. "And the rest of us miss you." She leaned into her grown-up son, relieved and proud of him.

"I've been wondering how to bring this up to you," he began softly, on a new tack. "Saturday is Dad's birthday."

Carla's hands flew to her cheeks and she bowed her head. "How could I forget?" Carlo stroked her back.

"I've made a plan," he began, "but only if you want to do it." Carla looked up hopefully.

"Remember when we all hiked that trail next to the waterfalls last March on Arturo's birthday and picnicked at the top?" Carla smiled despite herself, nodding.

"That was a hard hike but it was so worth it."

"I've lined up the whole family on Saturday. Marta is baking cupcakes for us all. We can celebrate Dad's 47th birthday and sing to him." Carla grabbed her son's ears gently the way she used to do when he was little.

"You are a perfect son."

On January 27, 2021, nearly everyone watched the Inauguration of Joe Biden and Kamala Harris. Don had been propped up even before breakfast, watching it unfold on the big screen, engrossed by the traditional dignity and order on display, paying close attention to the Chief Justice administering the oath without missing a word. He remembered in 2009, during Obama's first swearing-in, the Chief Justice's accidental omission of some of the phrases of the oath of office, unnoticed at the time but remedied privately later that same day. Probably Obama had caught the error, Don thought, and knew enough to protect himself against anyone challenging his legitimacy for this small error.

The halls of the Evergreen were nearly empty, its residents taking refuge in the ceremony of transition they had watched every four years since the fifties, when they had bought their first televisions. Erythea had taken the day off, staying home with Elissa to witness the changing of presidents. Elissa had prevailed on her to stay home and watch, and they were both equally fearful of some new national disaster – an assassination attempt -- or some stunt by the departing president. Even George, who never took a day off, remained at home in front of his own screen. Marta went from room to room, changing linens on the beds and scouring bathrooms as the inhabitants sat without stirring in front of their screens.

For Arturo, the day was oddly busy, and he had to snatch glimpses on a tiny screen as he and the rest of his team cooked, packed and handed food through the take-out counter to a line of customers who were not to be distracted by cooking on this day. Beto worked alongside his father, sautéing onions and garlic, his eyes tearing but his mind mirroring his hand, stirring up questions. Would things change? Would vaccinations come? Would people stop dying in droves? Carla toiled through the whole day, the rhythmic thrump of ventilators marking the moments for her patients. She could only glimpse the screen on the wall of the tiny, improvised COVID ward café as she took a quick break for lunch. But what she caught halted her -- a slim black woman with braids mounted higher than a turban, reciting

"That even as we grieved, we grew

That even as we hurt, we hoped

That even as we tired, we tried."

The hands of the young poet Amanda Gorman described graceful arcs in the air around her as she spoke. Carla could not move, arrested by the music in her words. This was the first music Carla could hear since Pedro died. She stood still throughout the whole delivery, wanting to watch it over and over again. The words "A country that is bruised but whole" echoed through her for the remainder of her workday. Only after she had removed her PPE, punched out, driven home, showered, changed her clothes, depositing today's into the washer, washed her hands, and joined her children in the kitchen did she realize she had missed lunch altogether. Carlo served her a steaming bowl of chili with cheese melting over the top, Luis passed her the chips he'd been crunching into, and Sabrina poured her a large glass of iced tea. Carla glanced around the table, led their daily prayer, and ate two bowls while her children babbled happily around her.

⸻ ◦●◦ ⸻

Simon headed north on Highway 1, winding along the coast, luxuriating in the undulation of the road itself, seeking the little town that had in the Sixties famously removed all road signs leading to it. Even with new road signs, the turnoff was tricky to find, as was the road to the coastal hike north of the obscure town. Talking to himself in his own head as usual, Simon declared himself in an 'unusually celebratory mood'. In the week after Biden's inauguration, the United States had rejoined the climate accords, re-opened its borders to asylum seekers, halted the Alaska pipeline and introduced a trillion-dollar bill to reboot the economy. These days he found himself basking in the news rather than dreading the headlines.

Surprised by the empty parking lot near the trailhead, Simon shrugged at his good luck and hoisted his backpack. Rain was forecast, but for a week it had been forecast daily with nothing but haze and sunshine ensuing. He had a poncho in his pack and boots on his feet. He pocketed the obligatory mask, knowing he could retrieve it if he met others along the way.

Within the forest, everything quieted, even his mind. His feet landed on the soft duff of the coastal fir that vaulted over him like a cathedral. With no wind, all was hushed below the canopy. He could hear the pattern of his own breath, more pronounced by the climb of the trail. He fell into a rhythm for the first few miles, completely undisturbed. When the canopy opened into a vast meadow, he could hear the sea below with its own rhythm of waves rolling placidly onto the shore. The gray sky was itself still, no buffeting clouds.

Simon's mind meandered like the trail tracing the shoreline.

His quiet mind lofted questions it would not ask in a more populated space. Had the pandemic helped rid the country of its last president? Could its incidence be explained, or had it arisen randomly? Would it change people's habits or culture in any positive ways? The newspapers droned on about the death toll exceeding that of this country in the two World Wars and Vietnam war combined, about the current hospitalization and vaccination rates, the political obstacles to vaccine delivery. But it was the big questions that had always preoccupied Simon. What had caused this? What would come of this?

Simon had read somewhere that modern scientists were researching climactic reasons for the Biblical plagues, such as the eruption of a distant volcano causing the sky to blacken for days. The notion comforted him, since it did not rely on the intention of a Supreme Being. In his classes, there were always students who insisted on tracing all the philosophical questions of existence back to a Supreme Being. Most cultures were premised on such a notion, with wars being fought over whose notion was correct. He had loved poking students' premises with his questions. But now he asked them for himself. Would he live long enough to see the answers played out? As if there were definitive answers.

Ahead of him on the trail, Simon spotted a doe, her head and ears suddenly erect after he had interrupted her quiet browse. Her belly bulged with new life she was carrying. When the doe saw that Simon was continuing toward her, she bounded off.

Simon hoped to see the shore below on this hike, but the trail continued to meander inland. In this vast open space, the grasses wore the temporary green of winter rains, and there were no trees, only rounds of dark green bushes dotting the terrain. Glancing ahead, he could glimpse beyond hills the bracelet of trail far ahead. Nowhere could he spot other people. Looking toward the ocean, he could see only a wash of gray. Now outside the shelter of the trees, he became aware of the moisture in the air by how damp his flannel shirt had become, and by the drips forming in the coiled nest of his hair. Wiping his hand over the top of his head yielded a spray of droplets. Not wanting to stop to retrieve his poncho, he let the moisture accumulate until his pants clung to his legs and his shirt sagged off his shoulders. After a few more miles, heated by his hike, Simon doffed his shirt, wrung it out and hung it from a strap on his pack. He suddenly felt freer, relishing his exposure to the air around him.

Finally, the trail wound closer to the brink of the cliff and he could discern the outlines of gentle surf on the beach far below. Simon stopped to drink from his canteen and found himself mesmerized by the white arcs of approaching and receding waves. Unable to stop watching, he took the poncho out of his pack and spread it on the ground. Impulsively, he removed his wet jeans and shorts and lay down on the poncho, fully exposed to the sky. What had been mist turned to droplets landing on his whole body, the gentlest shower he had ever taken. Closing his eyes, he drifted into the rhythm of the waves below.

When he reopened his eyes, he realized some time must have passed, for the sky had altered. No longer uniform gray, it revealed entire realms of light blue with clumps of clouds and rays of sunlight emanating from one of them. The shower had ended, and his naked body was nearly dry. Getting up on his elbows, Simon could finally see the horizon of sky and sea and the distinct arcs of the waves below. He redressed and ate his packed lunch, then headed back along the trail, energy restored to his legs and lungs.

His mind at peace, he listened to the keen of a hawk he could not see, and the trills of tiny birds clustered in the scrub. Spotting the forest far ahead of him, he marveled at the distance he had traveled and at his reserves of energy.

⚊⚫⚊

Japan coined the phrase *shinrin-yoku* – forest bathing – to describe the practice of walking contemplatively in forests, inhaling the pheromones of the trees. *Yugen* – feelings that are too deep for words, that cultivate the sense of beauty and mystery in the universe – are nurtured within the forest. One of the most densely populated regions of the world, Japan gave name to a practice that helps heal the soul of humans in a realm of concrete, artificial lights and sounds, congestion of all sorts, and rid ourselves of cortisol, the stress hormone. The term forest bathing has developed a small international cachet -- a small island off the coast of Sicily advertises its national park as a site of forest bathing in its effort to redevelop tourism post pandemic.

When a friend described forest bathing to Simon, he scoffed: "Japanese marketing."

⚊⚫⚊

In Ethiopia, churches preserve what remains of the once-prevailing forests. According to the ancient Amharic version of Christianity, a church cannot exist without a surrounding forest to protect and foster its spirituality. The circular churches are themselves encircled by their own small forests. The woods of those forests have been used to build the churches, and the barks, leaves and flowers from those forests have been used for the paints that decorate the inside walls. Eleven church forests remain in the Northern part of the country, a network of tiny green circles on a golden plain. Everywhere else in the region, the trees have been cut to create fields of grain to feed the people, and cattle graze the open fields. Now only these tiny green islands remain, and they are preserved against the encroaching grazing cows and grain fields by fences and rock borders created in recent times by volunteers and local religionists. The forests harbor varieties of trees and other plants that have otherwise vanished from the region. With the permission of the local church people, botanists from around the world have come to record and replenish ancient species that are now rarely seen anywhere else.

⸺ •◦• ⸺

Finally, at the end of January, the winter rains began — after all the lightning fires and tainted smoky skies of summer, after the deceptive sunny skies of December, after the hottest year on record -- the nights brought first the lashing winds that flung limbs and pine cones into window panes, then the lulling patter of night rains that enabled deep sleep. Tiny, winding cascades on the steep slopes of Mount Tamalpais began to gulp and plash and gurgle down the faces of the rocks, dripping through the needles of the coastal fir and dry-until-yesterday crackling leaves of the Eucalyptus, scenting the air with their soothing oil, settling the dusty trails into a wet mush and greening the land anew. The wet days felt cozy rather than confined, fostered reading in front of a fireplace or watching old movies. People took walks in the rain, welcoming it as much as their freedom to be outside after their long pent-up year.

The reservoirs in the forests gradually filled, the creeks created music again, and the salmon returned to spawn. In the forests, the pine needles dripped their nourishment into the soil, awakening the tiny flowerets of early spring. The earth began again to replenish itself.

The same corridor of ultra-moist air, the atmospheric river that washed the slopes of Mount Tamalpais, also collapsed a steep segment of Highway

1 along the ocean near Big Sur. Massive mudslides roared down hills where forests had burned the previous summer, sweeping away cars and homes at the bottom. Fortunately no one died in the nighttime swath of destruction, but the scenic highway would take years to rebuild.

It was a small version of the floods that destroyed much of Vernazza in the Cinque Terre on October 25, 2011, gullying the steep hillsides that defined this relatively inaccessible region. Watching the videos of the swift surge of flowing mud down the winding streets of narrow old buildings, one cannot be anything but astonished that the buildings themselves were not brought down and swept away in the destruction, like the buildings in Fukushima, Japan on March 11 of the same year, in the tsunami following the largest earthquake ever recorded. The city of Vernazza withstood the ravage. The ground floors of every building lay filled with mud and rubble when the surge subsided. The walking paths between Vernazza and its neighboring villages likewise washed away, leaving residents with only their boats as connection to their neighbors and their hillside vineyards. By hand and hydraulic machinery, residents carried away the rubble. Over the next two years, they rebuilt their town, refurbished their ancient homes and re-opened the restaurants. They cleaned the beaches and reformed the small harbor until only the memorial photos in the town and the still ravaged portions of hillside above it remained to tell the tale. In contrast, the town of Fukushima remains vacant, still radioactive from the tsunami damage to its nuclear power plant.

For every narrative, there is a counter narrative. We choose which one to tell.

———•◦•———

Author's Note

Like a journal, this novel was written in real time in 2020 and early 2021, with the information available at that time. Thus, for example, the author knew no more than the general public in early 2020 about the outcome of the U.S. Presidential election or the ways in which people would react to COVID-19 over time. With the exception of public political figures or identified writers, musicians or composers, all characters are fictitious, and any resemblance to real people is incidental or accidental. All characters and occurrences at The Evergreen are entirely invented. This is a work of fiction, though placed in real time. Thus, the occurrence of events in nature, such as earthquakes or fires, coincides with the real existence and timing of such events, though not always in the actual location. Statistics are intended to be accurate from reportage at the time. The author knew no more than anyone else of the ways in which COVID-19 would mutate in 2021 or of the fires and floods that would ensue in 2021. To the author, that is part of the magic of fiction – people's feelings and actions based on what no one did or could know at any given moment of time. Thus, each character must manage as he or she can with what is known at the moment of decision.